TIME THIEVES

Dale Mayer

Other Standalone Novels

In Cassie's Corner

Gem Stone (a Gemma Stone Mystery)

Time Thieves

TIME THIEVES
Beverly Dale Mayer
Valley Publishing Ltd.
Copyright © 2015

ISBN: 978-1-988315-91-1
Print Edition

About This Book

Time has a way of solving many problems – but it also has a way of creating many more…

Sari grew up with a secret that involved her missing father… The only other person who knows the truth refuses to acknowledge it. Sari can't forget what happened. Ever. She lost someone she loved.

Fifteen years later, the possibility of reversing the series of events drives her to keep searching for answers. Especially now that she's finally returned to where it all happened and with the people – one in particular – that she'd been forced to leave behind.

Fifteen years ago, Ward was devastated when Sari's mother fled to France with Sari. Even at ten, they'd been sweethearts. But the mystery of what happened back then had lain fallow… waiting for someone to stir up the soil. And damn if Sari wasn't the best at doing just that…

Sari and Ward are out of time. Can they solve the mystery of what happened? Or do they become the next victims…

Sign up to be notified of all Dale's releases here!

https://geni.us/DaleNews

PROLOGUE

SARI HARRODS RAN into her father's shop, excitement adding extra height to her bounce. At ten, she already loved that she was so much taller than that awful Jimmy but the exact same height as Ward. Perfect. She giggled.

"Daddy, Daddy!" She let the door slam shut behind her, remembering too late that she was supposed to be quiet. It was so hard to remember. So many rules.

"Hush, Sari." Her mother swept in behind her. "Your father is working."

"I know," Sari explained impatiently. "That's how I knew to find him here." How come adults needed to have everything explained to them?

"She's fine, Lisbeth. Let her be." Her father's voice rolled over them both with its deep timber tones.

Sari laughed. "Daddy, I made it through the spelling bee at school. I beat Ward with the word aquarium."

"Did you now? Now that's fine, that is." He stood up from his desk and came around the tall counter. Bending over, he swept her up into his arms. "I think that's worth a treat, isn't it, Lisbeth?"

"That's wonderful news, Sari." Her mother joined them, her warm and caring voice tickling Sari's ear. "I think hot chocolate is definitely in order." With a swift tickle of Sari's ribs, she disappeared into the main house at the back of the shop.

"Yay!" Sari loved hot chocolate. She wiggled free and ran deeper into their shop. "Did you get any new parcels today, Daddy?"

"I did. Brodin came by with one of his grandfather's watches. He's gone to pick up the matched set from the safety deposit box and will be back any moment. Then we're going to see just how special they are."

Sari glanced around at him. "Is it very nice?"

"It is." He pulled out a second chair to snug up against his desk chair before he sat down. Sari obediently hopped up beside him.

"Can I open it, pleeease?" She leaned forward, propping her elbows on the desk. "Please, Daddy?"

He laughed, opened a drawer, and pulled out a squat envelope. Shifting the mess on his desk back, he slipped the contents of the envelope onto the cleared spot.

"It doesn't look very pretty." Her voice reeked with disappointment. She'd been hoping for something with lots of shiny gold. Instead, this was a dingy tarnished color like Grandma's old silver set Mom hid in the back of the china cabinet.

"It's not always about the looks," her father said, his gaze narrowed on the timepiece in front of him. "And this one is very interesting in other ways."

"How? It looks very boring." Sari turned to look out the window, wishing Mom would hurry up with the hot chocolate.

"It's interesting because I've never seen anything quite like it."

That made it a little more interesting. Her daddy had been doing this for a long time. If he hadn't seen anything like it, then maybe it *was* special. She peered closer, astonished to see the metal piece open up. "It opens? Cool." She knelt on her chair to get a better look.

"Apparently. *Very* interesting." Her father leaned back, removing his glasses to stare off in the distance. Suddenly, he pushed his chair back and strode across the small room to the narrow bookshelf on the far side of the room. With his finger dragging against the spines, he went from one book to another looking for one in particular. On the second shelf, he found what he was looking for. He tugged the book out and flipped it open, his face alight with excitement. "It's here somewhere. Where is it?" He walked back to the desk, stopping every few feet to flip more pages.

"Where's what?" Sari poked at the metal piece, checking her finger afterwards to see if the gray dust had come off on her skin. "What is all this inside?"

"I don't know yet. Don't touch," he warned.

Sari lifted her gaze to see if he was watching. His glasses had slipped down the end of his nose, a sure sign that he was buried in whatever he'd found to read. "I won't touch anything."

Sounds of her mother's arrival with the promised hot chocolate had Sari glancing from one to the other and then back down at the odd-looking machinery in front of her. Her father was adjusting the inside of the watch, peering at papers beside him then looking back. He sat back with a satisfied grin. "Got it."

Cool. She leaned closer. "Got what, Daddy?"

Her father turned his head to stare at her, the intensity of his gaze a little unnerving. As if just realizing how vulnerable the timepiece was, he leaned toward her. "I mean it, Sari. That's a very delicate mechanism. It's worth a lot of money."

"Money?" Now that made it really interesting. They didn't have much money. "Can we keep it then?"

He reached for the box and went as if to scoop the timepiece back into the protective cloth when it slipped out of his fingers to the floor where it dropped and rolled. "Oh no."

Both Sari and her father bent at the same time to look for the missing watch.

"Where are you two? I bring hot chocolate and you're both gone." Her mother's footsteps sounded along the wooden floor.

Sari laughed. "We're right here, Mom. The watch dropped."

Then she saw it shining in the single ray of sunlight dashing across the floor. "There it is, Daddy." Sari stretched out her arm, but her father reached it first.

He glanced up at her, a big smile on his face as his fingers closed around it.

"I've got it," he said triumphantly. As the words left his mouth, an odd look came over his face. He swallowed once, then twice. His gaze went from Sari up to where his wife stood.

"Daddy?"

"Something's wrong," he whispered. His face thinned, paled to the point Sari could barely see him. She reached out to touch him, and just as her fingers would have made contact, he disappeared.

Her mother screamed, dropping the tray full of hot chocolate, the broken cups bleeding their dark chocolate contents. Sari stared as the liquid spread over the empty space where her beloved father had been.

CHAPTER 1

Fifteen years later

COULD THE AIRPORT get any more crowded? Sari struggled to find a clear passage through the hundreds of people blocking her way. The more she travelled, the more she wished for a pair of wings of her own. The fanciful thought made her smile. First time all day by her count. She came to a dead stop at the customs line up. Thankfully, she'd moved to the head of the crowd. *Please let this be simple.* She had her paperwork in order. And the paperwork for her bag of goodies.

She was in luck. She knew the agent and the agent knew her and her business.

"Hey, Sari. Back again, huh? What have you got this time?"

Breaking out a bigger, warmer smile than she felt, she gave the same response as always. "Junk most likely, but hopefully a few treasures too."

"Sure hope the treasures are worth the rest."

"Me too," she muttered as he went through her paperwork. Stamping everything, he handed the documents back. "Have a good day."

Relieved, her smile natural this time, she thanked him, picked up her bags, and walked out of the airport into the late afternoon sun. Now to collect her car, and if she was lucky, she'd be home in a half hour.

It was closer to an hour before she made it inside her front door. She couldn't resist a wiggle at knowing the old Victorian house with her father's original shop out front was now hers. Always had been apparently, except she hadn't found out until six weeks ago when the lawyers contacted her. Damn her mother anyway.

Since finding out that little tidbit, life had been chaotic as she moved across the ocean, all the while maintaining her crazy trips searching out hidden finds to repair and sell. This last trip had been her third since moving back to her old home. So far she hadn't even connected with her old friends, and she was dying to. And nervous about it. At ten, she'd been sure Ward Preston had been it. The one. He'd been her best friend and she was sure nothing would ever have changed that. Then her mother moved her across the ocean.

Time and distance had finished what the traumatic circumstances of the time had destroyed.

Checking the answering machine, she found a dozen calls from suppliers and clients, but none were urgent. Good thing. She was too damn tired. Tossing her keys on her dining room table, she draped her coat on the back of the closest chair and kicked off her shoes. Home sweet home.

Opening the fridge, she pulled out the single bottle of wine she'd stashed in there before her trip. There was no fresh food, so dinner would have to be cheese and crackers with wine to wash it down. Opening the bottle, she set about making herself a plate to carry into the living room.

Just as she set the wine glass and plate down on the coffee table, the phone rang. Her mother. Of course.

"Hi, Mom. Yes, I'm home safe and sound."

"Good. Why you couldn't have come to visit on this last

trip I'll never understand," Lisbeth said fretfully. "I hate worrying about you in that miserable hellhole."

"Mom, I'm fine. Nothing is going to happen to me here."

"You don't know that." The thin, critical voice made Sari wince. After her father's disappearance, her mother had lost the little warmth she'd had as she'd quickly moved her and her daughter back to the part of France she'd been from.

Sari had gone to a succession of boarding schools, then college, and as soon as she'd found out their old home was still theirs and sat untouched in the old part of Victoria, BC, she'd begged to have the use of it. Her mother had refused to discuss it in any way. Sari was ready to have another discussion about it, but then a lawyer contacted her when she'd turned twenty-five and Sari found out it had been left in trust for her all along.

"I'm happy here, Mom."

"How can you be? The city is small, the people are narrow-minded, and there couldn't possibly be enough business for you to make a living. Come back to France. You know Pierre and Josiah are hoping for you to return."

Like that was news. What her mother refused to see was that Pierre and Josiah were perfect…for each other. Neither male was willing to admit where their sexual orientation lay, and she had no intention of getting involved with either of them. They were good friends but nothing more. How could there be? Besides, setting up house and home as her mother's neighbor had to top the list of things she *never* wanted to do.

"I like it here. I love the ambiance, the water, the weather. I don't find the people narrow-minded, and my business isn't dependent on where I live." *Take that.*

"We have all that here too. Come home. It will be good

for us to spend time together."

Sari couldn't help but raise an eyebrow at that. Her mother had to be up to something. She never made gestures like this. "Not going to happen for a while. I just got home, remember? And speaking of which, I'm really tired. I need to go to bed and catch up on some much needed sleep. The jet lag hit me hard this time." A lie, but a perfectly reasonable one.

"Fine." Her mother gave a haughty sniff. "Then I want you home for my birthday next month."

Chills ran down Sari's spine. This was so not her mother's normal discussion. "What's going on? You never push to have me home."

"Can't I see my daughter for a visit? It's been years since you spent any time here."

Flopping her feet onto the coffee table, Sari slouched back onto the old couch. "I was at boarding school, then college." Although her mother managed to twist that fact to suit her needs any time it came up. "You wanted time to enjoy your men. Not spend time with me."

"That was then. This is now. I find the men are all boring anyway. But my daughter is growing up and away. I don't like that."

Too damn bad. It was a little late to want to have a cozy mother-daughter relationship. Like fifteen years too late. Since before her father's disappearance, in fact.

"Well, find a new boyfriend and those maternal feelings will fade away again." Sari knew that for a fact. Her mother's maternal feelings were dependent on how old she felt. With a new man, she felt younger and therefore had no need of her daughter. When the men left, then she felt older and more dependent on Sari. Or maybe more regretful of the things she'd let slip through her fingers. Like her daughter.

Hanging up the phone, Sari took a healthy drink of wine and settled back to try and forget about her wasted trip, her mother, and once again her failure to find a solution to the one thing that drove every action in her world – finding her father. Or at least finding answers to what happened to him.

And she knew she hadn't a hope in the world. Obsessed and delusional was what one doctor had called her. After that, she'd shut up about it and continued her search quietly. As she hadn't found out anything in the last fifteen years, chances were good she'd never find out.

Yet she couldn't give it up.

Speaking of which, she reached for her bag of treasures. There was one very interesting piece in there. Placing her wine glass down, she opened her leather bag and gently extracted several wrapped up bundles. As a jewelry maker with a penchant for antiques, she'd picked up a large clientele of both suppliers and customers. Unlike her father who focused only on timepieces, she focused on jewelry and of course any timepiece like the one her father held as he'd faded from her sight.

At least that's what her vague, shocked memory said had happened. Her dear mother Lisbeth had changed the story to him having walked out the door to meet someone and never returning.

Lisbeth knew the truth, but in typical fashion, she'd decided it to be too preposterous and had changed it to suit herself. It had gained her more sympathy and support from her friends and family. As it had been left unresolved, she'd never been pushed to remarry because her father had never been found. She said she couldn't be bothered to do the paperwork to have him declared dead when in truth, Sari suspected it was a way to keep her men around and not have to commit.

She loved her mother, but like one would a fine piece of china rather than a well-loved mug. Her mother was many things, but warm and caring wasn't part of her personality.

That had been her father.

And God, she missed him.

She studied the first bundle. It was an old, beaten gold neckpiece that sat on the collarbone. It was a beautiful piece that just needed a little care and attention. Sari knew she could restore it to its former glory. Smiling, she laid it down on a piece of cloth to admire.

She picked up the second piece and opened up a pair of platinum spider web earrings. These weren't nearly as old as the collar but were fascinating in the fine workmanship that had gone into creating the web of spun metal. A beautiful piece.

Her hand trembled as she reached for the third piece. Her trip to New York had not yielded many pieces, but the ones she'd returned with had been worth the trip. Especially this last one. Carefully, she unwrapped the one timepiece out of several hundred that had been presented at the show. Her colleagues had gushed over several fine pieces and had gone silent when they'd seen her purchase.

The vendor, however, an old English gentleman, hadn't. It seemed as if he'd recognized the desperation in her actions, the neediness in her voice as she'd searched for the watchmaker's special mark, hoping against hope to find one that matched her faded memories of her father's watch and his incomplete notes that she'd spent hundreds of hours poring over.

"It's reputed to always keep time. Who could ask for

anything more?" he'd murmured for her ears only.

She'd lifted a sharp gaze to assess the sly, knowing look on his face. "Indeed, what else could anyone want of a watch?" Coolly, she'd watched as amusement and a knowingness drifted across the old man's countenance.

That smile of his irked her, but it had been his next comment that had made the decision for her. He'd said, "Nothing at all. We're always losing things to Time, aren't we? Now if only we could regain all that we lost."

She'd frozen, her gaze locked on his face, analytically assessing the truth or gimmick of his voice and presentation. He was not the first to try and fool her. She hadn't gotten this far without being taken in at least once or twice. Maybe it was the old tweed, the almost dusty clothing, or the faded blue twinkle in his eyes that reminded her of her father, but whatever it was, it seemed as if the old guy knew something. Something that no one else knew. Something that could shed light on the driving mystery in her life.

Or he'd just heard the rumors about her obsession and was playing with her.

It hadn't been impulse that had made her pick up and study the one old, almost uncared-for piece out of so many he'd had on display. But when she did, it was almost as if he'd given her a magical silent pat of approval on her head.

A great sales technique. Conrad, one of her peers, had loved a more modern piece, laughing at her choice. She'd kept a smile on her face and her hand on the watch. No one would take it from her until she was done with it. And in this case, she thought as she pulled it out from its thick bubble wrap, she might never be done with it.

Getting up, she carried the watch to her desk and turned on the lamp. It appeared to be the same as the one her father had been working on when he'd disappeared, but she'd have to take it to her shop and dismantle it to find out for sure. Not tonight. She wrapped her prizes back up and placed them in the safe in the shop.

What she needed was sleep. She filled her glass with more wine, replaced the bottle in the fridge, and headed for bed. Maybe she'd actually be able to sleep tonight. Lord knew she was beat. Travelling, time changes, and no sleep in the hotel with their too-hard beds and too-stiff sheets all took their toll.

Hopefully the wine would help her sleep…and quickly.

After getting ready for the night, she carried her wine into her bedroom, changed into her cotton cami and pj bottoms, and sat on the edge of her bed to brush her hair. She yawned, and a small laugh escaped. Good. She was exhausted. Tossing back the last of her wine, she crawled under the covers.

It was good to be home.

Within minutes, she'd fallen into a deep sleep.

FIVE HOURS LATER she woke, a fine tremor ghosting across her skin. The air had chilled, stilled. She couldn't place what was wrong – just that something was. She rolled over and sat up. She'd left her window open, an unusual event in itself. With a storm brewing outside, the wind was tossing her curtains everywhere.

She threw back her covers and strode over to the window. With more effort than required, she pulled the window down, barely bringing it to a stop before it hit the wooden ledge. She did want a little fresh air. The old house needed big money poured into it. New windows and a better security system were at the top of the list. And the roof. It had sat empty all this time with well over a hundred years on its bones already.

Standing and gazing out into the black night, she realized an old truck had parked across the street at the empty lot. A man leaned against the box, a trail of smoke wisping around on the whim of the wind. He faced her house, staring up at her window – directly into her eyes.

Shit.

She slipped back out of sight.

There was no reason to be bothered; this small corner of downtown wasn't the best area of town, but she'd yet to have problems. Then why had she just remembered that she needed to upgrade the security system? Her house was bigger than many around, being an older three-story style. It offered lots of room but also lots of opportunity for anyone on the more sinister side of life. Leaning against the wall, she peered out from the side.

The man flicked his cigarette and opened his truck door. As she watched, he reached in and pulled out a takeout cup of coffee. Interesting. Anyone sitting out there with a hot drink must expect to be there for a while. She considered the rest of the street. Mostly old houses, mostly run down, at the edge of the commercial district of downtown but also right on the corner of where the downtown core started. It was a shabby area, but one now caught up in the midst of a big revitalization project. She had the only business here that she knew of, and even then she didn't use the storefront for the public. She saw the odd client who stopped in that way and had the shop as her workspace, but she hated the distractions of having a door the public could open on their whim.

Her shop was secured. Her safe was connected to a security system as per her insurance. She was a jewelry maker after all, and she stored gems below. Not many and not high grade, as she didn't have the funds to stockpile, but anyone looking for easy money would find a lot to sell for quick cash downstairs. She walked to her bedroom door and stuck her head out in the hallway.

As it was a split level the levels were confusing. She slept on the second floor, making it almost impossible to hear any activity on the first floor. Not impossible though. She walked back over to the window to find the stranger now talking on a cell phone.

Innocuous, but the sight made her skin crawl.

She couldn't throw off the feeling that he was watching her house, maybe talking to someone about her. The worst-case scenario was that someone was trying to get in or was already in, and this guy was warning him that she was up.

On the heels of that thought came a muffled sound followed by a voice.

Crap. She grabbed her cell phone and called 911. With her phone tucked into her shoulder, she pulled on jeans and tucked her cami top into the waistband. Snatching up her running jacket off the closet handle, she pulled it on as well. After explaining the situation to the dispatcher, and receiving instructions to get out of the house if she could, she hung up the phone and tucked it into her pocket. With a last glance out the window, she had to decide to either go downstairs and see what was going on or bail out via the upper deck and the fire escape ladder. The first could put her up against a dangerous intruder and the second could put her in the stranger's line of sight.

Neither appealed. She slipped into a pair of shoes and searched the hallway. Nothing appeared to be touched. She made a cursory check of the rest of her floor then opened the door to the downstairs. It was dark down there.

And not empty.

Shit.

WARD PRESTON DROVE slowly through the streets of Victoria; he didn't mind the night shift here. Working the night shift back east in the big cities? Not so much. It wasn't like he needed to be out cruising, but with the paperwork done, he wanted to get out and check out the streets.

And drive past Sarina's place. Or Sari, as he'd always called her. The pet name her father had kept for her.

He winced. He'd lost touch with her over the years, but the distance between them hadn't changed her place in his heart or mind. He'd kept her in the back of his head, always wondering if he'd see her again. Then he'd heard she'd returned. He'd waited, hoping she'd contact him while he tried to get up the nerve to see her. He'd been driving by her place at least once a week for the last month.

She wouldn't be pleased if she knew.

He grinned. Good thing he had no intention of telling her.

Heading instinctively in her direction, he thought back to the two of them in elementary school. She'd been his first crush. Even now, years later with one very short marriage behind him, he hadn't been able to get over her. Then he'd caught sight of her down at the beach about a month ago, and fantasy had jumped back into reality, and damned if he could get her out of his mind.

Victoria, at one end of Vancouver Island, offered almost any water sport imaginable. Sari had been standing in her bikini at the water's edge, watching as the waves from a speedboat washed over her feet. She'd been so free, so natural and so alone that he'd been desperate to go up to her and introduce himself. But it had been fifteen years…what if he'd been wrong about it being her?

He'd been on duty. He could have done it. He hadn't. He had driven past her old house that had stayed boarded up since the family had left and found lights on inside. It wasn't until his second or third time driving past that he'd caught sight of her a second time and confirmed it was her. To realize that she'd really come back.

He wondered why. He'd heard the rumors the same as everyone else. As her father was still a missing person case, it was still discussed both officially and unofficially. Supposedly her father had walked out on them – from one day to the next apparently – never to be heard from again. Ward had adored Sari's father. The mother he'd avoided. After Greg went missing, the mother – Lisbeth, he thought her name was – had stayed only long enough for Sari to finish her school year and then she'd pulled her out, taking Sari away. Gone overseas. Gone from his life. Never gone from his mind.

Sad.

He made a left turn that would take him onto her block. She lived in a quiet part of the city, but one that wasn't as nice as it used to be. Still, most of this city was decent. Sure, they had their fair share of drug dealers, biker gangs, and homeless people, but all in all it was a retirement tourist town. At least it used to be. Now that was slowly changing.

There it was. He smiled at the old hodgepodge of a house. It looked the same as always.

Except for the truck on the opposite side of the road and the guy standing outside and staring up at Sari's house. As

Ward watched, the guy checked his watch and glanced back again. His gaze was intent, as if he was standing watch. Or waiting…for someone that was being too slow.

It was in the middle of the night. Possibly he was waiting for Sari, but as he was parked out here and not in the driveway, he doubted it.

Someone was casing Sari's house.

Or worse…he was waiting for his partner to leave Sari's house. As in a breaking and entering in progress.

And if that was the case – where the hell was Sari?

CHAPTER 2

S ARI CROUCHED ON the first landing, her heart pounding so loud she could barely hear what was going on downstairs. A series of thuds and bangs was coming from her living room. Shit. She glanced down at her cell phone. Should she try calling 911 again and tell them she hadn't made it out of the house? No. The intruder might hear her talking. If she could scoot across the landing to the other side and get to the second stair landing with the outside exit, then maybe she would be better off.

"Where the fuck is it? She's only been home a couple of freaking hours. Not long enough to have sold it."

She froze. They were looking for something in particular? Something she hadn't had time to sell? So something she just brought home with her. How could they know?

And the bigger question – did she know who they were? Or was it only one man? No, the man outside had to be connected. Was there a third one out back? Damn. Knowing it was stupid but unable to help herself, she crept down to the bottom landing and peered around the corner. It was too dark to see much, but there was a dark form bent over her locked doorway to the shop.

Shit.

She couldn't let him in there. She didn't keep much in the way of valuables here, but there were enough. She couldn't afford to lose them.

Just then the guy straightened, his hand going into his pocket. She watched as he opened his cell phone and read a message.

"Shit." The voice was dark and gravelly but young. He raced to the front window and pulled the long drapes back slightly. Immediately, he dropped the material and flattened against the wall. For that brief moment, she caught a flash of red hair.

Too bad she couldn't see what was outside. She watched as he texted madly then waited, leaning tight against the wall. His face had a panicked look. Obviously not a pro. That was a good thing. Maybe he was just looking for an easy score. Except he sounded as if he was looking for something in particular.

She wished she could look outside. That would mean going back upstairs. And with the intruder not making a sound, he'd hear every step she took.

Then she saw a burst of color.

Outside the house, bright blue and red lights flashed. Cops. *Yes*. Her fingers clenched in a fist that she barely held back from doing a fist pump. There was a short blast of a siren then nothing but the flashing lights.

Even across the distance, she watched a sheen of sweat appear on the intruder's face. So that's what he'd panicked about. That also meant he had a partner who'd sent a warning. The stranger outside.

Why?

She crept back upstairs, holding her breath. At the top floor, she went to her bedroom window and stared out. A cop car sat parked at an angle in front of a pickup truck. One she didn't know. The officer stood speaking with the driver.

Just then, the officer turned to look at her house, the street light bright on his face.

There was something about that strong jaw, the light wave to that hair, and his profile...*Oh my.* She gasped in joy and shock. *Ward.*

She hadn't seen him in years – make that fifteen years. He was a cop? She couldn't imagine a better career for him. He'd always been a protector, even back then. Her lips curved in a warm smile. She was so proud of him. She went to wave at him, hoping to catch his attention. Ward heard something and spun around, his back to the stranger. Suddenly the stranger reached out and slugged Ward on the back of his head with something in his hand.

Ward dropped like a log.

Oh crap. This time she didn't hesitate. She dialed 911 again. As she waited, she double-checked that her bedroom door was locked before heading out to the small deck. Maybe she could get information on the truck. When the voice came on the phone, Sari quickly explained what had happened. The dispatcher wasted no time after Sari told her an officer was down, firing off a ton more questions. She answered as best she could. She was only minutes from the closest police station, but who knew how busy tonight was? Generally it was a quiet district, but shit happened...as she'd just found out. She stayed crouched by the railing, trying to keep an eye on what was going on outside. The stranger was now searching Ward's cruiser. The dispatcher didn't want her to hang up so Sari kept a running commentary of what was going on outside. The stranger pulled out a small book and flipped through the pages.

She sighed with relief when a man from her side ran across the road and hopped into the passenger side of the truck. The first man had gotten in already, book in hand. They reversed the truck and ripped away with squealing tires, leaving Ward prone on the pavement. She had just enough light to see the ram's head on the front hood. As for color – dark. Navy or black. She told the dispatcher the direction the two men took off in even as she raced down the stairs to her old friend.

She'd barely gotten the words out when the sounds of sirens filled the air. *Finally.*

She bolted out the front door, ignoring the dispatcher's orders to stay inside.

"Ward." She dropped to his side, snatching up his hand to hold it tight to her chest as the fire truck came to a screeching stop. The first cop vehicle ripped in behind. More sirens and vehicles arrived.

After that, it was complete chaos. She was shunted off to one side while Ward was checked over, loaded up, and whisked away in the ambulance.

An officer escorted her inside her house to talk. As soon as the door closed behind her she remembered the intruder, and with the officer helping, she searched around to see if anything had been stolen. Even though she'd seen the guy at her office door trying but not succeeding to get in, she unlocked it and checked anyway.

It was untouched as far as she could see. While she wandered around the house, she relayed the conversation as close as she could remember. The officer took notes and asked about what they might have been looking for.

"I honestly don't know. It could be any of many items. I deal in antiquities and have some semi-precious gems at home. The thing is, I've hardly lived here. I only came back a few months ago."

At his confused look, she had to explain about her father disappearing and her subsequent move out of the country.

When he finally left, the sun was breaking over the mountains. She loved this time of year, having forgotten how vivid the colors were on the island. Peach and pink bloomed skyward, lighting up the world around her.

She leaned against the front door and watched. When she finally turned to face her shop, she realized how old and dingy it looked. She'd been blinded by joy at being home, but now she could see how much work needed to be done.

Including installing a full-on security system. Inside, she wandered the shop where she'd spent so many enjoyable hours with her father. And that just brought her back to the past. There's no way he'd have left her behind…if he'd left willingly. She stuffed the old pain back inside, knowing nothing good could come of hashing over the same nasty scenarios of what had happened that day so long ago.

She sighed, tears once again coming to her eyes. She wondered if they'd ever stop.

She'd tried year after year on the anniversary of his disappearance to duplicate the exact set of events that had happened when her father had vanished. So far she'd had no luck. This year would be the first time she'd have a chance to repeat the ritual in the same physical location in which he'd disappeared.

In just over a week's time. She'd repeat her ritual soon enough. No need to do it early.

Realizing how fatigue had caught up with her, she locked the safe and her office and slowly climbed to her bedroom. Crawling under her covers, her last thought was to wonder what Ward had been doing at her house. And did he still remember her?

WARD SAT UP in his hospital bed and clutched at his head.

"Whoa. Where do you think you're going?"

Ward peered through half-closed eyes to see an old friend. "Well, Dr. Janz Coran, are you on tonight? Fancy meeting you here."

"Yeah, fancy that. You come into Emergency and meet an emergency doctor. How odd."

His grin belied his sarcasm. Not that Ward would have listened. They'd been friends far too long for that.

"How's my head, Doc?" Ward asked.

"Looking pretty sore from where I'm sitting. What did you do this time?"

"Someone hit me from behind." And stupid of him to let that asshole get the drop on him. He straightened suddenly. "Did I come in alone? There wasn't a woman with me, was there?" He looked around for his phone. He needed to make sure Sari was okay.

Dr. Coran laughed and grabbed him by the shoulders to gently force him back down again to lie on the bed. "This isn't exactly a two-person activity. You came in alone."

"There was someone parked suspiciously outside a friend's house. I was talking to the guy in the truck, heard something odd, turned to look and was hit from behind. I need to make sure she's safe."

"There is an officer outside. I'll let him inside in a few minutes."

While Ward stewed and fumed at the slowness, Dr. Coran checked him over thoroughly. Standing back slightly, he smiled and said, "Now I'll let your partner in."

True enough, Jeremy came around the curtain almost instantly. "Hey, talk about giving us a scare."

"Did you guys catch the asshole?" Ward asked, trying to throw his sheet off and drop his legs over the side of the bed. "And did anyone check on Sari? The truck was parked at her house."

"Easy – let someone else do their job too." Jeremy pushed Ward gently backward until he was resting again. "Sari is actually the one who called us to *your* rescue. Apparently she saw the whole thing. There'd been an intruder in her house and then you showed up. The inside man was contacted and he waited for his partner outside to knock you down, then they both ran. She couldn't give us many details on the men or the truck though."

"A Dodge Ram with duallies and a sprayed-on box liner with a beat-up toolbox in the back. Black, I think…I wrote the license plate down in my notebook. It had oversized tires on it."

"A lot of truck for some punk that's going to raise it."

"There's a lot of money in this town." Sitting on the ocean in the province, this was considered a retirement city by many. But that also included retirees that had enough money to get out of the rat race early. It also meant lots of offspring with plenty of disposable income. "Where's my jacket?"

They both looked around, but there was no sign of it.

"My notebook was in the pocket."

"Are you sure you had it on you when you were hit?"

Ward frowned uncertainly. "I thought so, but I'm not sure. I might have tossed the notebook on the passenger seat of my cruiser."

"Hmmm. Sari noted that the man who hit you checked out your vehicle before he got back into the truck and drove away."

Ward groaned. "So he probably grabbed my notebook. Damn it, that book had a bunch of numbers I needed."

"Your cruiser has been taken to the lot, so I'll go and see if the notebook is still in there. You stay here and rest."

Ward snorted. "Hell no. If I'm going to rest, it will be in my own home and in my own bed." He struggled back up to a sitting position. "My head's taken a beating before. I feel fine."

"A blow on the head is nothing to laugh off. Why don't you stay here until morning?"

Forget that shit. Ward hopped off the bed and stood facing his friend. "Hell no. I'm outta here. Besides, the doc just gave me a warning – he didn't admit me. So let's go." He didn't wait to hear any more protests. He led the way from the building, which was almost too silent. Then again, it was dawn and the whole town should be asleep.

Outside, he got into Jeremy's truck. "I should probably stop in at the station, huh?"

"Nope. I'm taking you home." Jeremy started up the big diesel engine and pulled out onto the main road. "I was afraid you were going to insist on going back to Sari's house to make sure she's all right."

Ward glanced over at him. "Did you see her?"

"Hell yes. And yes, she's just as gorgeous as before. That short dark hair, huge baby blues, and that same gamine grin." Jeremy smirked, but his smile fell away. "She didn't recognize me though."

"Yeah, I'm not surprised. It's been years. She won't likely recognize me either."

Jeremy shot him a sideways look. "Except she called you by name when she called it in. Not only did she recognize you, she's the one that alerted the cavalry to come to the rescue."

A warm bloom heated Ward's insides. It made him feel good to think that after all this time, she still remembered him. They'd been best friends. If she'd stayed here, he'd have done his damned best to keep her as a friend and eventually something more. He'd always planned to take her to the prom. Her leaving had devastated him.

"Hey, you okay there, buddy? You went kind of quiet."

"Just remembering the shock of her leaving. First her father's weird disappearance, then her up and moving like that." He sighed and dropped his head back on the head rest and closed his eyes. "I never stopped thinking about her."

"Yeah. I wasn't as close with her as you were, but it seemed like her mother had been a bit different back then. She'd been almost cold."

Ward barely held back the disgust in his voice. "She was reserved. But Sari's old man – well, I really liked him. He reminded me of my own." Even now he couldn't imagine what the loss of her father had done to Sari's mental state. She'd been the light in her father's eyes. The open adoration between the two had probably contributed to the sense of her mother being the odd one out. He'd asked Sari about her mother once, and she'd just shrugged as if to say *what can I do?*

"So are you going to ask her out?"

Ward looked over at Jeremy and frowned. "A little early, isn't it? I'll definitely stop by and thank her, but for all we know, she's married and has children."

"Nope, she's not and never has been." Jeremy's smug grin had Ward narrowing his eyes at him. "I checked."

"Really?" *In that case…*Ward smiled a little sheepishly. "If she's interested in spending time with an old friend, then I might. Have to wait and see. Fifteen years is a long time."

CHAPTER 3

"I'M SORRY, BUT the house needs more than a Band-Aid."

Sari frowned as she looked over the house inspector's report. She'd figured it was really the only way to see what kind of repairs she'd need to be making.

"A new roof is the priority, I'm presuming."

"Yes, and get an electrician in to check the wiring. That electrical panel needs to be upgraded. Particularly if you're planning on putting in a sophisticated alarm system. You don't want the alarms to go off when you plug the teakettle in or some other such nonsense." He grinned good–naturedly.

"No, I really don't." She glanced down at the report again. "Thanks for this."

"That's just the rough stuff. I'll email you a full report this afternoon when I get my notes written up. That gives you a place to start though."

"Good enough." She stood on the porch until he left then wandered the house, matching the report with some of the problem areas. The old cedar siding needed to be repaired on the back, or she could redo the whole house with the newer siding. She was partial to keeping the house the way she remembered, but there was no point in being stupid. Memories couldn't replace common sense.

Back inside, she started the tedious job of looking up and calling contractors for quotes.

By the time she finished the ones on her list, she was badly in need of a cup of tea. Her mother would be sipping a glass of wine at this hour, having returned to the French way of life immediately. Sari still preferred tea. So had her father.

Busy filling the teakettle, she barely heard the knocking on the door. When it sounded the second time, she ran to the front door and opened it.

She gasped. Ward. She cried, "Are you supposed to be out of hospital?" He grinned and opened his arms.

She didn't hesitate. She leaned in, loving the way his arms wrapped around her and held her tight. She burrowed closer, burying her face in his shirt. God, she'd missed him. Stupid really – she didn't even know him. Not anymore. Feeling slightly self-conscious, she pulled back with a sheepish grin.

"I guess you can tell I missed you, huh?"

"As I missed you." His arms tugged her close, squeezed her tight, then released her slightly. She loved that he kept his hands on her as if not wanting to lose contact again. "Damn it. I've hardly heard from you in all this time. First a few letters, then emails, but lately not much. Where was the 'hey, I'm coming home in September – be nice to see you' or something?"

She laughed. "I sat and wrote and rewrote that damn note a dozen times, then thought screw it. I'll just surprise him."

"Well, you did that. I swore I heard your voice when I was lying on the cement last night. I'd heard you were back, but damn it, you didn't let me know."

Her smile turned melancholy. "I'm sorry. I was planning

on it. But being back wasn't exactly being back. I've been gone more than I've been here."

He dropped his arms. "Well, seeing as how you rescued me last night, you're forgiven."

She led the way back to her kitchen. "I think you probably rescued me first." She glanced back at him. "I had an intruder and didn't quite know what to do."

"Get out of the house to safety is always first."

She shrugged. "Yes, but as I quickly found out, the guy's partner was watching outside. I was afraid there was a third one out back."

Ward grabbed a kitchen chair, spun it around, and sat on it, facing her over the backrest. "Any idea what they were looking for?"

"Not really, except from the little bit I heard. I got the impression they were looking for something in particular." As she made tea and carried over the pot and teacups to the table, she shared what she remembered. "The thing is, I deal in antiquities and jewelry, so in theory they could have been looking for any number of pieces." She added slowly, "Not to mention the multitude of semi-precious stones I keep on hand."

"Ouch." He winced. "That's a lot of reasons for an intruder to case your place."

"Except since I've only been back for a few weeks and been gone for most of that time, how would anyone know? It's not like I've had a chance to reconnect with the community in any way. I seem to be dashing to and from the airport constantly."

"Do you do any business locally?"

"Not yet. I plan to eventually, but I'm global."

"It's possible these two were hired to do this job by

someone out of town. If they are looking for something particularly valuable…please tell me you don't keep anything really valuable in the house."

"Not *really* valuable. Several pieces run in the thousands, but I have a safety deposit box where I keep a couple of the more interesting pieces. I'm getting repairs done on the house and plan to put in a high-end security system at the same time. I have a safe here, but it's old."

"The same one your dad used?" At her nod, he grinned. "I remember trying to open that thing every time I was here. Your dad was the best."

Silence. She dropped her gaze to the teapot as if suddenly remembering she hadn't poured it and immediately filled two cups with the hot brew.

"I'm sorry. It's still painful?"

Glancing over at him, she admitted, "Even more since coming home. I hadn't expected it to hit me so hard, but it's almost like looking over my shoulder and expecting to see him sitting at his desk like he always used to." She cupped the hot cup in her now chilled hands. "As if the time in between never happened. Like we went on an extended European visit without him."

"I'm sorry. I'd have expected to have him show up, his body at least somewhere over the years. But it's like he disappeared into thin air. There's never been any sign of him since."

Sari kept her gaze on the tea, not daring to let him see into her eyes. He'd always been very perceptive, and being a cop should have amplified that instinct over the years. She knew what she'd seen all those years ago, but there was no way she could share it with him.

Unfortunately.

"Sorry to dredge up bad memories." Ward's voice turned brisk. "What kind of repairs are you having done?"

She smiled at the change of subject and started laying out her plans to him.

He left soon after, leaving her wanting more. They'd left it open and casual. She just hoped he came back soon, or she'd have to track him down and take the next step. She'd really missed him. And they'd already lost enough time. She wasn't up for losing too much more.

SEVERAL DAYS LATER, she watched the huge crane truck carefully drop long packages of roofing tiles on her roof. The one half had been stripped bare; her front lawn showed the evidence of the many attempts from the workmen to toss the ripped pieces into the supersized dumpster that had been delivered and was sitting in her driveway.

Soon the new roof would be finished. She'd been fascinated at the speedy coordination between men, equipment, and supplies. They were fast. Of course, the forecast was for rain and they wanted it done beforehand. So did she.

Several other contractors had come and gone, giving her estimates on various projects. The biggest one she had to decide on was the flooring. It would be expensive to do the entire house at once, not to mention a major pain as the house was fully furnished, but the old wooden flooring in the shop was looking a little dubious at this point.

She wandered inside to the shop. She needed a garbage bin out front like the roofers had. Honestly, had her mother tossed anything away before running off to Europe?

There were dishes in the shop, clean but just stacked on the one side. There was equipment hiding under years of dust. Books lined one wall, and she could almost peel the dust off them – it was so old. Speaking of which, she was likely to need a new furnace. Oh joy. Not for the first time, she wondered if the savings she'd set aside was going to be enough to bring the house back to order.

She wandered through the shop, letting herself pick up old books from her father's collection and thumb through the yellowed pages. The titles intrigued her. *Time Encapsulated. Facts on Time Travel. Timepieces. Alternate Dimensions.* She'd always assumed the books had to do with her father's favorite hobby – watches. Sure, some did, but some were more fantastical in nature. Or esoteric maybe. She'd pondered the concept of time travel a lot over the years; how could she not after what she'd seen and experienced? She'd haunted websites, libraries, and databases while at university, but nothing had ever been able to explain the most defining moment in her life.

Finding out her father had apparently been fascinated by the topic made her wonder if he'd learned something important or had accidentally triggered something in that one timepiece – sending him somewhere else. She'd hated staring at old watches, feeling like her father was caught like a prisoner inside one. And no, she wasn't ready for the nuthouse. But she'd racked her brain endlessly and that was the only conclusion she'd been able to come up with. It had really made it difficult to sit through some of her classes in school. She knew something they had no explanation for. Not that she'd brought the subject up. She'd tried several times with her mother, but Lisbeth had stuck to her version. That her father, instead of waiting for her to return with their hot chocolate, had gotten up from his chair and walked out the door – forever.

She also told Sari that she had to stop making up stories about her father.

Except Sari hadn't been *that* young. If Sari hadn't been home beside her father when he'd vanished in front of the two of them, hadn't been searching then reaching for the same watch at the same time as her father, if she hadn't been old enough to understand that he'd disappeared then…maybe. But she had been there. She had been about to pick up the timepiece. She had watched him disappear. Her mother had searched the room frantically as if that would give them a crevasse, a hole, a container, something that had held her father.

She'd screamed at the time, frantic. Sari hadn't. She'd known even then how devastatingly wrong the whole mess was.

That was another mystery that Sari hoped to solve now that she was home.

Home?

Her mother's place was just that – her mother's place, never Sari's home. Yes, it finally felt like she was home.

CHAPTER 4

L ATER THAT AFTERNOON, she was in her father's shop when she looked up through the window to see one of the workmen walking toward her. She met him at the front door.

"Sorry, but there's some damage to the room directly above the shop. We're going to need to take a closer look. Can we get inside the attic, please?" He motioned upward to the area of concern.

Sari stepped out and looked up. With the roofing tiles off of this side, she could see the underneath looked blackish to a dark brown. She wrinkled up her nose. It was just the one area, a bit bigger than a sheet of plywood. "I hope that isn't mold."

"We're not sure what it is, actually." He shook his head. "There wasn't any damage on the surface of the roofing tiles to indicate this was below. Good thing we found it now though. We'll have to get some wood in and replace these boards."

"Come inside. The attic is actually accessible from this room. I just haven't ever been in it."

"Most people don't go to their attics unless they have to. It's too bad. If you keep an eye on it like the other rooms in your house, you'll get an early warning that problems are starting."

"I never even thought of it. Then again, I haven't been in the house more than a few weeks." She led the way into the front of the shop and pointed upward. In the corner of the room by the hallway was a large rectangular shaped door on the ceiling. "I don't even know how to get up there."

They walked closer. Sari stared at the door like she'd never seen it before. It was right above where her father had disappeared. How could something so important have been overlooked? All the time they'd searched for her father, they'd looked down. Had they even considered looking up? The workman strode over to stand underneath. "You've also got high ceilings. Is there a second floor here?"

She blinked. "There is on the rest of the house, but I don't think there's anything above us."

"Except when we look at this area from the outside, it appears like there should be a room here."

Had her father ever mentioned the attic? Not as far as she could remember. "Honestly, I've been away from this house since I was ten. I can't remember ever seeing anyone go up in there. You're welcome to look at the rest of the house. It's a bit of a designer's nightmare. It's a split level with stairs going up in all directions. However, what would be the closest room to this is this way." She led him out of the shop and into the main room. She took the first set of stairs on the left that went up to a landing and then up another small set of stairs. At the top, she opened a door on the right. "It's the spare room. But as you can see, it's got the dormer window." She pointed it out, and with the slanted roof, there was no attic here.

He walked over to the window and looked out. They were on the right side of the damaged area. He went to the second window that overlooked the side street then walked back to stare at the solid wall on the right. He tapped the wall several times and frowned. "Weird. There's a space here. The access panel must be what we're thinking of as the attic door from downstairs."

As they trooped down the stairs and back into the shop, the workman shook his head at the sight of two other small staircases leading in opposite directions. "Either this place has been renovated to hell and back again, or the original designer was nuts."

She laughed. "Probably both are true."

"There's not even a handle for that trapdoor?" He stared in wonder up at the door just above his head. "I'll go get the ladder off my truck."

She watched him as he strode out and crossed the street to where his big truck sporting the name *Island Roofers* in large white letters across the side was parked. He unloaded a ladder mounted on the box.

Effortlessly, he carried the ladder inside and opened it up just below the attic door. He climbed up and pushed on the door.

It wouldn't budge.

He stepped up another stair and put his shoulder into the next heave. There was an odd cracking, grunting noise as if the house itself was giving way. The door shifted and lifted. The workman eased back so he could change his hand position and lifted the door, shifting it sideways to open the area up wider.

"Well, that didn't seem too bad."

"Just seems stiff from disuse." He unhooked a flashlight from his belt and stepped up higher, his head and shoulders disappearing into the attic. "Well, that's interesting."

"What is?" Sari waited anxiously. She could only watch

his legs and torso as he twisted and shone the light in different directions. She moved closer, hoping to see what was up there.

"What's up there?" Still no answer. She waited another minute. "Can you see anything?"

He bent over slightly enough, and his head popped below the ceiling so he could see her. "There's lots of stuff up here. Come on up if you want. It appears to have a floor in here as well. There aren't any windows, although I can see light through the damaged boards." He straightened and with the simple maneuver of a man who lived a physical lifestyle, he hopped up inside her attic.

She stepped around to the rungs on the ladder and climbed up behind him. He was taller than her so she had to stand on the very top of the ladder in order to haul herself up higher into the attic. Once sitting on the floor, her legs dangling down, she saw that the attic door had levers that should have allowed it to drop down. It was obviously broken, but as it had a simple staircase attached, it would be a much easier way to get up and down. Something else she'd have to fix. She should have written a better list.

Her priorities were going to need to be re-evaluated. She stared into the gloomy interior, only able to see what the workman shone his light on. "Any idea if there is power here?" The light shifted around the room to a spot on the far wall. He walked over and hit a light switch. Immediately the room was lit up. She hopped to her feet and stared, fascinated at the room she'd had no idea existed. And it was full.

"Wow. I wonder what all this stuff is."

"I don't know how long your family lived here, but some of this stuff looks really old. How old did you say the house is?"

"The original part is supposed to be from the 1850s." She wandered, looking at old seaworthy trunks and tables and the odd chair. There were a few odder-looking chairs sitting in the corner as well. In fact, the place was brimming full of history, and she couldn't help but feel excited at the idea of learning more about her family. This house had been in her father's family since it was built. "Amazing."

The workman stood under the damaged part of the room and studied the warped wood. "This is the problem here."

She looked up to see him pointing in one area. "Is there mold?"

"Not that I can see. We'll need to replace this wood." His voiced deepened at the end as he checked something else. "No, the struts and supports all look good." He pounded the damaged wood lightly with his hand and the wood broke, letting splinters of light in. He hit it again, and a large piece broke off in his hand.

"Wow," she whispered as the dense sunlight shone deep inside the room. "Sunlight would be so nice."

"Pardon?" He turned to look at her, puzzled. "What did you say? Something about letting the sun in?" He stepped back and appraised the slanting roof. "Are you wanting a window or maybe a skylight in here instead?"

"Yes," she almost shouted. "I'd really like a big window in here. I don't know why it's separated off from the rest of the house, but it's a great space. All it needs is natural light."

"Well, we'd need the work done pretty quickly, so you need to let me know the size you'd want it to be."

"I'd have to find someone to come and give me an estimate."

The workman flipped his phone open. "That's easy. My

brother owns a glass shop. He's almost done for the day. He can come and give you an idea."

While he made the arrangements, Sari wandered the room, wondering why it was only accessible from the downstairs. How hard would it be to punch through to the hallway or another bedroom, giving a normal doorway access? She'd have to find someone to do that work too. So much for her budget.

But for all the financial stresses, she couldn't get over the find. What joy and what gold. There might even been some antiques in here valuable enough that if she sold them, they would pay for the work. Like a kid with a treasure, she danced in place.

"He's here?"

She spun around to look at the workman who'd been busy tearing off the rotten wood and dropping it to the ground below.

With the opening wide enough for his head and shoulders to pop through, she only just now noticed he stood on an old wooden crate of some kind and was waving to someone down below.

"Jimmy, come in and turn left. Up the ladder."

She heard a muffled response below. Then another head popped up. A younger man than the first one clambered inside the attic and introduced himself.

"Hello, I'm Jimmy. My brother John says you're looking at putting in a new window."

She nodded and pointed out the large opening in her roof. He walked over and studied the area. "No problem."

They discussed style, insulation factors, and cost, and Sari had a promise to get a new window installed in the morning. John had wanted him to do the job right now, but he couldn't fit it in. After he left, having sorted out the materials with his brother, John came down and walked out to his truck. The rest of the workmen looked to be close to calling it a day.

Several came in and helped John secure the hole for the night while he promised to come in and finish the job when his brother was done. Then he walked around the house to check on the rest of the roof. Sari, standing out front, couldn't believe they'd managed to get the entire roof done except for the area by the attic. She should get the gutters replaced too, damn it. There went her budget again. Although, for a window in a secret room, no problem. She'd find the money somewhere.

Somehow.

WARD WAS PISSED. There was no sign of the guy who had attacked him. He'd disappeared. Although they'd found the vehicle abandoned on the road leading to the other end of the island. At least his notebook was recovered at the scene.

Of the driver and passenger – nothing.

Breaking and entering was one thing; attacking a cop another thing altogether.

He so wanted to slam their asses behind bars. Not the least of which had to do with Sari possibly being in danger, too.

After checking the time, he decided to run by her house and give her an update; not much of one, but still it gave him an excuse to see her. Several trucks were just pulling away as he drove up. One he recognized. He played soccer with Jimmy. He waved as his friend drove off. Was Sari planning on getting new windows too? He assessed the old heritage house. They didn't make them like that anymore. This place was out of the way slightly and set back off the road, and with the high fence of cedars and lilac bushes, not much was visible from the street. Of course the bright blue tarp on her roof was hard to miss.

He knocked on the open door, then pushed it open and stuck his head inside. "Sari, are you here?"

No answer.

"Sari?"

"Hello?"

Sari's voice, oddly distant sounding, came from inside. Ward pushed the door open wider and walked in. "Where are you?"

"Over here."

He followed the sound into the shop to see very shapely bare legs dangling from an open hole in the ceiling. At least she had sandals on her feet. He walked to where he could look up and see her face. "What are you doing?"

She peered down, a huge grin on her face. "You so have to come up and see this."

He glanced around the shop. "I would if I knew how." A chair stood underneath, but surely it wasn't high enough to climb up.

"John the roofer guy brought the ladder originally, but I guess he took it with him when he left. You'll have to find something higher to stand on. It will make it easier for me to get down too."

Shaking his head, Ward dragged a heavy wooden workbench under the opening. He hopped onto the chair, then to the workbench. His head poked through enough to be able to see the interior. "The attic, I presume."

"Sorta. Come all the way up." Sari scrambled to her feet

and backed up to give him room. She loved the way Ward's shoulder muscles rippled as he pulled himself up. Damn, she must be in a man drought for her to even have noticed. She'd like to blame it on appreciation for a beautiful male specimen – she was an artist, after all. But she wasn't sure that excuse would fly. Not that her hormones cared.

They were already sitting up and taking notice.

Ward brushed the dirt from his clothes then straightened. He peered around the room in surprise. The air was dark and gloomy as the light no longer shone in. She shone the flashlight over the light switch. Ward stepped and flicked it on.

"I had no idea this room existed. John found the rotten board when he pulled the roofing tiles off."

Ward looked at her in surprise. "Really? It's an attic."

She laughed. "I know. But I'd never been up here and from the outside, you can't see this space. There are bedrooms up on either side of those two walls." She pointed them out. "So why has this room been walled off? And why isn't there a door for access from the bedrooms or even the hallway?"

Ward walked over to the first wall and tapped lightly. "How interesting."

"I know, right?"

He glanced at the items stacked high all around. "Do you know what any of this stuff is?"

"No, but I'm looking forward to figuring it out. This house has been in my family forever. It's an awesome find."

"Or a huge bin full of trash."

She gave him a wry grin. "True enough. I need to get this thing fixed." She motioned at something beside him. "It's like a drop down ladder staircase thingy. But it's broken, I think." She walked over to the mechanism. "See here?"

He examined the ladder door system. "Cool. I've only ever seen one of these in the movies." He made a couple of adjustments. "I think we just have to figure out how it works."

"Really? That would be great."

She backed away as Ward extended the stairway slightly. The door was meant to drop down and lock into place. Ward extended the stairway and from where she sat, it looked to almost reach the floor. He had to jump down and move the worktable then fully extend the ladder. "Oh, excellent."

She watched as he checked the bottom of the ladder. "Do you think it's safe?"

"Let's find out." Ward cautiously stepped onto the first step and bounced ever so slightly. Except for the metal squeaking on metal, it held.

He climbed all the way up, turned and stepped down the rungs until he was standing on the shop floor. "Come on down."

Excited like a kid with another new toy, Sari cautiously climbed down. "That is so sweet. I love this."

"I can't believe you didn't know."

"I'm sure my father did, but my mother – well, I'm not so sure. She hates dark cramped spaces, and I just can't see her caring about an attic in the first place. She'd never lower herself to sorting through all that old stuff for the odd treasure," she said thoughtfully, then shook her head at the image. "No, definitely not."

"She's more the hire-someone-to-clean-that-out type of person, I gather."

A lopsided smile slipped out of Sari's lips. "Yeah, you could say that. She's a good person in her own way, but definitely not the hands-on type."

"I remember her vaguely. She seemed more like a china doll to me back then."

"Perfect description and now she's just a little older, she'd say a little more valuable because of it."

He laughed, and she had to grin. "Don't get me wrong. I love her, but she's not the person I'd like living next door."

"Me either. Now your dad was wonderful. He was always so down to earth."

"The exact opposite of my mother. And you're right. My dad could talk about anything with anyone. He never put on airs and could always be counted on to give a helping hand when needed." The warm memories were bringing tears to her eyes. She sniffled them back. "I still miss him. Every single day of the last fifteen years, I have felt like some part of me is also missing."

A warm hand landed on her shoulder, gently squeezing. She smiled through her tears. "I'm fine. But there's nothing like coming home to find how, although stuffed away, the memories have never been forgotten."

"You don't want to forget him. He was a good man. He deserves to be remembered."

"Thanks."

In the distance, a phone sounded. Sari groaned. "That will most likely be my mother. France is not far enough away."

He laughed. "Answer it then. You can ask about the attic."

"Stay. I'll put on coffee," she said over her shoulder as she raced to answer her cell phone still sitting on her desk.

Picking it up, she groaned at the number. "Hi, Mom."

She rolled her eyes at Ward.

Ward grinned and wandered through into the kitchen. There was a new coffee maker sitting on the counter. With minimal effort, he managed to get a pot dripping.

He stood at the back door lost in thoughts of his childhood and what might have been if she'd stayed behind when he heard her come to stand behind him. "I'd planned to take you to prom, you know."

He felt her startled pause, heard her gasp. He turned to face her, a melancholic smile on his face. "Leaving like you did hurt more than just you."

The smile in her eyes shone at him, but the serious look on her face agreed. "If I'd been anything but a kid, caught by the decisions of adults, I'd have stayed. And I'd have gone to the prom with you."

They smiled, a rekindling, a reconnection, a resolve firming between them.

"Then I suggest we pick up where we left off." His grin was contagious.

She laughed. "As I recall, I'd just beaten you at the spelling bee."

At least that had been the last highlight, the last normal day she remembered. After that her life had been a blur.

He laughed. "Actually, you tromped me."

"Another round?"

"So not. Once was enough for me. But how about a cup of coffee to catch up on old times?"

Damn. That's the best offer she'd had in a long time. Her heart swelled with the sense of reconnection. "Sounds good."

CHAPTER 5

BY THE TIME Ward left, Sari actually felt like another piece of her had come home. A piece she hadn't been fully aware had been lost in limbo. She'd been devastated by all the changes that had happened so fast in her life. Crushed. Losing her best friend at the time had been just another blow she'd struggled to deal with.

To know he'd missed her as much as she missed him made her all warm and fuzzy inside. Yes, they had stayed in contact at first only, but it had a distance to it. Some of that distance had remained after their first visit. Not now. The distance was gone in an instant as if it hadn't ever existed. Now…she felt like she'd fully come home.

That attic was yet another homecoming. Her mother couldn't remember there being an attic and said it wouldn't have mattered since she'd never go inside the damn thing anyways. And Sari had better stay out too. The floorboards were probably rotten. Sari had explained about the roof, and her mother told her she'd send over some money to help with the repairs.

"If I can't get you to come home where you belong, then I'd damn well better make sure you're safe over there. That house is a ruin. Sitting empty for all this time. The stove is liable to blow up the first time you use it."

Sari hadn't had the strength to tell her mother that she

hadn't turned it on yet. In the back of her mind, she had wondered if all the electrical wiring was safe. She'd liked to have done this alone without her mother's financial aid, but there was no doubt this house could eat away all her savings at the rate it was disappearing. And how sad was that? She needed to leave again soon too. She had a trip to Washington DC in a week. There was much to do first, including laundry from her last trip.

At least she'd put out the money for a washer and dryer when she'd first moved in. Those units worked, so in theory the electrical system was just fine. That didn't mean she'd trust all the wiring. She'd have that checked as soon as she got back. Tomorrow was the window and the roof.

Then the rest.

First, sleep.

She tried, but it was difficult to sleep that night. She couldn't get the little room out of her mind. She'd taken a quick glance through some of the boxes up there and had Ward haul a couple down before he left, but nothing had given a clear indication of why the room had been left as is. Storage? Then why not put a door into the upstairs where it was more accessible? Sure there'd been the weird attic door, but there could have been so much more.

Then again, maybe money or speed had been a factor with intentions to make changes down the road.

After Ward had left, she'd gone through the first box, only it had contained nothing but old clothes, relatively all the same size. As if one woman had cleaned out her closets and found it easier to throw the unwanted clothing in the attic instead of giving it away to Goodwill. Then again, from the age of the clothing, maybe being frugal was the sign of the times and they were the ones in need of Goodwill. Sari was no clothing specialist, but these articles didn't appear to be of great quality.

She'd tossed and turned before finally falling into a troubled sleep.

Somewhere in the middle of the night, she woke and bolted upright. Something moved in the house. She'd planned on getting a cat to keep her company eventually. And that's what it sounded like; a soft, gentle padding across the floor.

She scooted to the edge of the bed, grabbed up her housecoat, and walked silently to her open bedroom door. Peering down the hallway, she realized that for all the odd sound, there was no sense of an intruder like last time. She wasn't afraid – she was curious.

Intrigued.

And that was just plain dumb. She'd already gone through a terrible break-in, so why this time was different she didn't know.

She walked down the hallway to the top of the stairs and listened intently.

Silent. No voices, no footsteps, no sound at all. She straightened and looked around. The attic was behind the wall to her left. She laid her head against the plaster and thought she heard something. She frowned. Could an animal have gotten into the attic? With the window due to be installed in the morning, the hole in the roof, while tarped, was relatively open to an animal. Squirrels came to mind. She laughed lightly. That's exactly what it would be. She'd seen many big gray squirrels outside. One had probably come inside to investigate.

Nothing to worry about.

She returned to her bed, content.

IN THE MORNING, Sari didn't have a chance to look if a squirrel had gotten in. If he had, he wouldn't have stayed as the window guy, Jimmy, arrived before seven with a beautiful unit that had small panes and lots of small wooden dividers. It was old looking and matched the house perfectly. She grinned. The roofers were back, and John was helping Jimmy put the window in. They'd been delighted at the drop down stair system.

"Don't see many of those units around town."

"They probably wouldn't pass inspection," John said. He seemed the more dour of the two, but both men were friendly and appeared competent. That was all she cared about. Still, having the window in was glorious. Beautiful daylight shone into the room.

"Are you going to put a door from the hallway into here?" Jimmy asked.

"You probably should. Better for safety. Just in case, you know."

"That means finding someone who can do the job though." Sari glanced over at the two brothers, a grin on her face, "Don't suppose you have third brother who does renovations like this, do you?"

They laughed. "Nope, just the two of us."

John pulled out his notepad. "This is a guy who does this stuff. I've seen a bunch of his work. Looks good. And even better, he doesn't chintz on the job. He's a craftsman."

"Does that make him expensive?"

"Nah. Not for something this small. A door is a hundred or so, the labor another hundred maybe. I'm sure it wouldn't cost much more than that. Of course, some painting might be required after the work is all done, but likely just touch ups."

"I need to do a bit of painting anyway, so I'll see what he says." She accepted the piece of paper and tucked it into her pocket. "Thanks." Leaving them to their work, she went downstairs and finished doing her laundry.

They came back after a couple of hours for her to see the finished job.

She loved it. Ten minutes later Jimmy had been paid and he left, leaving her alone. Now she could go and inspect the small room. She refilled her coffee, slipped her cell phone into her pocket, grabbed a notebook, and headed to her shop. She struggled to get the stairs down but once the movement started, it slid down nicely. She carefully climbed with the coffee cup in her hand and the notebook between her teeth. At the top, she stood clear of the opening and turned to look at her new window. Stunning. Sunlight streamed into the small room, lighting up all the shadowy places. Now she could easily see the contents of the room. The electric light helped, but it was not anywhere near as effective as natural light.

She placed her coffee cup down on top of a small worn table, figuring it wasn't valuable, then turned to see where she could start. The room had piles as if different items belonged to different people, each claiming a different corner in the storage room. There appeared to be five separate piles, at least five that she could see. Who knew if more were underneath? A smallish heap sat on her left. That looked like a good place to start. She sat down on the floor and started going through the small stack. In her notebook she kept track of what she was doing, how she was proceeding and what she found.

The first box held more clothes belonging to a tall male,

judging from the length of the pant leg. And a different era, from the pinstriped look and winged shoes as well. She frowned. She'd need to do more research if she planned on finding out who these people were. Had this house even been built when these shoes were in fashion?

She kept digging. The pockets were all empty, and the first box held no other treasures. She reached for the second box. This appeared to be more personal items like socks and underclothes. She went through everything carefully, writing a list of what she found before moving onto the next. It was weird. It was as if these people were gone and this was all their belongings. Of course that was all too possible. She knew almost nothing of her father's family history. Maybe these people had died, and someone not wanting to get rid of their belongings put it all in here. Not that it made any sense for generations to repeat this system.

She shrugged and kept going. There were all kinds of little items like a knife, a small bell, an old book. She flicked through the book, wondering at the spidery writing. It didn't look like a man's script, but could have been his mother's or girlfriend's for that matter. She could barely make out the words, but it appeared to be a diary of some sort. Interesting. She put that in a different pile to take downstairs and continued.

By the time she finished the small pile of boxes and glanced at her watch, she realized it was almost lunchtime. Her coffee cup had long been empty. Straightening, she walked back downstairs with the journal.

She'd yet to eat. In the kitchen she made herself a small chef's salad, using up the fresh ingredients in her fridge. With a trip coming up in a couple of days, she needed to keep an eye on waste. She hated throwing food out. Unlike her mother, who was so picky she'd get up and walk away from a dinner party if she didn't like the food. She really was a trial.

Not to mention rude.

Sari smiled at the thought. She did love her mother, but she was such a perfectionist. She couldn't imagine how her crumpled-looking father had hooked up with her never-a-hair-out-of-place mother.

Still, they'd done well together.

Until her father's disappearance.

Her glance fell on the journal she'd brought down. She opened it up in her hand and started flicking through the pages. No dates, no months, no year mentioned. Some pages appeared to have a formula on them as if the owner had been a budding chemist. Other pages appeared to be rants of temper. It was worth reading, but she had so much to do she'd have to put it off for later. She had to get to work. The real work. The one that paid the bills.

In her shop, she opened her safe and pulled out the couple of items she had picked up on her last trip.

The first one was an antique necklace she hadn't been able to leave behind. Deep amber stones laced a neck collar piece connected to an older-looking chain. It was probably not the original combination and not likely worth anything, but it was beautiful nonetheless. She busied herself cleaning it up, testing the closures, and double-checking the settings. It was a wonderful piece and ready to go.

She had a buyer in mind for this one. Charlotte Donste was a diehard for the necklace collar style. Living in the South, she bought items from anywhere, but they had to be collars. Sari took several pictures of the necklace in different lights and angles then set up to email the pictures off to

Charlotte.

With that done, she pulled out the small jade statue she'd found on her last trip as well. It appeared to be a fertility statue; only it had diamonds for eyes – another unusual combination. She loved the unique. It always gave her a thrill.

She went through the same process with the statue, but instead of emailing them off to a buyer, she uploaded the best of the pictures to her website and inserted another copy to her catalog in progress.

She sat back with a sense of satisfaction. Now she could pull out the timepiece. She could never resist buying them when she found ones like the one her father had. They always were a disappointment in that they were never exactly what she was looking for, but like a moth to a flame, she kept picking them up.

Carefully, she unwrapped this one. It had a soft cleaning cloth around it when she'd first seen it; that alone had made her want to snatch it up. Peeling back the soft cloth, she turned on her special lamp and took a careful look at the markings on the outside of the timepiece. Excitement churned inside her stomach. It had similar markings to her father's piece. Or rather, the piece her father had been working on when he'd disappeared.

She snatched up her camera and snapped several photos of the exterior of the watch. She'd compare the images to the ones her father had taken years ago of his watch.

Then she opened it up.

A plain clock face, a simple design, but…it had the same markings inside as her father's old piece. Excitement clawed at her. This was the first one she'd seen since. She swallowed hard and took more photos. She hadn't really imagined that there'd be a double of the same watch. She'd hoped there would be, she'd dreamt there would be, but inside after all this time she hadn't really believed it would be possible.

Now she couldn't contain her excitement. It was so great she had to get up and walk around a bit and calm down. On impulse, she returned to the safe and pulled out the old notes and photos her father had made of the watch he'd vanished with and spread them out gently on her second table. She studied the two watches, comparing the similarities and the differences.

According to the notes and what she could see, both were made of silver, both with aged patina. Both were found wrapped in soft cleaning cloths from a more modern era. She hadn't been able to locate the artist's name of her father's watch listed anywhere; however, it appeared similar to this second watch. So they were likely from the same watchmaker or an apprentice.

The interiors were similar but not identical. The hands on the new timepiece had sharp points off the side as if showing some artistic license. The one her father had been working on had straight, no-nonsense points.

A minor difference showed the second watch was intended for a different class of client. The first was meant for a working man, and the second for a businessman or a wealthy man who needed something a little more special. Typical.

She wondered if the original watchmaker had any idea where his watches would end up or the amount of trouble the first one would cause.

She shook her head at the fanciful thought. These pieces were old; now if only she could figure out how old. There were these inconsistencies about them that had kept her and the specialists she'd consulted guessing. And that didn't make her happy.

It should be possible to say it was made in the early 1800s, for instance. And true enough, it might have been, but she couldn't prove it.

She walked back to her new piece. It appeared to be just an updated model of her father's, yet just as old. She pulled out her tools and sat down in front of it. Her hand trembled so badly she was forced to put the tools back down again.

"Nuts!" She sat back and took a deep breath. "It shouldn't be this hard." But it was. She hadn't been able to shake what she'd seen happen to her father all these years, and the memory sat beside her every day since.

That the same fate might happen to her wasn't an issue; it was the hope of finding out what had happened to her father. To know for sure. To put that ghost to rest.

To be able to move on in life.

To move forward.

She picked up her tools and deliberately took the face off the timepiece. Lifting it away carefully, she placed it on top of the soft cleaning cloth then tilted the light so she could look at the insides of the machine.

Unlike the others she'd seen in the last fifteen years, this one looked…different. She sat back, puzzled. It was busier. But how? Then she saw it. There were markings on the casing underneath the working pieces similar to the outside of the timepiece.

Odd. She walked over to her father's notes and studied the photos again. She should have them remembered by heart by now.

Disappointment made her stomach clench. No, wait. She bent to study the interior closer. She still couldn't see.

She tilted the lamp slightly and moved her big magnifying glass closer over the image and gasped. There, when the light hit it just right…it had the same markings as the new timepiece. Only fainter, softer, or more worn away. She couldn't quite tell.

Fascinating. Exciting and terrifying.

She'd finally found a watch similar to the one her father had all those years ago. Similar, but not the same. And she had no idea what to do with it now. She didn't know how similar either – or rather, how different.

She got up and walked to the window of the shop. Her hands shook so badly she wanted to stuff them into her mouth to hold back the building scream threatening to pour forth. Was this the moment she'd been waiting for? Since her father's disappearance, every moment in time had come down to this one. She'd searched, planned, tried to find a matching unit to her father's piece.

But why? Did she really feel like she could bring him back? Or that a matching one would give her a matching experience – and take her to wherever the first one had taken her father?

All of it was ludicrous. She loved her father, but he was gone.

And she wasn't going to be able to get him back.

She spun around, narrowing her gaze at the new time-piece. She shuddered. Or was she?

CHAPTER 6

IT WAS LUDICROUS, and still she couldn't get the idea out of her mind.

Should she try it now or wait for the anniversary day? No. She needed to wait.

She stared at the markings that were so much clearer on this timepiece. She grabbed her notepad and camera and took a series of close up shots for her computer. She wanted to research the markings to see if there were any language or meanings she could find. They had to mean something.

The phone rang. She groaned, not wanting to leave what she was doing. Her mother. She ignored the call, hoping she'd give up. After fifteen rings, she finally did. Sari glanced at her voicemail, playing the recording. Her mother's voice was disturbingly high-pitched. "Call me. Something odd has happened. I know you're there. Please call me."

Shit. Something was wrong. Her mother never said please.

Sari dialed, waiting impatiently for her mother to pick up. Nothing. Sari dialed again, this time fear making it hard to punch the right buttons. Thankfully her mother answered. "Mom, what's the matter?"

"We had a break-in. I'm okay, just a little nervous. The police have just left. Boris is staying to keep me company."

Boris? Sari didn't want to know. "Did they take anything?"

"I don't know. I tried to take a close look, but it's so hard. They were in my bedroom. *My bedroom.*"

Sari could almost see her mother's delicate shudders. This time, she was in full agreement. "I'm so sorry, Mom. I had one a couple of days ago and know exactly how you feel."

"What?" her mother shrieked. "Why didn't you tell me?"

"I didn't want to worry you. I'm getting a new security system installed, and that should deter anyone else looking for quick cash."

"That's terrible." Her mother's voice was outraged. "Both of us in the span of a couple of days? How unbelievable."

Yeah, a little too unbelievable. It was a big coincidence, something Sari had a hard time believing in anyway. Surely the two break-ins couldn't be connected. "Mom, any idea if they were looking for anything specific?"

"The police asked the same thing. I don't know. Of all the rooms in this house, why my bedroom?"

"What do you keep there?"

"Nothing expensive. My clothes and a few personal trinkets from your father. Everything valuable is in the safe, you know that."

"Obviously the intruders didn't, though." But her mind had glommed onto the personal trinket comment. Since when did her mother have anything personal of her father's? And if she had, why keep them a secret from Sari?

"Harrumph. I don't like it, I can tell you. I feel violated. And I have a security system." She sniffed. "Little good that did."

"Did it not go off?"

"They cut the wires or something like that. Disabled it, I think the police said. Now I'll have to get that fixed, too."

Sari couldn't shake the idea that was hammering away in the back of her mind. "What kind of trinkets from Dad do you have, and did they take any?"

"I never checked. Why would I – it's not like they are worth anything. Your father never had any money to spend on the good stuff." There was that *born with money, raised with money*, and with the exception of the years she lived with Sari's father, *lived with money* snobbery.

"No, but he had the house, Mom. It's not like he had nothing. Many people have so much less." Sari rubbed the bridge of her nose. "Could you check to see if any of those trinkets are missing, please?" She waited a moment for her mother to sigh heavily. "And how come I don't know anything about them?"

"Because you are too obsessed as it is about your father's disappearance, that's why. I didn't want to show you anything that would set you off on another of your rampages."

Rampages? Sari rolled her eyes. She dared any other child to have experienced what she'd gone through and not be obsessed. But there's no way she'd gone on any rampages. Trust her mother to exaggerate.

"I'm looking now. I don't know that the thieves would have even gotten to this drawer. I'm sure they were looking for cash or jewelry or electronics."

"Maybe, but one never knows these days what people are thinking. They might have known about Dad."

"So what if they did? Your dad was a jewelry repairman, and that's all he was."

"He was so much more, Mom." The waspish tone of

voice set Sari's back up. "I'm sorry you weren't happy with him, but he was a good man."

"Well, he's been gone a long time, so whatever he was no longer matters."

But it does, the small child who'd watched him disappear cried out. *He matters.* Sari knew the old echo wouldn't be well received by her mother. Lisbeth had moved on, and that's what she wanted Sari to do.

And Sari would, as soon as she found out what happened to her father.

"I can't see anything missing. There was only an old ring of his, and his first watch that he got from his great-grandfather."

"A watch?" Sari hopped to her feet and stormed around the small room. "He left you a watch?" Her heart threatened to jump out of her throat. Why was she just hearing about his now? "Do you still have it?"

"I just said so, didn't I?" Lisbeth snapped. "Besides, they wouldn't have found it anyway – it was under an old set of books of his. I'm sure they weren't anything of interest."

"What kind of books?" Sari marched over to the bookshelf in the shop. The top shelf was only three quarters full. She'd often wondered if more had belonged there. In her memories, the bookshelf was stuffed full.

"They were books from his great-grandfather. The only reason I took them was he told me they were very valuable." She snorted. "I had them appraised when we first arrived in France. Worthless. They are all worthless. Like everything else he had."

Oh good Lord. Sari closed her eyes against her mother's mercenary streak. Her mother was *so* wrong.

"Then if they are worthless, can I have them?" Sari held

her breath. Her mother had a crafty mind. She wasn't the most open and generous soul around when it came to something you really wanted. If it was money, now that she handed over in buckets. But something sentimental, as if understanding it was worth so much more…you were so not going to get it.

"Why?"

This was the tricky part. "I'd like to keep his stuff all together. I just put everything on the one wall in the shop. It's behind glass so I don't have to dust it."

She winced. It was also behind glass so she could lock it up. Not that a thief wouldn't be happy to break glass to get at it. "The books should join his other books. Who knows, maybe someone will need them one day."

Lisbeth sniffed again. "I suppose. At least it's one less thing for me to cart around. Don't be thinking they have any value though. I told you they were assessed."

"That's fine. I don't care."

Her mother grudgingly agreed. "Fine, then. But you'll have to come home to pick them up."

Sari rolled her eyes. Of course she would. "I might be in England next week." She mentally calculated the time she had at the end of her trip as to how she could swing home and get her father's stuff. In truth, she wanted to rush across the ocean today and get it. She couldn't believe her mother had been keeping this from her all these years. When she went home this time, she'd make her mother hand over everything.

It could very likely be what the thieves had wanted after all.

WARD DROVE UP to Sari's house and parked in the driveway. He got out and walked to the front of the house, staring up at the new window. From where he stood, there was no way anyone could have known that small room had existed. Now with the window already in place, he had a hard time imagining it had never been there.

As he stood there, Sari opened the front door. "Admiring my new window?"

"And roof."

She smiled and joined him on the front lawn, turning to look up at the front of the house. "It looks good, doesn't it?"

"Yup. Find anything of value in the attic?"

She shook her head and led the way back inside. "Not really. There appears to be old clothes and belongings from people long gone. I'm hoping to trace some of them and learn more about my family history, but they didn't leave much behind."

"If you have anything recent, I might be able to run them at the office. Of course, if they've never had any run-ins with the law, nothing is liable to pop."

"True, but it would be a place to start. Some of the stuff appears to be quite old. Maybe fifty years. It's hard to say at this point. I've only gone through one pile of stuff. A tall male is about all I know." She grinned. "I doubt there's a database for that, huh?"

"Only if he's missing, then we have a height and weight description along with any other discerning marks."

"Hmmm, but how far back? Computers have only been around for what – fifteen, twenty years?"

"Some of the other material is in microfiche, and some of it is in files."

"Actually, the library is probably a good place to look –

after the Internet."

"And don't forget to check genealogy sites. They would probably be the best resource."

"I'd never thought of that." She grinned. "This is great. I could learn all kinds of things there."

He smiled. God, she was pretty. Then again he was biased, having been smitten for years. And it showed no signs of easing now. "What are you up to today?"

She glanced at the shop. "I'm leaving for England and France in a few days and have a few pieces to work on, so I'll be taking them with me."

"Jewelry pieces?"

"In this case, yes." She smiled. "I'll be gone for three to four days this time."

"Did you get your security system set up in the meantime? After the last break-in, it would be a shame to leave the house wide open for them to have a second try."

She winced. "Thanks for the reminder."

"Just trying to be careful."

"Well, I'm happy to say the security system upgrade is supposed to happen tomorrow."

He grinned. "Good." He hesitated a brief moment. "Are you going to see your mother on this trip?"

That made her wince. Sari sighed, propping her chin on the palm of one hand. "I hadn't planned on it, but I just found out that my mother's house was broken into last night as well. She's finally told me she has some of my father's belongings she's been keeping safe all these years. I'm going to retrieve them."

"Valuable?"

"My father said they were, but she had them appraised and found them to be worthless."

"But not to you?"

Her face softened. "No, not to me. I'm wondering if the books she has of his are the ones from that shelf." She pointed up to the open space in the bookshelf.

"Does it matter?"

She shook her head. "No, not really. It would be just another mystery solved. In my head, I see the bookshelf full from the last time I saw it as a child. When I came back, the shelf was no longer full."

"Then it probably is those books." Ward walked over to take a look at the volumes. "Wow – time travel, time space continuum, timepiece repair. Crossing time." He turned back to look at her. "Really? He believed in time travel?"

She shrugged. "I don't know what he believed. I was too young back then to discuss it with him. Now I'd give anything for a day with him." She sighed. "The things we don't value until it's gone."

"Except you did value him. And he knew it," Ward said seriously.

She smiled, the shadows in her eyes lightening. "Thanks. I hope he did."

CHAPTER 7

BEFORE HE LEFT, Ward helped Sari to haul more boxes from the small attic down to her shop. She'd planned to give away or recycle anything that was of no value, and hopefully she could find something personal to identify those who'd owned the various belongings. She had a family tree somewhere around, but she didn't think it went back very far. Maybe four generations. She spun around in the shop, wondering where it had last been.

Her eyes lit on the half empty bookshelf. She needed to get those items back from her mother. Who knew what information her father had deemed valuable? She would have them in a couple of days, but that was too long. Maybe she should have had her mother priority ship them. No, they were too valuable. What if something went wrong and they were lost or damaged?

In the meantime, she stared at the orderly mess in her shop. Maybe she should have left everything upstairs like Ward had suggested. No, of course she couldn't do that. It would have been the easy answer.

Time to get to work. She packed the clothing and other items she wasn't keeping neatly into boxes, then set them against the back wall to deal with later. Grabbing another box, she opened it up and dug in. This set of belongings all appeared to be from a woman. There were dresses, underclothes, shoes, hair clips, and handkerchiefs, putting the belongings somewhere in the sixties as far she could see. Interesting. This person should be on the family tree then. She continued to go through box after box, but outside of a few trinkets, there were no books, journals, pictures, or any other identifying items. There was a beautiful handheld mirror. It appeared to be real silver, and there were tiny jewels or cut glass pieces inlaid in a delicate pattern around the edge and the front of the handle. On the back in a big ornately carved circle were the initials *MH*.

Sari sat back on her heels. MH? Offhand, she couldn't think of any relative with a name starting with that letter. Not that there were many relatives. Her father had been an only child. His mother had also been an only child. His father had a sister though, who'd died as a young woman. Damn, she couldn't remember her name, but she'd have lived about the right time. Sari stared down at the mirror.

This was likely to be her belongings.

Maybe the parents couldn't bear to part with them. As Sari surveyed the sad pile, she decided there wasn't much here to remember a child by. As she repacked the various items of clothing, she searched pockets and creases, looking for anything she might have missed. Still nothing. She shrugged and packed it all away again – except for the mirror.

The mirror was special. She laid it out on her shop desk and studied it. She had no plans to sell it, not when it was from a family member long gone, but it looked old. Very old.

Sari realized that although she'd barely started in on the piles of stored belongings, she was already tired. Tea time, then. Maybe she'd recoup enough energy to continue. She wandered into the kitchen and filled the teakettle, and as she waited, she checked her emails. There were several responses she'd been looking for, one from the customer she'd emailed about the necklace and another about a small statue. Good…sales.

There were several business emails that she took a moment to answer before she clicked on the last one. It was from Brodin, her father's old friend. She'd kept in touch with him over the years. In fact, he'd been a big help to her and her mom back when her father disappeared. He'd been on the fringe, not quite a friend but also not quite a stranger.

She read the message. Stopped, leaned forward, and read it again. "*Found any interesting watches lately? I hear you came home with a special one from your last trip. Interested, as always.*"

Not possible. How could he have known? Then Sari laughed. The collector's world was small and if she'd been at the show, chances were good he'd been there too. Maybe not at the same time, but who knew – although she'd like to think he'd have come up and said hi to her.

She read the short three-sentence message again then started to type out her response. "Not sure how you knew, but I did indeed make an interesting find on my last trip. Too early to tell how interesting," and she sent it off. He was also one of the few people to have heard her and her mother's garbled version of events as he'd come by with the second watch in the set soon after her father disappeared. Her father was supposed to wait for his return so they could compare the two watches. Instead, her father had been so interested he'd taken an early look.

Lucky for Brodin that he hadn't been there at the time. Maybe they'd both have disappeared.

Brodin had given her and her mother both long, disbelieving looks at the time, deciding they were hysterical females, and that her father had finally washed his hands of them. He proceeded to come up with a more factual version.

Then he'd called the police.

As she'd grown older, she hadn't been able to forget his watch had supposedly been one of the matched set. She'd asked him about it early on, but his had been stolen a few years after her father's disappearance. He'd been looking for it ever since.

So had she. It was likely her closest link to finding out what happened to her father.

FOUR DAYS LATER, she sat back in her plane seat and waited for the hubbub around her to die down. She'd finished her business in England and should be at her mother's in time for dinner. She patted her oversized purse in her lap. Business had gone well. Very well, actually. She grinned. In fact, it had gone excellent, if her new purchases turned out to be half as good as she thought they would. Now if only her mother's visit went half as well.

After stowing away her bag, she leaned back and closed her eyes. To her surprise, she slept. She came awake at the sound of the *Fasten seatbelts* signs coming on and the captain's voice pouring through the cabin.

She blinked several times to reorient herself. Straightening her seat, she buckled up. Looking out the window, she saw the bright lights below. Sunlight twinkled and caught on the glass surfaces.

A beautiful sight, and still nothing inside called to her. For her entire life, she'd been trying to get back home. The home she'd grown up in. The home she'd been forced to leave. The home she'd loved.

She'd always be just a visitor here.

And a reluctant one at that.

Hours later, one of the reasons for her reluctance was in full force.

"I've changed my mind. It's my right," her mother pouted. Her lips literally curled and her voice became childlike. Sari stared, and in spite of her mother's words, humor crinkled her insides. The older her mother got, the more obstinate and manipulative she became.

A part of her hated it. Another part recognized it for what it was – an attempt to bind her to her mother. Her father's possessions were one more thing she could hold over Sari's head.

And she loved to play mind games like that. Sari hated them. And with every passing year, she hated it a little more.

"It's not yours anymore. You gave them to me. Therefore you can't change your mind. I will take the items home with me. If you continue to try to stop me, you can bet it will be a long time before I return." Sari kept her voice even and flat, letting her voice show how she really felt over her mother's tricks.

"But I didn't hand them over. So you can't take them." Coolly, her mother walked over to the side table and refilled her wine glass then walked out onto the patio. Cool evening air wafted across Sari's face as she joined her.

"I'm sorry you feel that you have to do things like this in order to keep control over me. It's not going to work. My father's items are not yours, and I will not allow you to play games with them. You know how important they are to me."

"And I know that you won't ever visit unless I have

something to give you."

Considering she'd only been gone from France for six weeks, that was hardly fair. But it was so typical of her drama queen mother. "I would have come to visit, but it would be on my time, not by you jerking the family strings just because you can."

Lisbeth sniffed. "I didn't do that."

Sari laughed. "Yes, you did. You always do. You're very generous, but you like to keep dragging me back. I need to be home and get my house in order. It won't be long, a couple of months, but with my business trips already taking me away, I can't afford the time."

This time, it was Lisbeth's turn to laugh and it was much colder. In an icy voice, she said, "What you mean is that it's almost the anniversary of your father's disappearance, and you want his things to once again try to figure out what happened."

Sari's gaze sharpened. She studied her mother's face before turning away abruptly. She walked to the edge of the patio and stared out into the blackness of the evening, the lights of the neighbors the only illumination in the sky. After a long moment she tried to explain, knowing her mother had yet to listen. "I have to. I need to know what happened."

"Nothing happened," her mother cried. "Your father walked out the door one day and never came home."

Sari spun on her heels. "Really? After all this time, you're still trying to stuff that garbage down my throat?" She glared in disbelief. "You might want to rewrite history to suit you, but I was there, remember? I saw him pick up the watch and disappear like a puff of smoke in front of me. I saw it. And for all your lies you've tried to feed me in the years since, I've not forgotten it."

Her mother tried to stuff her fist in her mouth as she looked at Sari with wounded eyes.

Sari closed hers briefly. "Mom, I can't forget. I loved him. And I miss him so much."

"He's gone. Can't you accept that?"

"No." Sari stared into her mother's eyes, willing her to understand. "I can't. I have to explain what I saw, and I want to know where my father is."

"He's gone. That's all there is to know."

Sari clenched her jaw. As she stared into her mother's face, she realized it was fear that hid in the back of her eyes. Whatever had happened, she was afraid of something happening again. She was most likely afraid for Sari herself. "Are you afraid that whatever happened to Dad might also happen to me?"

Her mother's gaze widened in shock. She swallowed hard. "You're playing with something you don't understand. You can't know what forces are coming into play. If he disappeared, what will keep you safe?"

"Oh, Mom." Sari understood her mother's fear. "Isn't it better to find out now so I can finally put the past to rest?"

"Not if I lose you too."

She wanted to be able to reassure her mother that all would be well, but how could she when she'd been living with the one inexplicable fact – it hadn't gone so well for her father. "Do you know anything about all the goods stored in the attic?"

Her mother's headshake was too fast to be believable. Sari studied her face, only her mother refused to meet her gaze.

"You do know something. What?"

At her mother's continued silence, Sari started to get

angry. "You know something and you won't tell me. Really? Knowing that I've spent my entire life looking for him? Even now that I am of age, you're still holding out on me?" Her anger built. "What do you know?" she snapped. "Tell me."

Lisbeth lifted her head higher. "I don't know anything for sure. Just some stories your father shared years ago."

"Tell me, please." Sari tried to tamp down her impatience.

"I can't remember," Lisbeth whined. She lifted her wine glass and took a long sip.

"Mom, please."

Lisbeth looked at Sari. "Oh, all right. But I don't know that I recall everything."

"I'll take what you can."

With an abrupt move, Lisbeth turned and walked back inside the well-lit room, her heels clicking on the Italian marble tiles. "In that case, I need another glass of wine."

Sari hid her smile. Her mother wasn't looking for fortification as much as she was looking for an excuse to come up with a way out. She knew her too well. However, if Sari had made some headway with her here, she didn't want to lose it.

She followed her mother inside.

With her back to Sari, Lisbeth took a drink of wine. "I only know that some people in your father's line have disappeared...died, you might say, under suspicious circumstances over the years."

"Really?" Why had she waited until now to mention this? Sari waited impatiently. When nothing more was forthcoming, she prodded slightly. "And? What else?"

Her mother turned slightly and lifted her shoulders. "Nothing, really. They never had any answers. And if you were to check his family line against any other family line, you'd find his is completely normal. Every family has some oddities in their history." She raised a cool eyebrow then sat down on the leather couch, crossing her legs in a sophisticated movement.

The grace, the regal tone to her actions caught Sari's attention. She frowned. "Mom, I've always wanted to ask you something." She took the seat across from her mother. She probably shouldn't ask this, but the sight of her mother's cool richness brought back the puzzle she'd wondered about in her mind a lot over the last few years.

"What's that?" Lisbeth raised her wine glass again.

"Why did you marry Father?"

The wine glass stopped in mid-air. Lisbeth eyes cooled to an iciness Sari hadn't seen directed at her much in life. She stared back blandly. "I don't mean to be rude, but look at you. Wine and pearls, marble and leather, expensive and classy."

The ice in her mother's gaze eased. Sari continued. "Father was rumpled cotton t-shirts and jeans. A cup of tea or a cold beer. He loved that old house and you…you hated it."

Lisbeth smiled, a chill to her patrician features. "Yes, I did."

"So why Father? He wasn't your type at all." Should she ask the question that she'd always wanted to ask but hadn't dared? "Were you pregnant? Is that why you married him?"

Silence.

Her mother refused to meet her gaze. Sari was afraid that meant yes.

"Mother?" Sari narrowed her gaze. "What was he – a quick dip into the ocean of lower class peons for you or something?"

Lisbeth's nostrils pinched at her words. "It's none of

your business."

"I'm not so sure about that. Maybe I'm adopted." She'd often wondered if Lisbeth was even her birth mother but hadn't been able to come up with a scenario that explained her keeping Sari with her if she wasn't. They looked nothing alike. Inside, they couldn't be more opposite. In her bad times, she'd hoped she'd been adopted. In her good times, she'd still wondered.

"How dare you say that to me?" Lisbeth glared at her. "I am your birth mother. You know that. If you are going to insult me, then I will say good night."

"And I'll head to the airport. I need to get home soon anyway." Sari stood up and walked to the front door where her coat and bags were standing. "I'll take Father's belongings now too, please."

The two women stood in an icy standoff.

Finally, Lisbeth's shoulders eased back and her voice when she spoke had a conciliatory tone. "Stay overnight, please."

Sari stared at her, knowing that to back down without having established her position was a mistake. "If – and only if – you hand over *all* of Father's belongings right now."

Relief washed over her mother's face. But she couldn't give in quite so easily. "Fine. Then follow me." Her nose in the air, she led the way to her bedroom. Sari followed curiously. She'd not been welcome into her mother's lair very often.

She didn't know when it would happen again. She gazed around the opulent bedroom with red velvet walls and chocolate with gold embroidered bedding. The floor was a lush cream carpet to help the impression along.

To Sari it was her mother all over again, and for Sari it

was way too much. She loved clean wood lines and light. Sunshine. She'd put a skylight in here and open up the darkness to the bright light of day.

Her mother walked over to the large picture hanging on the wall and flipped it back and away. A small safe could be seen. Sari raised an eyebrow in surprise. She hadn't known about that.

Within a few minutes, her mother had the door open and was reaching into the depths. She pulled out a dark cloth bag and several books. Lisbeth peered inside, and satisfied she had what she'd come for, she closed and locked the safe behind her. Flipping the picture back to hide the safe, she shifted the items in her arms. After a moment, she turned and walked over to Sari. She stared down at the items for a long moment then held them out for Sari. "Take them. I don't want them any longer anyway."

An odd look on her face, Lisbeth stared at the books now clutched tight against Sari's chest. She said, "I never wanted them."

"Did you hate him so much then?" Sari couldn't help asking. She hated the thought that her father might have not been well loved. He'd been such a wonderful man, and it hurt to think he'd been unhappy. At least from her mother. Sari had loved him; maybe that had been enough.

"No, I didn't hate him." She gazed at some past issue over Sari's head. "But I wasn't very happily married to him."

"Were you happy when he disappeared?"

Lisbeth's gaze narrowed once again, a muscle ticking away to a steady beat in her jaw. "Happy? No. I was left with a huge mess. There were bills to pay, police wandering around asking questions, and I had no answers."

Ouch. Sari winced. For all her mother's areas of skills,

handling questions wasn't one of them. She didn't remember much of her mother's behavior in the days immediately following her father's disappearance. She'd been in shock, so busy trying to find her father she'd not been paying attention to her mother's difficulties.

Her own thoughts turning back in time, Sari frowned. In fact, she'd not been very easy to get along with at all. Screaming and crying out for her Poppy. Her mother hadn't had answers or been capable of handling their now-turbulent relationship that had never been close, but up until then, with Poppy to keep the balance, had always been loving. Just not adoring.

"I'm sorry. As a child, I'd been focused only on my father," she began, intending to say more, when her mother's harsh laugh interrupted her.

"What's your excuse now?" Lisbeth sneered. "You're *still* only focused on your father's disappearance."

A hard truth. Sari swallowed. "I know that, but I'm not obsessed with it." At her mother's disbelieving snort, she cried out, "I'm not, but I can't let it go. If he disappeared, then maybe he can return."

Shocked silence filled the room, widening the distance between them.

Her mother's sorrow-filled gaze locked on her. "No, honey, don't ever think that. He can't come back. It's not possible."

"Why? How do you know that? He wouldn't be so old now. He's only been gone fifteen years. Maybe he's in another part of the world or something. Someplace he can return from." Even Sari could hear the little child in her voice, hoping against all hope that the impossible could happen.

"Is this what you have been working toward, focusing on, waiting for? Sari, you have to accept the truth…he's gone. If he could have come back, he would have."

It was an undeniably logical answer, but one that Sari couldn't accept. "He might not have been able to. Did you ever *try* to find him? To help him?" She couldn't believe they were finally having this conversation she'd been pushing for after so many years. She'd needed to ask these questions for so long, and her mother had always clammed up over the subject. Not today. She pushed forward. "The police, did they have any idea? Is he listed as a missing person? Is his file still open?"

"I don't know." Lisbeth tugged at the sleeves of her dress, straightening the already-perfect material. "I didn't know what to tell them. What could I say? That he'd vanished into a puff of smoke? If it hadn't been for Brodin, I'd likely have been locked up in a psych ward or arrested for his murder."

"But he did disappear into a puff of smoke – more or less. He snatched up the watch before I could and a weird look came over his face and he just faded away in front of me."

"Do you understand how crazy you sound?" Lisbeth stared at Sari, fearful concern in her eyes. "You know what the police are going to say if you tell them that story – right?"

"I know. But the way you told it, everyone would have assumed you two had a fight, so he's run off somewhere else to get away."

"Some people did believe that. When a family member disappears like your father did, you certainly find out who your friends are. Everyone would point at me, whisper behind my back." She gave a delicate shudder. "It was horrible."

And for her mother who held pride up as a shield, it would have been. No wonder they'd left within weeks. "If we hadn't left so fast, I might not have felt like I needed to go back."

"I doubt it." As if suddenly weary of the conversation, Lisbeth walked over to the sideboard and set her wine glass down. "I had no choice but to leave fast. I couldn't sleep for fear of the police showing up at my door to arrest me. I was the last one to have seen him alive."

She shuddered. "I hated your father for a long time. Hated that he'd left me alone to deal with the mess." Bitterness deepened the lines of her face. "You were a child. You were never a suspect. You had no idea what I went through all those years ago. But that didn't stop you from judging me and hating me." She spun around to stare at Sari. "You were everything to your father and he was everything to you. Do you know what that was like for me? I was a third wheel. You were my daughter but only wanted to spend time with him."

Her harsh gaze suddenly switched to an ageless weariness. "And nothing has changed. You're still focused only on him. You never could spare me a few moments of your time. Look at you. You wanted to go to boarding school to get away, live in residence at university to stay away, and as soon as you could, you moved back to his house." She closed her eyes. "And you're only here now because you wanted your father's possessions. It wasn't to see me. It wasn't because you cared to spend time with your mother – no, it was once again due to your father. Even dead, he steals all you have to give."

Sari didn't know what to say as the tirade rolled free. How long had her mother been holding that mess in? Forever. She sagged into the closest chair. Had it really been that bad for her mother? If she listened to her words right now, then maybe. It couldn't have been easy being the one left behind. No answers to give people, no answers to give her daughter. She hadn't been a manager before her father's disappearance, so after he'd gone, she'd been forced to cope. No wonder she'd run back home…it would have felt safe.

"Why did we leave so quickly?"

Her mother shook her head, a broken laugh escaping. "It wasn't quick, Sari. You just don't remember. We stayed almost two months. Two whole months where I wanted to escape every day. Two months of hell. Finally, I couldn't take it anymore. I figured if he could have returned, he would have, and when he didn't, he was gone forever. I woke up one morning and realized it was over. He was gone and I was going to have to carry on – alone. You were impossible. The neighbors were falsely solicitous and the police – well, they were just plain suspicious."

"I'm sorry." And she was. It was the first time she'd really understood how difficult it had been for her mother so long ago. Sari had missed a lot of it. "Honestly, I am. I hadn't considered the difficulties from your viewpoint."

"I know. You've always been very narrow-minded on the subject of your father. You refused to forget him, and I'd do anything to do so."

"And that brings back the question of why you married him. I know he and I were close and you were out of the loop somewhat, but I find it hard to believe that you were happy before I was born."

Her mother's face pinched tighter again. She stared at

Sari, then off in the distance. "I wanted to live in France. Your father refused."

"Surely you knew his home wasn't here. He had the house, the business…"

"The business was nothing. We barely made a living." Her lips thinned. "It was no living at all."

Sari frowned. "You mean it wasn't the life you were accustomed to."

"No, it wasn't. And what's wrong with having a comfortable lifestyle?"

"Nothing, if you have it to enjoy."

"Well I did, obviously."

"But why not enjoy your money over there? Why not invest it in the business or in the house or for the comforts you wanted?"

"Not there. Not in *that* house," she snapped. "I wanted *my* life back."

Sari shook her head. "So what – Father was a one-night stand and you ended up pregnant? Felt you had to marry him or something? You had money. You could have come home."

"Not without a husband. My parents would have cut me off. I'd have had nothing. Not a penny. But your father wouldn't listen to reason. He wouldn't move. He kept saying we didn't need anything but ourselves. That it would all work out. That we were happy and that was all counted."

"And he was right." Sari remembered her father's joyous attitude to life. He'd been an optimist but not necessarily a good businessman. He'd help out a neighbor in need and hand over the food in his cupboards to anyone who needed a meal. "His heart had been in the right place."

"He was a fool. Our house could have been so much more. Our life could have been so much more."

"No, Mom, we had all we needed. Only for you, it was never enough."

"No, it was not. There was so much more we could have had. He refused. He didn't want to live at my parents' home."

Sari choked up at that. "Of course not. He was a man with a home – a family – of his own. He wouldn't want to live here. He had a business, a life there. He didn't even speak French."

"So, he could have learned. He was smart, capable."

"He was a man. And you were his wife."

"You make that sound like a prison sentence." She snorted. "And I guess it was. I couldn't make him change, but neither could I stay and live that way."

Sari hated the thoughts that filled her head. Her tongue had no such problem. It blurted out, "Then his disappearance was a blessing."

That earned her a grim look. "Don't you say that. A divorce would have been a better answer. I could have taken you and come home. My parents might not have been happy, but they would have provided for us."

"Is that all you've wanted out of life? To be provided for? Did you never want to do something with your life? Be something?"

Lisbeth snorted. "I am someone. I don't need to go to school or to do anything to become someone. I am someone just the way I am."

Her mother had never lacked self-confidence. And seeing that lightened the mood for Sari. Her mother was who she was. And in truth, she did love her. She felt sorry for her father though. And for the first time, she wondered what would have happened to the family unit if her father hadn't disappeared. "True enough. And now I need to go to bed." She stood up. "I'll see you in the morning."

Lisbeth smiled and stood to hug her daughter lightly. "Sleep well."

"You too." Sari smiled and walked up to her bedroom, the same bedroom she'd had since they'd arrived so long ago.

She stared at the childish room, wondering why she'd refused her mother's offers to redecorate. The same pink walls and frilly curtains from decades ago framed the pink bedding and teddy bears that decorated the pillows.

Then of course she knew. Changing her room would have been saying goodbye to her childhood, and that would have meant saying goodbye to her childhood dream – the return of her father.

And that was something she could never do.

CHAPTER 8

SARI UNLOCKED THE door to her home gratefully. It had been a short and emotionally draining trip.

"Hey Sari."

Startled, she spun around, almost dropping her bag.

"Whoa. Sorry. I didn't mean to scare you." Ward raced up the last step to take the leather satchel from her arms. "I was coming to update you on the case when I saw you arrive."

"I just flew in."

"I would have picked you up." Ward pushed the door open for her. She stepped across into the hallway, and he picked up her overnight bag to bring it inside.

"Thanks. You can just leave the bag there in the hallway." She smiled at him over her shoulder.

He placed the bag at the bottom of the stairs. "How was your trip?"

"Both good and bad. I picked up a couple of gems in London and then went to see my mother."

He glanced over at her. She smiled wryly. "My mother is a piece of work. She wouldn't give me my father's possessions if I didn't fly there and get them."

"Sounds like a normal mother." He grinned.

"I guess." Sari grimaced. "Maybe she is at that. I haven't been close to many other mothers to know if they also coddle and contrive situations to suit themselves."

"That's exactly what they do." He chuckled. "At least mine does." He pulled out a chair and sat down at the kitchen table. "They aren't all bad. They usually do it out of love."

"It's that *usually* part."

He studied her intently. Even as she turned away to put on a much-needed cup of coffee, she could feel the intensity burning her back.

"Do you not get along with your mother?"

She sighed, staring out the window over the sink. "I don't know if we ever did. I was very close to my father. And since his disappearance…well, you'd think she and I would have pulled together to get over it, but…"

"But instead it's divided you further, correct?"

She spun around. At his compassionate look, her lips quirked. "Yeah, something like that. I'm more like my father and she's so very different."

"Which is maybe a good thing."

"Maybe." She straightened, turning to open the cupboard door to pull out coffee cups. She placed them on the table. "Do you take cream? I haven't been shopping in a while, so I'm not sure what I have." But there was a small carton of cream. She opened it and sniffed it experimentally.

"Smells sweet." She handed it over to him. He grinned and poured it into his coffee.

"Did you find anything special on this trip?" he asked, stirring his cup.

"Not shopping wise, but I did get a watch of my father's that my mother has been hoarding all these years."

"Oh, interesting." He studied her across the table. "Any idea why she didn't let you know about it before this?"

"Yeah, she says I was devoted to him when he was alive and became obsessed after his disappearance." She met Ward's compassionate gaze. "She didn't want to add to it."

"Back to that whole mother thing again. And what they do in the name of love."

She smiled crookedly. "Especially as I've been hunting for watches similar to the ones my father loved."

"What do they look like?" he asked.

Never sorry to show off her passion, she raced to her bags at the front stairs where he'd dropped them.

"You could have waited until tomorrow," he said, laughing by her side as he watched her dig through her carry-on bag.

"I'm happy to show you. I wanted to take a closer look as it is." She shrugged. "I didn't even take a look at my mother's place for fear she'd catch me and try to snag it away from me." She grinned as she pulled the bag free.

"Do you have a place to keep this stuff safe here? Considering you've already had one break-in."

Pointing toward the office, she said, "In my safe. And thanks for the reminder. That damn security system isn't fully operational yet." She rubbed her temple. "I'll need to check in with them immediately." She glanced around at the old but lovingly used room. "Now I have to admit I wished I had it installed before. But with the roof, window, and attic, I had a lot going on already."

SHE STARTED BACK toward the kitchen when she realized Ward wasn't following her. She glanced behind to see him studying the door handle to the shop. She froze, her pulse jolting. "What's the matter?"

"It looks like someone was trying to get in here."

"What?" She ran back and saw the gouges around the knob and the dented metal of the actual lock. As she watched, Ward grabbed the handle and tried to open the door. The lock held.

"Oh thank heavens," she murmured. She quickly unlocked the door and walked in, taking a quick look around. "It doesn't look like the intruder made it in."

"Is everything insured?"

She winced. "Yes and no. There's a top dollar amount for the plan I'm on, but my goods come and go on a regular basis so that amount could be high or low depending on the day." At his raised eyebrow, she added, "We're not talking hundreds of thousands here. Closer to thirty thousand maybe on a regular day."

"Hmmm. Do you want to take a closer look to see if anything is missing?" He looked around the shop. "Has anything been disturbed?"

"I have no idea." She groaned. "I've only begun to find out what is here in the first place." She walked over to the far desk and bent down to find her safe closed and locked. "I need to make an inventory, but I haven't got there yet. The safe is locked but that doesn't mean much. Anyone who knows safes could break in." She quickly twisted the dial first one way, then the other. When she finished, an audible click sounded. She twisted the handle and popped the door open.

She peered inside. "It's all here. Or appears to be." She rustled inside, sorting through the items she'd placed in there before she left along with the small bit of cash and gems. She stood up and opened the bag she'd taken from her luggage, tumbling the contents into her hand. Looking at it carefully, relief swept through her as she noted some of the similar markings on the watch she'd seen in her father's notes. "It looks right, at least from first glance.”

Holding it out for him to see she grinned at the look on his eyes. “See, isn’t it beautiful?”

“This is valuable?”

Her gaze widened as she whispered, staring at the watch, “Very.”

“Interesting.” He shrugged. “I’ll write this up and add it to your file. I’ll send someone over to fingerprint the door, but chances are good they used gloves. The first intruder did. What’s the chance he came back for a second look around?”

“Quite likely. Yes, please do what you need to do.” She stared down at the watch in her hand. “I want to keep this safe.”

“OKAY, BUT IT looks like any other pocket watch to me.” He grinned at the look of disgust she shot his way. “I really don’t know anything about them.”

She laughed as she carefully repackaged the watch and set it beside them on the table. She gave him a big fat grin. “It is. And it’s a great find. But I’ll need time to take it apart and photograph and catalogue the insides. There are a lot of similarities to my father’s piece, but I suspect the internal markings are different.”

“Do the markings identify the maker?”

“His signature marks are here, but the other marks are an identification system I haven’t been able to figure out yet.”

“Must be fun.”

“It is, actually.” She gave a deprecating laugh. “My life might have gone in a different direction if my father had lived, but as it was, I became obsessed with his passion.”

"You most likely would have if he'd been there all your life anyway. You were close back then – I doubt that would have changed."

He hoped that was true, because he'd been very close to Sari and he really didn't want *that* to change. He wanted to get to know her again. So far, so good. He did like that she hadn't had a recent relationship. He hated the idea of her having any. Still, she was here and they were both single. It was their time.

"So what did you say about updating me on the case?"

He stared blankly at her. "What? Oh," he flushed slightly. "I was just looking for an excuse to come by to see you."

She smiled sweetly. "You don't need an excuse. Just stop by anytime."

He couldn't help the self-conscious grin. "Thanks. I'll remember that. However, I do know that we are working on the case, but there's no sign of the guys."

She nodded. "I'm not surprised. I'm sure they're long gone. And thanks for coming by."

He took that as his cue. She was itching to get at the watch, obviously. "I'll head out and get this started." He motioned in the direction of the shop. "Take care of yourself. And I'm glad you're home safe."

"Dinner tomorrow, maybe?"

He raised an eyebrow, barely holding back a cheer. "Sure, that sounds great."

"I'll need the rest of today to get caught up and go shopping." She stood up and walked him to the front door.

He walked out into the bright sun, smiling.

Life was good.

CHAPTER 9

S ARI WALKED BACK inside, closed and locked the door behind Ward. First thing tomorrow, she needed to get that security system functional.

She picked up the watch she'd brought home, desperate to see what that marking had been. Back in her shop, she turned on the lights over the desk and sat down. Her hands were almost shaking as she took pictures of each layer as she carefully took it apart, carefully documenting each step.

Inside were similar markings to the original. Similar but unique.

She photographed everything then locked it all away in the safe. She'd thought the process would only take a few moments, but it ended up intense and detailed. Of course she got caught up in her work and lost hours.

A yawn caught her by surprise.

Jet lag was catching up. She secured the shop then grabbed her bag and headed up to her room.

Everything appeared undisturbed. And yet someone had been inside the house…and could have been several times before for all she knew. It made her uneasy. Even though she'd walked the house with Ward and there'd been no one hiding in it, she couldn't shake that sense of violation. She hadn't mentioned anything to him, but now that she was alone again, the feeling was amplified.

She crawled into bed and tried to sleep. But although she was tired, her mind couldn't stop spinning. She thought she drifted off to sleep, at least her clock said hours had passed. It wasn't enough though. She needed more. She dozed.

Until she heard something…off.

Her breath caught in her throat, she waited. And there it was again. She sat up. What could it have been? Finally, she realized she had to know.

Standing beside her bed in her pajamas, she realized there was one place she hadn't checked with Ward. As the shop had been locked, she hadn't considered an intruder up in the attic. Then again, no one knew about the attic.

Unless the two contractors had said something.

It's not like people cared about her old house, but the attic was a curiosity that could have been mentioned in passing. And pricked someone's interest. Shit.

She stepped into her slippers, grabbed a housecoat, and walked back downstairs. She unlocked the shop and entered, heading straight for the attic door. Using the long pole she'd left close by, she pulled open the door and climbed up the staircase. It was dark inside. She should have grabbed her flashlight, damn it. She carefully made her way over to the light switch and flicked it on.

Sari turned to look around and gasped in shock.

An old woman huddled in the far corner of the attic, her eyes closed, her shoulders trembling. How she got into Sari's home – and the attic, no less – Sari had no idea.

"Jesus." Sari took a quick look around, realizing that the woman might not be alone. But it appeared that she was.

"Who are you? And how did you get here?" She wanted to know why she was there, but from the sounds of it, the woman wouldn't be able to say much, being on the edge of collapse.

"Hiding," the old woman whispered, her voice shaky and thin. "Please…hide me."

"Huh?" Sari rushed over to her. "I can't imagine any place you'd be better hidden than here."

The woman clutched at her clothing, "Not safe. Help me, please."

"Hush, of course I'll help you." Sari wrapped an arm around her tiny body, worried at the shivers wracking the bone-thin frame. "Let's take you back downstairs and get you warm."

"No, no. I can't be seen."

"Why not?"

"Scared. Can't go back." She started to cry and buried her face in her hands. "Please help."

"Shh. We'll take care of it." Looking around, Sari found a blanket folded up on top of a box. She snatched it up and shook it free. Returning to the woman, she wrapped it up snug around her. "That should help you to warm up." She couldn't leave the woman. It was freezing up here. The heat didn't reach into the room. "Please let me take you downstairs. Or to one of the bedrooms. You can't stay here."

"No, no. They'll find me." The woman hunched up smaller and tighter into a ball. "Please help me."

"Sure. Okay, don't get upset." Only what was she to do with her unexpected and unwelcome visitor?

"What's your name?"

"Madge." The lady lifted her head and looked up slightly. "My name is Madge."

"Well, hello Madge. I'm going to go downstairs and make you a cup of tea, okay?"

Madge nodded slightly, her face losing some of its pinched look. "Thank you," she whispered. "Tea would be lovely."

Hating to leave her, Sari slipped down the ladder and ran into the kitchen. She put on the teakettle and grabbed up the phone. She called Ward.

The phone rang, then rang again.

She shifted on her feet then peered out in the direction of the hallway. She didn't want Madge to come down and panic at Sari talking to someone else.

"Come on, hurry up and answer," she muttered. She glanced at the clock on the stove and winced. It was two a.m. No wonder he wasn't answering.

"Hello," Ward said, his voice deep, husky. He cleared his throat. "Hello?"

"Ward, it's Sari."

"Sari?" Suddenly he sounded wide-awake. "What's wrong?"

"Oh, thank God you're there. I don't know what to do."

"Whoa, hang on. First off, are you in danger?"

"No. Not now. I mean, I thought I was but now it's fine. Except I don't know if it's fine because she says she has to hide, so maybe it's not all good." Sari blew a stray strand of hair out of her face, taking a deep breath. She was babbling, for Christ's sake.

"Calm down and talk to me. I'm getting dressed and I'll be there in five, but don't hang up."

She took a deep breath. "I'm sorry. I'm making a mess of this. Yes, please come over. I don't know what to do with her."

"With who?" he damn near shouted through the lines.

"Madge! Didn't I say that already?"

"Who in the blazes is Madge?"

"She's the woman I found hiding in the attic."

Silence.

In the background, she could hear doors opening and closing and the sound of an engine starting up. Then he took a deep breath and asked very quietly, "Sari, are you telling me there is a strange woman in your attic and you didn't let her in there?"

"Yes, exactly." Sari grinned, her shoulders sagging with relief. He did understand.

"Jesus. Get out the house right now until I get there, do you hear me?" His voice roared across the sound of the engine.

"I can't do that. I'm making her a cup of tea."

Shocked silence filled the line. "Sari! Stop. Please go out in the backyard until I arrive. You don't know who this woman is. You don't know what she wants or where she came from." His voice turned pleading. "Please leave right now. I'm almost there. Just stay outside until I get there."

He was serious. Something in his voice had her turning nervously to look again in the direction of the shop. Was she dangerous? Surely not. Then again, how had she gotten there and had she come with someone? That made her spin around and look outside.

"Sari?"

"I'm going."

"You should be out already," he snapped.

She let the kitchen door slam behind her. "Did you hear that? That was the kitchen door slamming behind me."

"Good. I'm almost there." He hung up.

Standing outside in the cool night air, she realized how late it was. There'd be no sleep for her this night. Damn. She could really use it too. The sound of squealing tires had her racing around the outside of her house.

Ward.

Grinning, she picked up her feet and ran around her house to the front door. He opened his arms. She rushed in and they closed tightly around her. She soaked in his loving concern like a sponge then reared back and hit him lightly on the shoulder.

"That's for scaring me half to death."

He rolled his eyes. "*I* scared you? But a person hiding out in your attic didn't?" He reached out and shook her shoulders lightly. "Do you even think about that? How did she get in? Did she come alone? Or is she a distraction?"

"A distraction? For what?" But she did understand. She stared at him in amazement. "Wow, I don't think I like the way your mind works."

He shook his head and gave her shoulders a second shake before dropping his hands. "Too many years on the force."

"That's got to be tough." Her smile sobered. "Come on. Now that you're here, we'll take a cup of tea up to Madge. Then you'll see that she needs our help, not our suspicion."

She led the way around the back of the house and in through the kitchen. While he waited, tapping his toe on the linoleum floor, she made the tea. "I forgot to ask her if she takes anything in it."

"I don't think that's the issue right now. Let's go talk to her first before we worry about her comforts."

She shot him a hard look. "You do realize she could have just wandered into my house because she's lost? Confused, even?"

"Then I can apologize. Right now I doubt her story."

Shaking her head, Sari picked up the mug of hot tea and led the way. As they came to the shop door, Ward asked, "Was this door locked?"

"Locked?" Sari stopped to consider. "I'm not sure. I usually do, but I can't remember if it was this time or not."

He nodded his head at the front door ahead of him. "What about the front door? Have you touched it?"

She shook her head. "No."

He walked over to see if it was locked. He didn't touch it, just noted that the bolt on top had been locked up tight. "And you locked it last night?"

"I'm sure I did. I always do."

Ward searched her face for a moment, then as if satisfied, he motioned for her to lead the way. Inside the shop, he walked along the front wall, checking that all the windows were secure.

"What are you looking for?"

He spun around, surprise on his face. "How do you think this woman got in?"

"I figured she broke in. That I must have left the door unlocked." She shrugged. The how wasn't bothering her as much as trying to get back and make sure the woman was still there. If she'd disappeared as suddenly as she'd appeared, Sari would be frantic with worry. The poor dear hadn't been in good shape.

"Madge? I'm coming up with a cup of tea. Sorry it took so long to make and return."

Ward, his voice low, asked, "And the stairs – were they down?"

She frowned and shook her head.

There wasn't a sound from above their heads. Madge hadn't answered.

"Shit." Sari knew she should have made it back faster. She handed the mug to Ward and clambered up the ladder. At the top, she spun around, looking for Madge. Ward came up the stairs, mug in hand, right behind her.

Madge was gone.

WARD CLIMBED THE last few steps, handing the mug over to Sari. He didn't doubt her word; it bothered him more that the woman might have taken off and hidden somewhere else in the house. Or that she'd run out the back door when they weren't looking. Sari's house had a chaotic layout. Nothing made any sense or logic. The last set of renovations made a mockery of the floor plan.

He carefully searched the small space. There was no sign of the supposed nocturnal visitor. He walked forward. At the crumpled blanket, he stopped and sent a questioning look at Sari.

"That's the blanket I wrapped around her." She chewed on her bottom lip. "Where could she have gone? It doesn't make sense. I knew I shouldn't have left her alone."

"It's not your fault." He straightened without touching the blanket. After he walked the rest of the small space, he said, "Let's check the rest of the house."

Silently they went down to the shop and made their way through every room in the house. They turned up nothing on the ground floor. Sari led the way upstairs to the left wing. The first bedroom was empty, as were the closets and bathroom. "This is useless. She's not here."

"Until we finish the search, we don't know that." He nudged her forward slightly. "Let's keep looking."

With a heavy sigh, she walked back down to the other

rooms and back to the staircase leading to her bedroom. At her bedroom, she flung the door open wide, hoping she'd picked up her clothes last night. She'd rushed out earlier without thinking she'd be bringing someone back inside.

Ward walked in, strode over to the closet, and double-checked that it was also empty. He made a half-strangled noise and crouched down.

"Sari?"

She rushed over. "Is she here?" Sari bent down. "Madge!"

The tiny woman stared up at her in terror. "Please don't hurt me."

"How did you get here?"

But Madge wasn't listening. She was too busy gnawing on the fist in her mouth, staring blindly at Ward.

"It's all right, Madge. This is a friend. He can help protect you."

Madge's gaze switched to Sari's then swiveled back again to lock onto Ward. She whimpered.

"Ward, move back slowly." Sari sat down in front of Madge and belatedly held out the cup of tea for her. "Here, take this. It will help warm you up."

The woman's gaze never wavered as Ward slowly backed up, leaving the field open for Sari. "He's not going to hurt you. He's here to help."

Madge's gaze never softened. Neither did it leave its position on Ward.

"Look at me, Madge?" Sari raised her voice sharply.

Madge spun her head to look at Sari, her eyes wild.

"Here, take your tea. Now just calm down."

The old woman stared at the cup in Sari's hands. She licked her lips.

"That's right. Take it. It will help you to relax. We're not going to hurt you."

Madge reached out a shaky hand and tried to grasp the cup. It shook so severely Sari reached over and clasped both of her hands over Madge's, steadying the cup. Madge took a deep breath, and some of the tension seemed to drain out of her. Her shoulders eased back and her gaze lost some of its wariness.

"That's it. Take it a sip. It can't be too hot after all this time. We carried it while searching for you," Sari said with a gentle smile. "I'd love to know how you found my bedroom, too."

Madge dropped her gaze and stared into the depths of the cup. Then she lifted it to her lips and took a sip, then a bigger sip. She closed her eyes and sighed. She dropped her knees and leaned back against the back of the closet wall. "Thank you."

Settling deeper into her position, Sari smiled. "You're welcome. See, isn't that better?"

"Not much," murmured Ward beside her. He'd sat down into a cross-legged position at her side. He held up his hands at the woman. "I'm not here to hurt you."

His tone of voice was somewhat lacking. Madge whimpered and Sari shot Ward a warning look. "It's to be expected that I'm concerned about her sudden arrival. She might be a danger to you."

Madge's gaze widened. She shook her head frantically. "No. I'm not going to hurt anyone. I'm trying to stay safe. To hide."

"But by breaking into Sari's house, you put her in danger too."

Madge's eyes filled with tears. She shook her head so

rapidly the tears flew off to the side. "I didn't mean to. Sorry. Sorry. So sorry."

"Shh, it's all right." Sari laid a hand on Madge's knees. "It's all right. It's going to be okay. He's here to help you. To help me. We aren't going to hurt you."

Madge huddled into a tight ball, the hand holding the tea shaking uncontrollably. The liquid sloshed up the sides to spill onto the floor below. Sari removed the cup from her shaking fingers and handed it off to Ward. She grabbed Madge's hand and held it tight. "Madge. You have nowhere else to go and no one to help you. Let us…please."

But Madge curled into a tighter ball on her side and rocked back and forth. She refused to answer.

Finally, after failing to reach into Madge's psyche and get a cognizant response, Sari turned to face Ward. "What do we do?"

He stared down at the tiny woman, pity lining his face. "I'm going to call for help."

Sari looked from Madge to Ward and then finally bowed her head. "All right. I guess that's the only thing left to do."

"She needs care. Medical help. Psychological help." He reached over and stroked her shoulder. "It's the best thing. We can't leave her here on the floor. She could die in the shape she's in."

She smiled sadly. "I know that. Make your calls. Help her." She sighed. "I just wished I didn't feel like I was betraying her."

CHAPTER 10

SARI SAT IN her shop several hours later. A fresh pot of tea sat on her desk beside her. Tired and dispirited, she couldn't help but wonder how Madge was doing every time she saw the teacup. Madge had been catatonic by the time the paramedics arrived. She hadn't moved when they'd lifted her birdlike frame onto the stretcher.

It had been sad yet reassuring to have the ambulance take her away. Surely they'd be able to help her. Ward had left soon after, stating he had paperwork to do about the incident. Now alone, she realized that they hadn't gotten to the bottom of the problem of why Madge was so scared…and who she'd been hiding from.

Ward's last words were to get the security system working today. Immediately.

The company was working on it now. She hoped they'd finish today. She didn't think she'd sleep tonight after last night's events. Then again, she wasn't doing so well today. Tired and stressed, Sari knew she should have a nap, but her bedroom didn't feel right. Her room needed to be cleaned up as soon as possible from the scene with Madge – she wasn't going to want to deal with the mess later tonight.

"Excuse me."

She spun around. The security guy was standing at her shop doorway. "Oh, hi. Sorry, I didn't hear you come in."

"No problem. I have to go and pick up a couple of things. Two of my men are working on the installations. I should be back in an hour or so."

"Will the system be done today?"

"Yes, it will – providing we have everything with us here. We'll do our best though. No worries." With a bright smile, he walked out the front door. She stood at the front window, teacup in hand, and stared out. She couldn't focus on anything. She just wanted to lie down and sleep.

Sighing heavily, she walked over to the stairs and went up. At the entrance to her room, she stopped and grimaced. How could the simple act of picking up one tiny woman cause such a mess? There were plastic wrappers and dirt from the paramedics' shoes. Her bed had been moved to make way for the stretcher, her shoes and clothing had been shoved to one side to reach Madge. Small she might have been, but she'd nestled deep into the space she'd chosen.

Sari put her tea down on her night table and proceeded to get to work.

Twenty minutes later, she'd stripped the bed and remade it, cleaned up the garbage, and had vacuumed the floor. She walked over to her closet and bent down to straighten that section of her room. Shoes first. She paired them up and moved a couple to the far side, then moved the hangers over to where they'd been before. As she went to straighten them, she thought she saw something on the floor. She bent deeper into the small space. It was a clasp. Not on the floor but on the back wall, right at the floor. She frowned. It was almost impossible to see. There was a fine crack leading upward, and she pushed the hangers as far back as they'd go. She'd automatically taken her same bedroom when she came back and had yet to go through her childhood belongings. She shoved the way too small clothing out of her way. There. The crack ended about halfway up the closet at another latch. This clasp was painted yellow, the same as the wall. And it was broken open.

Excited, she pushed on the wall. A small door opened.

WARD SHOOK HIS head. The woman in the bed in front of him was absolutely tiny. And frail. He couldn't give her an age, but would guess her to be in her early eighties or thereabouts. In fact, she could be in her sixties. Her skin was thin and translucent, her veins giving a gray cast to the skin covering them. According to the doctors, she was dehydrated and desperately in need of nutrients, but was in essence healthy.

Her mental state was yet to be determined. She hadn't spoken since she'd left Sari's house.

He had a report to write up and as it stood right now, he couldn't say much. Sari had woken up in the middle of the night to find a complete stranger hiding out in her attic. There was no explanation as to who she was or how she'd gotten in.

He ran his fingers through his hair.

Bizarre.

"Hey, Ward. Your girlfriend is keeping you busy." Jeremy walked over. "I didn't figure you'd still be here."

"Hmmm?" Ward refocused on his partner. "What was that about a girlfriend?" He finally clued in. "Oh, you mean Sari. As much as I'd like it to be, she's not my girlfriend."

"Sure. Like I'm going to listen to that." Jeremy smacked him on the shoulder. "And what kind of weird shit is this?" He nodded to the woman lying in front of them. "Is that correct – Sari found her in the attic, freezing and terrified?"

"And when Sari took me to where she'd seen her last, she wasn't there. We searched the house and Madge here," Ward tilted his head at the sleeping woman, "was hiding in the back of Sari's bedroom closet. Now how the hell she found her way there in that mess of a house, I don't know."

His friend grinned. "I've heard the house is haunted."

"It's a whole lot more than that. From the outside, you'd have no idea. Even inside, unless you know where you're going, it's easy to get turned around. The place is old and it's huge."

"I wonder how she got inside in the first place. It's not like Sari lives downtown or that the house is easily accessible. It's fenced, it's set back from the curb, and although there are neighbors on either side, the property is big enough that it's as if there was no one around." He shook his head. "And how could she have gotten into the attic?"

"Many people knew her family from before. Her father was well loved – he was a character, but a friendly one. I used to spend hours in his shop." Ward shrugged. "Maybe more people know about it than I thought."

"Oh, and here I thought that you were spending that time with Sari."

Ward grinned. "We were ten. Spending time with Sari back then *was* spending time with her father. And vice versa."

"Not the mother." Jeremy frowned. "I don't remember hearing much about her."

"She's a different sort. As reserved as Sari's father was friendly. She was one of those women with perfect makeup in place at seven in the morning and at eleven at night – whereas Sari's father would look rumpled at seven in the morning and eleven at night. They were chalk and cheese."

"Funny how opposites attract, isn't it?"

"Yes. But I don't know how well the relationship was working. Would it have survived the years if he hadn't disappeared? I don't know."

"Do you suspect the wife of having something to do with his disappearance?"

Ward twisted his lips. "I've certainly considered the possibility over the years, but I just don't see it. She's not likely to get her hands dirty."

"She could have hired someone."

With a grimace, Ward nodded. "Which is why I considered it. He's gone. He hasn't popped up in another city as far as we can tell. There's no sign of a body. It's like he just vanished into thin air."

"It happens sometimes. Cold cases are terrible. For everyone."

They both stared silently at the sleeping woman. "This is one strange turn of events."

"No," Ward said. "This is a second strange turn of events. Remember, Sari's house was broken into a week ago as well. We haven't found those two men either."

"True enough. Back to the office then. Check the missing persons files. Maybe she'll show up there."

With a backward glance at Madge, Ward walked out of the hospital and headed to the office. It was going to be a long day.

"WHAT'S WRONG WITH me?" Sari sat staring at the dark deep space in front of her. The hidden cupboard door was propped open with her shoes, and she'd shifted everything from that side of the closet to the other side. There was no sign to indicate where it went or what it was used for. And for the life of her, she couldn't find her flashlight. She'd used it several times last night when she'd found Madge but not since. She'd searched the shop and the attic. Maybe Ward had accidentally taken it with him when he'd left.

She pulled out her phone and called him. She hated to disturb him again, but she so didn't want to go into the passage without light. Not that she knew it was a passage. It could just be a storage space, but if so, then why couldn't she see a back wall? She'd known her house had secrets, but this was getting ridiculous. She wondered if her mother knew…if that's why her mother had packed up and left, never to return.

"Sari? How are you?" he asked, his tone lightening at her voice. "I was hoping you'd gone to bed and stayed there."

Sari smiled as his gravelly voice slid through the phone. What a turn on. "I'm good – at least I think I'm good. Still a little tired. How is Madge?"

"Still asleep, but she appears to be doing fine."

"Do you remember putting my flashlight away somewhere? I've been looking all morning but haven't come across it. And I kinda need it." Her voice dropped at the end. She really wanted him to come and help her explore, but that was asking a little much. The guy had a job to do, and she'd stolen his sleep as it was.

"I think the last time I saw it, the flashlight was on your bed. It might have dropped and the bed might have been rolled over it when the paramedics arrived."

"Oh, I never thought of that." Sari hopped to her feet and walked the few steps to her bed. She bent down, tugging up the bedding. There, high under the head of her bed, was the flashlight. "Oh, it is there. Now if only I can reach it."

"Roll the bed instead of hurting yourself. I never thought about it – we left your bedroom in a mess, didn't we? Sorry about that. I left with Madge and honestly never gave it another thought."

Sari smiled. "Not to worry. Madge was the priority. But you should see what I found just now."

"What?" His lively voice teemed with curiosity.

"A few minutes ago. I was straightening up the closet and found a cupboard hidden in the back."

"What? Like a closet?"

"Yeah, I don't know about that. That's why I wanted the flashlight. I can't see a back to this space."

"Whoa," he snapped. "Hang on there. I don't like the sound of this. We were trying to figure out how Madge got into your room, remember? What if that connects to your attic? You were wondering why there was no exit from there in the first place."

"Oh." Sari snatched up the flashlight and raced over to the closet. She shone the light inside. "Jesus. I can't see the back here. It's so dark. It's big enough to crawl into."

"Stop. Don't you go in there. I'm just leaving the hospital. Put on some coffee and I'll swing by on my way to the office."

"Ha. You just want to explore my crazy house some more."

"You're right. You also dragged me out of deep sleep, so I need a caffeine hit before I drop." The laughter in his voice brought an answering grin to her face. "I'm already at the parking lot. Be there in ten. Close the damn cupboard and wait for me. There might be clues about Madge there, so don't touch."

Sari rolled her eyes. "So now my closet is a police issue. Right."

"It was the minute a strange woman showed up in your house."

"Right. I'm closing the damn door and going to put coffee on. But you're spoiling my fun, you know. You owe me lunch for this."

"Done. Actually, it's almost lunchtime now."

"Not today." Sari sighed. "I'm too tired to enjoy going out right now."

"Coffee. We need coffee. Be there in five."

Sari hung up and stared at the open doorway, considering. Should she go in and explore?

CHAPTER 11

W ARD PULLED OFF the main road and turned into Sari's curving driveway.

He hoped she'd listened. He'd been through enough this morning. According to his partner, there was no one matching Madge's description in the missing person files for the last year. He'd suggested Jeremy look further back. Madge, although skinny and starved, was relatively healthy. It appeared she'd been someplace where she was taken care of, or at least had been able to care for herself.

He turned off the engine and hopped out. The house rose with spirals and columns. The front shop had a sloping roof all its own. The new roof looked good. The new window looked even better as it shone out from above, the glass panes twinkling in the light.

"Hey, there you are." Sari stood in the doorway grinning at him. "You were longer than five minutes."

Ward reached inside and pulled out a white bakery bag. "I stopped off at Nino Bakery and picked up fresh cinnamon buns to have with the coffee."

She rolled her eyes, looking lovely as she leaned against the door frame. So relaxed; no one would know the mess she'd gone through the night before. She had a natural grace about her. Gentle but resilient. She'd learned how to bend to life's punches, and still she stood straight.

"Are you trying to fatten me up?"

"You could stand to gain a pound or two. You were skinny as a kid, too."

"I was a scrawny beanpole back then. Thank God I've filled out some."

"Yeah, thank God," he whispered under his breath. She'd filled out in a beautiful series of graceful feminine curves. Model thin and centerfold built. A man's dream girl. At least for him.

Only she heard him. She snatched the bag out of his hand. "You also used to bug me about my bony knees. Did you think I'd forget?"

He laughed. "Why not? I did. But thanks for the memory."

She grinned as she led the way to the kitchen. "School was fun back then. I hated France in the beginning. My French sucked – I did terrible in school for years, then I finally got over myself and started to do really well."

He looked at her sideways. "I think you deserved recovery time. I'd have failed every course if I had to do them in another language."

She grinned. "I could speak French; it was more an attitude adjustment. I hated that we left home…left my dad. I desperately wanted him to come home. Figured if we weren't here, he wouldn't come back. Even when I was flying here almost two months ago, I couldn't stop the spark of hope that he might have come home and would be sitting here waiting for me." She smiled sadly.

"I'm sorry, Sari. I can't imagine."

She looked up at him. "How is your mother? I only remember meeting her once."

"Yeah, at the spelling bee."

"Right. The last day I saw my father."

Silence.

"I hadn't realized." Ward stared off into space. "That day wasn't remarkable to me. I can hardly remember."

"I beat you in the last round with the word *aquarium*."

He grinned. "Now I remember. My mother bugged me about missing that one for days. I let you win."

She gasped in surprise then in outrage. "You did not. I won that fair and square."

He laughed and laughed. She reached out and clipped him on the shoulder. "Oh, you. You were always the biggest tease."

"I was sweet on you back then. There's no way I'd have been able to beat you and live with it."

She poured coffee and handed him a cup. "Like I'm going to believe that. You might have been sweet on me just so you could come and visit with my father."

"Your dad was the greatest." He took a sip of coffee. "I just wish we had answers to his disappearance."

There was an awkward silence.

He peered at her over the rim of his mug. She wore such an odd look on her face. "What's the matter?"

She looked like she was about to speak, then changed her mind. She smiled brightly. "Come on. Let me show you the hidden door."

Knowing she'd held back but not sure he should try to push her to talk about her father's disappearance, he nodded and said, "Sounds good. Let's go."

LEADING THE WAY to her bedroom, Sari wondered if she'd missed the right moment. She felt like she needed to tell someone what had happened to her father. Not that Ward would believe her. Like who would? On top of that, her memory was sketchy. It *had* been fifteen years ago. She'd been just a child, and she'd had her memories poked and denied by her mother for all that time. How sad was that?

At her bedroom, she stopped automatically to survey her space. It had been invaded several times.

Maybe it was time to move to the master bedroom. Before that could happen, she'd have a huge mess of cleaning to do. Her mother had literally packed Sari's clothes, a few personal possessions, and they'd left, leaving all the furniture, dishes, and remaining personal possessions. For Sari, coming home had been like a trip backwards in time.

"Where is the cupboard?" Ward strode to the closet, crouching down in front of it.

Sari, at his side, pointed out the hard-to-see clasp on the bottom. "See, it's been painted the same color as the wall."

He bent closer. "Was there anything in front of this earlier? It's almost directly behind where we found Madge."

"I know. I don't know if there was there before. But there is still so much here that was left from before. I've got so much going on that I can't figure out where to start. I should have cleaned this room out before, but every time I start I get sidetracked by memories."

"Understandable. It's like a time capsule."

"I know. It was a bit of a shock returning."

Pulling the hidden door open wider, he stuck his head in. "Whoever built this did a good job. It's a hell of a hiding place. I can see the end here. It's only a few short feet over."

Sari stilled then winced. "Thanks for that thought. I might never sleep in here again."

"I'm surprised that finding Madge didn't freak you out.

How is the security system coming along?"

"Oh, I forgot they were still working out there. At least I presume they are – I haven't seen anyone in a while."

"The truck is out there. How many doors and windows are you getting done? To do the whole thing would be incredibly expensive."

"It is, but they said it was a comprehensive system and my mother is paying for it in a roundabout way. She offered to pay for the roof, but I'd just finished paying that bill so I'm applying her money to this."

"That makes sense." The door stood open in front of him and he shook his head. "Who'd have thought this house had so many secrets?" He leaned back to survey the closet as a whole then glanced out the bedroom window. "This is the front of the house. You saw me get struck down from that window, so this closet should go into the attic. It's the only thing that makes sense."

"And does it?" she asked sensibly.

"I don't know. Let's go see." With that he crawled into the cupboard, his flashlight showing the way.

Not wanting to be left behind, Sari followed slowly. The closet was barely high enough for her to stand slightly bent over. Ward didn't bother trying to stand. "The connecting door is slightly open, as if Madge came through and just pushed it closed."

"There can't be room in here for it to be anything else." She could barely see in front of him as he disappeared into the opening.

"It is the attic." He chuckled. "So that answers the question of Madge." His voice turned serious. "But there appears to be another door here as well."

"What?" Sari crowded closer. "This house is a bloody

maze. I wish I knew about all these hidden corridors. I hate to think someone could hide in here and I wouldn't know."

Ward glanced back at her. "Like Madge."

"Little terrified old ladies are the least of my worries. There was that break-in last week. What if one of them had been looking to hide out in here?"

"Let's not think that way. If it really bothers you, it could be boarded up. Sealed off so that no one has access. Or better yet, get someone in here to take down some walls and open the space up. Add it to the attic so you have more space in there. Put a door in from this side so you can access it easily. Make it a sitting room or something. With that new window in there, it's quite a nice space."

"That's not a bad idea." She peered in the direction of the flashlight shining on the bare wood wall. "Is that the second door? Open it."

Another heavy grating noise sounded. "Whew, I don't think this one has been used in a long time."

He shone the light into the other side of the door. "It's another bedroom."

"The spare room?"

"I don't know." He crawled through and finally stood up. Sari had to crouch down to come out the doorway. She stood up straight and stared in surprise at her parents' old bedroom. "Really?"

"What?"

"This is the master bedroom. Why would there be a secret door from their room to my room?"

"In the olden days, the master of the house often had a secret passageway to his current mistress that might have been a maid or someone visiting." Sari wrinkled up her nose. "That's just wrong. With his wife sleeping right here? How would he hide what he was doing?"

Ward grinned. "I don't know. I can't imagine it happening at all, but men have always found a way."

"So true. Still, it's an odd space. Let's go into the attic and see how Madge might have opened the door from her end. I certainly hadn't seen a doorway when I was in there."

With a last glance at the still-full bedroom, Sari followed Ward back into the short passageway and stood up on the other side. She glanced around, but everything appeared to be the same as before. "It looks the same."

"Stand over here." Ward stood on the other side of the ladder. "You'll see how the doorway blends perfectly into the wall." She walked over to join him and turned around to take a look. True enough. "I would never have seen that from this side. That's also exactly where I found Madge. She was curled up at the base of the door."

"It might have opened up under her weight if she'd been leaning against it. It's hard to know. It still doesn't explain how she got into your house in the first place, but it does explain how she made it to your room."

Sari shook her head. "I wonder if my mother knew about this passage. Or my father?"

"I don't know. Ask her."

"Yeah, later. She's not happy with me as it is."

"Oh, more problems?" Ward opened the hatch door and dropped the ladder. He slipped down and waited for her to join him.

"Not really. The same ones. Just the things he'd asked her to keep safe in case anything happened to him. I showed you his watch already."

She was rambling. It took a moment for the odd silence to filter in. She glanced up at Ward. "What?"

"He gave her some items for safekeeping in case anything happened to him?" At her confused nod, he continued in a controlled voice, "And when he disappeared, without a trace and with no explanation, she didn't think she should tell the police about it?" His control broke, his voice rising slightly at the end.

Sari grimaced. "This is my mother we're talking about here. She thinks differently than you and me. She didn't think the items would have anything to do with his disappearance – she had enough to deal with at the time, so I'm sure she never gave it a thought."

He glared at her. "And you? Did it ever occur to you to mention it?"

She rolled her eyes. "Give me a break, I haven't had time to breathe, let alone fill you in on my mother's odd behavior."

"Maybe you should take a closer look at what she gave you."

She sighed, hiding her grin. She'd really like a chance to do just that. "Now, I suppose?"

He smiled. "Now that would be the smart thing to do."

"THEY ARE OVER here." She led the way to the bookshelf where she'd placed her father's books.

Ward watched her stretch. "Do you need help?"

"No. I just put these up yesterday. I was going to look, but I needed them back where they belonged."

"Those books were part of what your mother was keeping safe?" And why would that be? It wasn't like anything important enough to kill over would be in there. He didn't see how it could be. He walked over and held out his arms to help. She gave him two books and reached for the third. As she was pulling it down, one flap opened and papers fluttered to the floor.

"Damn." She bent down and carefully picked up the loose pieces. Straightening, she sighed. "I haven't had a chance to go over these notes yet. I can't imagine why he'd have asked her to keep them safe, too."

"Was he a collector? These books might be valuable." Ward looked down at the spines of the two books in his hands. The leather-bound editions might be valuable first editions. The monetary value could be what her father had meant.

"I hadn't thought so, but I haven't had a chance to research them. They are old, but I'm not sure they are collector's items. After the appraisal, my mother deemed them worthless."

"What's the possibility that her concept of worthless and mine are different?"

"I'd say they are miles apart."

"Is this all your mother handed you?" He almost missed the fleeting look crossing her face. He waited a moment. She hesitated. "This is most of it along with my father's watch, that you saw yesterday and his ring." She stared down at the sheafs of paper in her hands. "It's all valuable to me just because it was his."

A gentle silence filled the air, then Sari walked over to desk and placed the papers and books down. She pulled out a chair and motioned for him to sit. "Let's see what's here."

Ward sat down and put down the first book. The second one he opened. "*The Art of Time Travel.*"

Sari laughed. "Yes, my father's pet hobby. It used to drive my mother nuts."

Her laughter was so infectious. He grinned. "An odd interest."

"Not really. His specialty was timepieces after all." She held up the spine of the book in her hand. "*Delving Into Time.*"

Glancing at the book he'd placed down, he read the title. "*Beyond Time.*" He shook his head. "Wow, who'd have thought?" He looked up at the full bookcase. "Surely those aren't all the same?"

She twisted to look in the direction he was. "No, most of those are on timepieces. He collected a lot of specialty books."

"Makes sense." He nodded to the papers. "Is there anything important in there?"

She picked up several pages and turned them to try and read them. "This one isn't in English and this one appears to be notes on a repair job." She frowned as she picked up the other papers and shuffled through them. "They all appear to be the same. His handwriting, but some of it nonsensical."

"No idea why they were singled out?"

"No, chances are he thought they would be a nest egg for Mom. He was dreaming." And that gave her an odd adult look into who her father was. Maybe they were valuable. But maybe he was just dreaming, hoping they were.

"How did you survive after leaving here? I'd have thought she'd have sold the house in order to re-establish herself somewhere else."

"My grandparents. They were delighted she went home. They were wealthy and she was an only child."

"Ah, I see." And he did. The money would have been a big inducement for a woman suddenly alone with a child to support and no marketable skills. And the wealthy parents would have been only too happy to use money to bring to their child home.

She shrugged. "Besides, she could never sell the house – it was in a trust for me." A flicker of anger crossed her face. "It became mine when I turned twenty-five, but she didn't let me know. I found out when a lawyer contacted me."

Ward watched as she flicked through her father's items, a melancholy look on her face. "You still miss him, don't you?"

"There's no closure." She closed the book in her hand and leaned back. "I have no answers, no body to bury. Nothing to prove he's gone."

He could understand that. She wasn't alone. Any family with a missing person went through the same issues. "I'm sorry."

She motioned to the books. "Now you can see why my mother didn't bother the police with these."

Standing up, he nodded. "True enough. Do you want me to put them back up?"

"No. I'll do a bit of research. See if I can find out more about them."

"Okay. I'm heading back to the office."

"Thanks for coming and checking out the passage for me." She stood up and walked him to the front door. "This house has to be out of secrets by now." She grinned. "It was good to see you again."

"I'm here a lot lately. Glad you came home and enlivened my world."

She laughed. "Not exactly the way I'd have liked to. Aren't we supposed to be doing dinner soon?"

"Absolutely. It was supposed to be tonight, but I presume we were going to push it back due to a lack of sleep."

She looked so cute standing there he couldn't resist. He leaned forward and dropped a kiss on her cheek.

"Hey."

He looked at her in surprise. "What?"

"You could at least do that right." She smirked, then grasped his face with both hands and kissed him properly.

After the initial surprise, Ward stepped closer and wrapped her in his arms. Her lithe frame snuggled closer. He deepened the kiss, forgetting that he was standing on her front doorstep, forgetting that he was on his way to work and forgetting all the years they'd lost. She was here. In his arms. And she'd gotten there herself.

It took a moment to sense her withdrawal. He fought the urge to hold her closer, knowing it wasn't the time.

He stepped back and grinned. "Now that's a goodbye kiss."

"Actually, that's an 'until I see you again' kiss.'" She smirked and stepped back. "Have a great day." She closed the door in his face.

Ward turned, unable to wipe the silly grin off his face.

Damn, he was glad she'd finally come home.

CHAPTER 12

A S SOON AS Ward drove off, Sari walked back inside her shop. She didn't know what she'd found, but she hadn't wanted him around while she figured it out. She hadn't determined what to tell him yet.

The notes from her father were some kind of formula. She didn't know for what, but she thought the numbers and figures looked familiar. Locking the front door, she headed to her desk and computer. She had to wonder what her father had been up to. She also hadn't solved the issue of the last timepiece.

She'd seen the same markings on her father's notes and maybe inside the one book. She went to her safe and removed the last few items she'd gotten from her mother.

It was long past time to solve the mystery.

An hour later, she had no idea what to do next. She'd confirmed the same markings on her father's watch; however, there were different markings there as well. What could the markings mean? Or had her father not had a chance to record the other markings? She got up and went to the kitchen where she put on the teakettle. She needed to sit down and read the book.

An hour later, she found it. She read the material out loud as if that would clarify its meaning.

"The markings determine the time period the watch

can travel. Understanding the markings is imperative to determine the final location of the owner of the watch. If the watch changes hands, there is grave danger to the new unsuspecting owner. There have only been two watchmakers known to have the ability to write the language of time dimension into their pieces — Tooley and Dunne, who were partners for forty years until Dunne disappeared without a trace from his shop in 1803."

And that was it. Nothing more.

Yet it was a hell of a lot.

She went to her computer to look up Tooley and Dunne. The one name sounded familiar, but she couldn't place it. The whole time concept it hinted at was too unbelievable. She grabbed her father's notes and studied the odd lettering. Latin, maybe? She opened up a web page and as best she could, she typed one of the sentences into Google. There. A historical watch society out of England had several old manuscripts uploaded containing detailed diagrams of some old watches, timing mechanisms, and common repairs. She loved the site. It was full of information. Further searching found a contact email.

She quickly fired off a message asking for more information.

Feeling somewhat better, she sat back and took a sip of tea.

Her phone rang. Cautiously, she picked it up. "Hello?"

"Well, there you are. I heard you'd moved back to your father's house. Wondered if you'd contact me."

Sari frowned, her gaze automatically going to her email. "Who is this?"

"Your old friend Brodin Wilson."

WARD KNEW HE'D been shuffled out the door; he just didn't know why. She'd seen something. Understood something. Something she hadn't wanted to share. He understood – somewhat. But his curiosity had been piqued.

She'd kissed him to throw him off.

And it had worked. He'd walked out like a love-struck puppy.

She'd done it on purpose. Not that she'd been uninvolved in that kiss. She might have started it that way, but she'd not been as unaffected as she'd started out to be by the end.

Good.

But what had she been up to? He pulled into the parking lot at the office and parked. Walking in, he said hi to several friends. Jeremy looked up. "There you are. I figured you'd gone home to sleep."

Ward shook his head. "I wish. I went back to Sari's house from the hospital." Sitting down, he filled Jeremy in on the passageway. "At least we know how Madge made it into Sari's bedroom."

"Now that is a weird house. She should have someone go through that place and see if there are any other hidden corridors." Jeremy shook his head. "Can't say I'd feel very comfortable sleeping in there myself."

"It is weird. So," he turned to face him. "Any news on Madge?"

"Nope. I called a half hour ago and she was still asleep."

"And that's another weird thing about that house. How the hell did that tiny woman get into Sari's house, through the shop, find the ladder, and climb up it? Who'd have even known about the attic? Christ. You're sure Sari isn't some kind of hidden psycho that kidnaps people and keeps them as a captive?"

The smile fell from Ward's face. He glared at Jeremy. "You might be joking, but I don't want to hear that ever again."

Jeremy held up his hands. "Sorry. I know she isn't. But you have to admit that whatever is going on is weird. And it surrounds her." He dropped his feet and leaned forward. "Think about it. The house has been empty since doomsday. She comes home, what…four to six weeks ago? Then within two weeks, there's a break-in, you're attacked, now an old woman is found hiding out and strange corridors show up."

Laid out that way, Ward could see his point. "Have there been any break-ins at her house over the last umpteen years?" He clicked on his computer and logged in. "I don't remember anything about it."

"I already checked. No incidents involving that address between Sari's father's disappearance and Sari's return." He grinned. "You gotta admit it's beyond weird."

Ward didn't have to admit anything. Staring at his screen, instinct kicked in yet again. Sari knew more than she was sharing. That would have to change.

She could be in danger. He'd lost her once; there was no way he was going to let her go again.

CHAPTER 13

"**B**RODIN WILSON?" SARI said. "Really?" She hadn't even had a chance to answer his latest email. Speaking of which, why'd he call? She hadn't given him her number, but her mother would have in a heartbeat. She laughed. "What's up? Must be big for you to call me."

"Yes." The voice sounded quietly amused. "But only to check up on you. I hear you've moved back to your old home. Greg's home, Sari."

"It sounds odd to hear his name. I keep forgetting you knew my father," she replied softly, pensive. How many of her father's old friends knew about what had happened to him? She hadn't informed anyone.

"I knew him well. We were joined by a common interest. Even on that last day we were supposed to work together, but he disappeared before I returned."

Sari straightened in her chair. She'd had so few details of her father's last day. He'd disappeared right before her, so she hadn't considered what might have happened before her arrival home from school. "When that day?" She tried to minimize the sharpness of her tone and failed.

He laughed. "The last thing he said to me was he wanted to finish studying the watch before you got home."

She swallowed heavily. "I wished I had seen the watch better. I only have his old notes to go on."

"Old notes?" he asked curiously, his voice slightly raised. "Figures. That watch fascinated him. He said he'd found something very special in it. He often took pictures and notes with unique items."

"I haven't found most of them." Her gaze went to the dusty bookshelf. "But the ones he made of that watch were as detailed as any I've seen," she admitted softly. Her gaze kept drifting to the safe that held her latest acquisitions, including the watch her father had given her mother for safekeeping. "Only they are unfinished."

"Unfinished?" Brodin asked, his voice sharp, cutting across the miles as if it were nothing. "Are you sure?"

"Yes."

"Too bad. I wish mine hadn't been stolen. I can't know for sure it was identical, but with his notes, we could have had a comparison. Now we have nothing," he said, a tinge of bitterness in his voice.

She understood. There was more than a tinge of it inside her. "Sorry. I've been looking but haven't seen anything like it." She wondered if she should mention the one she got from her mother.

"It's probably sitting in a private collection. Collectors are an unscrupulous lot." Brodin laughed. "At least that's the term your father would have used."

"And you – what would you call yourself?"

"Obsessed." His voice turned flat. "Weird things happen around obsessed people."

"Tell me about it. I've had enough weird things happening in the last week for a lifetime."

"Like what?" he asked worriedly. "Nothing dangerous, I hope."

"A break-in after I returned from purchasing a second

watch like my father's. One of the men was a redhead. His partner attacked a cop on a street outside my house. Then I wake up to a strange little old lady hiding out in my attic." She sighed. "So I don't know that any of it is dangerous, but it's definitely weird."

"Wow." There was an odd silence as they both digested the strange mess of happenings. "I don't know if it's related, but your father's research bordered on the shady side."

"Shady?" Sari was outraged. "There's no way my father was involved in anything illegal."

"I didn't mean illegal, but his interest…our interests…were a little odd."

"Odd?" she asked cautiously. "How odd?"

"We were fascinated by the concept of time. I admit I still am."

"Oh." Relieved, Sari gave a small laugh. "That's what you meant."

"Not many people shared our interests." He laughed, a mocking sound that made her wince. "Your father's particular interests were time and dimension."

She stared at her phone. Had he been that obsessed? She'd been too young to know at the time. "At least he didn't hurt anyone with it."

"Just himself. And tore his family apart by disappearing into his obsession."

With that, Brodin hung up.

Sari stared at the phone in shock. "Wait…" But she was way too late. He was gone.

Could her father have really disappeared into the watch? No, what had Brodin said? Something about her father disappearing into his obsession. His obsession had been about time and dimension. So had her father disappeared in time? Like a black hole. Or traveled in time? Dimensions. What did she even know about dimensions? She understood the basics, but that was it.

She turned to stare at her father's bookshelf. They should be able to tell her what she needed to know. She strode over and grabbed the first three and sat down to read. After an hour, she sat back and stared off in space. Could other dimensions exist in the same place? Simultaneously? According to this book, there were places where the distance between dimensions were thinner than other places. Where some overlap could occur. There were locations all around the world where there'd been issues of this type; towns that were on meridian lines that made them more likely. The book listed several likely locations. Her town wasn't one of them.

Duh.

She slammed the book close, watching as dust floated into the air. This was too bizarre.

Even if the layer between time, dimensions, or whatever you wanted to call it was thinner here, did she really think her father had crossed to some other reality? That he was living with another family, or even alone, living out an existence on another plane – happily? No, not happily. Her father would be trying to get back to her.

WARD WORKED HIS way through the emails stacked up in his inbox. He'd been at it for a good half hour already. "Hey, buddy." Jeremy said. "The hospital called. The old woman is awake."

Ward glanced over, his mind not computing the shift of topic from the emails to Jeremy's conversation. "What?"

"Let's go to the hospital. Madge. Now."

He blinked and stood up. "She's awake? Great. I was afraid she wasn't going to make it."

"I wouldn't count on it still. But if we can get her to talk, maybe we can find out who the hell she is."

True enough. With a last backward glance at everything on his desk once again left in limbo, Ward shrugged and raced outside. Priorities.

At the hospital, they walked in and went straight into Madge's room. Ward frowned as he realized no one stopped them or even questioned their presence. Cutbacks these last couple of years had been brutal, but surely there should be someone around here.

At the doorway to the room, he stopped and studied the tiny woman. She didn't look awake to him.

Then she shifted slightly and opened her eyes. She stared straight at him.

Her gaze widened. She made a tiny squeaking sound and huddled against the headboard.

He held up his hands. "Sorry, we didn't mean to startle you. Madge, do you recognize me?"

She made a tiny head shaking motion, her fingers gripping the sheet up close to her chin.

"I'm a police officer. Sari called me when she found you hiding in her house." His words had no effect; she stared at him in confusion. He tried again. "I'm here to help you. Do you have any family we could call for you? I'm sure someone must be worried about you."

He didn't think it was possible, but her gaze widened yet again. She didn't answer.

Ward approached the bed cautiously. She looked like she was ready to bolt.

"Madge? That's your name, correct?"

She gave a tiny, almost imperceptible nod.

"Good. What's your last name?" He'd almost reached the chair sitting beside her bed. "Do you remember your last name?"

"Harrods."

"Harrods?" As in related to Sari? He frowned, watching the expressions flit across her face: surprise, confusion, doubt. "Is your name Madge Harrods?"

She gave another nod, but with a hint of hesitation behind it, as if she didn't really know.

"Good. Now, do you have a husband, Madge? A child? Someone close to you that we can call?"

She frowned slightly then shook her head.

Not good. "Do you live alone?"

She shook her head.

Ward tried to relax his shoulders and appear less tense. His partner walked up beside him. "Hi Madge, I'm Jeremy. I'm Ward's partner."

She stared at both of them.

Jeremy tried again. Both men stayed where they were, not wanting her to run, which was something she appeared ready to do any minute.

"Who do you live with, Madge?"

She stared fixedly at him then shrugged her shoulders.

"So not helpful," Jeremy whispered, only loud enough for Ward to hear.

"Madge, can you tell us anything about how you got to Sari's house? According to her, you said you had to hide. You were scared of being found."

Madge made a tiny noise and pulled the covers up over her head.

"Damn."

"Yeah."

"Excuse me."

Ward turned to find a doctor standing in the doorway, two nurses flanking him. Ward pulled out his badge for them to see, and the doctor nodded. "She's in good shape, health wise." He smiled at Madge, who had the sheet down just low enough that they could see her face. "She's recovering nicely from her ordeal. Aren't you, Madge?"

She offered him a tiny smile.

"Has she said anything to you two?" the doctor asked curiously. "We haven't been able to get her to speak."

Ward turned to stare at the tiny woman. "She gave us her last name."

"So she does speak, good," one of the nurses spoke up as she smiled at Madge. "We haven't been able to get her to talk to us."

"But she is doing better. Find out where she belongs and she can leave in a few days time." With a nod, the doctor left and the nurses followed.

Jeremy gave a small laugh. "So not helpful."

"True enough." He glanced back over at Madge.

She'd fallen asleep again, or at least was pretending. Either way, she wasn't any more help at the moment.

Ward said to Jeremy, "Let's go run her name and see if we can find out anything."

CHAPTER 14

S ARI CLOSED THE book in front of her. Multiple tabs of paper stuck out from between the pages in places where she'd marked the location of interesting information. Still, from the looks of the number of tabs, going back through those specific pages wasn't going to be a quick hop either. This was one of the three books her father had given her mother for safekeeping, and she could see why. It wasn't just about time and dimension. It was theories; formulas for crossing the dimensional barrier. She didn't know if her father had believed this stuff or had actively participated in it, but should any of this far-fetched gibberish work, it would explain her father's disappearance.

Like nothing else would.

She still didn't quite understand how she'd come to believe her father had shifted through dimensions, but with her own eyes, she'd seen him disappear before her and he'd never shown up again. Whether he'd chosen to go, circumstances had mysteriously been right, or things just happened without him knowing it was going to – he'd disappeared.

She hated to think he was looking to come home. It would almost be easier to think of him as dead instead of locked in another reality and trying hard to come back. He didn't have his books or his research wherever he was now.

And she didn't know that she could get to him. Who

said there was only one other reality? What if there were hundreds? Anything she did could possibly send her into an altogether different place. Then they'd both be lost.

But she couldn't leave her father missing if she knew of a way to help him.

Her phone rang, startling her out of her deep thoughts.

Ward. "Hello." She smiled at the warm voice on the other end.

"I wanted to tell you that Madge is awake."

"That's great news." And it was. One less thing to worry about. "She's recovering then?"

"Yes, only she's not talking much. She told us her name was Harrods. Which, considering where she ended up, means she's likely one of your relatives. She doesn't know how she came to be in your house or why she was scared and hiding out."

"Wow, really? Oh dear. That's not good."

"No. Do you recognize the name?"

"I don't know any Madge at all." Sari frowned, thinking for a minute. "Our family tree is very sparse. I'll see if I can find it and let you know."

They talked for another few minutes and hung up.

Sari frowned as she closed her cell phone. "Madge Harrods." Then it hit her. She got up and headed to the bookshelf where she'd stacked the journal she'd found in the attic.

There'd been a family tree in there. It took twenty minutes of frantic scrambling to find what she was looking for. Using her finger, she went over each line on the tree. There. M. Harrods. Born in Victoria in 1935 and deceased thirty-one years later.

Stunned, Sari sat down at her desk and tried to work

through the logic. M. Harrods didn't mean Madge Harrods. Harrods was a common name. There had to be thousands of people with that name. Surely.

Still, the fact was Madge was found inside her house. Her gaze automatically shifted to the book on her desk full of tabs. Surely not.

Her gaze switched to the note on M. Harrods's death. Ward should be able to confirm that this person actually died and not just…disappeared.

She winced. Ward was a good friend, a potential lover even – but asking him to believe in someone accidentally or intentionally crossing some kind of dimensional barrier would be asking a bit much of anyone.

Still, her hand automatically pulled out her cell phone, dialing all on its own.

"Sari?"

"Yes, it's me again, sorry. I found something a bit odd," she added sheepishly. "In the family history that I found in the attic is a listing for a woman named M. Harrods."

"What? So that could be Madge? And that would make her your kin."

"I don't know that." She took a deep breath and told him the rest. "Because right after that entry of her birth, there is a date for her death."

Silence.

Yeah, this was all a bit much. When he still didn't speak after a few moments, she murmured, "I did say it was a bit odd."

He sighed. "You're wondering if the date written for this M. Harrods's death could be a mistake?"

"I'm sure this person is dead and there's no connection. But…"

"But, given that we have an M. Harrods found inside your house and she has no idea how or where she got there or who she's hiding from…and now in another place someone of similar name has died?"

"But not similar age."

"What? Explain."

"If I did the math correctly, she died at thirty-one." She read the numbers back out to him.

He mumbled away to himself as he calculated out the math himself. "And if she hadn't died at that time, she'd be close to ninety now."

"Which is possibly correct for Madge?"

"Damn. I'll look into this and call you back. Oh, can you scan that family tree into the computer and send it to me? I might need the parents' names, not to mention others in the family in order to find the old records. Nothing back then was computerized."

"Right. I'll send it in a few minutes."

She clicked off her phone and walked over to her scanner. Holding the book flat in place, she scanned in the page and sent it to Ward's email. As she stood there looking at the book, she noticed the spine was thicker in one spot. And so was the lower half of the back cover. Frowning, she walked over to her workshop and turned on her lamp. Under the intense light, she could see the inside of the back flap had been repaired over time. Repaired, or had someone actually added something to the back flap? This was a little out of her expertise, but she hadn't planned on selling her father's things anyway. Deciding quickly, she sat down and got to work. Slicing through the glue that held the back flap in place, she lifted off the outside layer of the inside of the back cover.

She gently worked to open the layer of cloth that bound the back flap. It was open on the inside of the book, but to remove any more would damage the back of the book as well. Staring at it, she realized she'd have to cut the binding at the bottom in order to get at the back.

Oh, wait. Further inspection at the center spine showed it had been cut and repaired once already. She gently opened the repair job. It took another ten minutes to open it up. She held the book up and gave it a shake, hoping to slide down whatever was inside the back of the binding. That it could be just a shoddy repair job wasn't something she wanted to consider.

No, there. A small metallic item poked through.

She grabbed her pliers. A small slim piece of maybe tin came out. It had little to no markings on it. She put it down carefully and turned to look at the book. The tin might have been there to support a broken spine. Still, there was something on the back. She grabbed her tiny needle-nosed pliers and carefully maneuvered them in the right area. It took several minutes before she could grasp the item. Tugging carefully, she pulled it toward the small opening. "Shit." She winced at the sound of ripping.

Making a sudden decision, she put the pliers down and then picked up her knife. Seconds later, the opening at the base of the spine was twice as big.

Another careful few moments later and she had the folded sheet of paper out and open on her desk.

"What the hell?" Sari sat back against her chair and studied the rice-paper thin sheet. It appeared to be a weird set of figures like a formula. Even after having read two of the three books from her father, she realized this was nothing like she'd ever seen before. This was something else entirely. And it made no sense.

Picking it up carefully by the corner, she walked over to her printer and scanned it in. She didn't want the single copy to go missing. And with all the weird happenings going on in her life lately, that was an all-too likely event, unfortunately. She saved the document in several places then emailed a copy to herself. Paranoid? Maybe. Still, she couldn't help worrying.

Back at the book, she carefully refolded it and inserted it into an envelope. Then she got up, walked over, and locked the envelope in the safe.

What were the chances this was what the intruder had been looking for? He'd been through the books on the bookshelf. She'd had to put them back herself. But this book hadn't been there. It had been thousands of miles away in France. And they couldn't have known that. Although if they had found that out, it might explain the break-in at her mother's house.

Turning back to the book, she searched the back spine for any other deformity, but the rest looked normal except for a slight loosening of the binding with the single page missing. Inspiration struck. She took a piece of printer paper, cut it roughly to the same size as the folded piece she'd removed, and carefully inserted it to fill the space. It took several attempts to fit it and even then it wasn't perfect. It was enough to fool most people though. She carefully replaced the metal bar and closed the bottom seal with tiny drops of glue.

Then she sat and stared at it.

Was the book important enough that she should be copying it too? Page by page? Or would it be safe locked up as well? She had no idea. It was old and fragile and would take hours of tedium standing there at the copier and turning the pages. Or she could give up the value of the book, cut off the binding, and feed the pages into the machine one at a time. That would work, but…it went against the grain to destroy an old book. There was more value if she kept it whole, but money wasn't the drive at the moment.

Turning away, she headed back into the kitchen. She stopped at the doorway, hesitating. She couldn't help herself; she returned and locked the shop door behind her. Yes, she was paranoid.

In the kitchen, she put on the teakettle, wondering how the day had disappeared. It was almost dinnertime and that she hadn't even thought about. She opened her fridge and groaned. As close as possible to empty. That meant she had to go out. Or she could order in. Making a pot of tea, she checked her laptop. As she had several computers, one had started to 'live' in the kitchen. Convenient. And addicting. She brought up her email, and there was a response from Brodin. She ignored it, not sure what she wanted to do about him. If anything.

Checking the rest of her emails, she smiled, realizing her long-term client was excited about the last piece she'd emailed. Good, because that neck collar was a pricey trinket. This sale would keep her going for quite a while. Well, as long as she didn't plan on more expensive renovations. She answered happily, making arrangements for payment and shipping.

Buoyed by the sale, she quickly scanned through her other emails, surprised and delighted to see one from Ward. She'd forgotten she'd emailed the scanned family tree to him.

She clicked on the reply, disappointed to see it was only

a brief thanks. She'd hoped for more. And what did that say about her? Besides the fact that she wanted to go back fifteen years to when they'd been children and pick up where they'd left off? Only this time fast forward to adult feelings and adult actions. She grinned. There was nothing wrong with it. They'd been the best of friends, so taking that relationship another step forward was a normal step. They were both free and both adults. So why was she hesitating?

Another decision to make.

She picked up her phone. When he answered, she said, "If you are as tired as I am, you've made no plans for dinner tonight."

He gave a mock groan. "Food – I'm soooo hungry."

"Liar," she laughed lightly at his spluttering response. "We were supposed to do dinner, but somehow that didn't pan out. I'm going shopping to buy groceries as my cupboards are bare. I'd like to cook for you as a thank you for always coming when I call."

"Now how could I refuse without making a lie out of your reason?"

It took her a moment to understand, then she chuckled. "Good. Red meat or fish?"

"Red meat," he said instantly.

She rolled her eyes. Figured. "Okay, but then you're going to get lots of veggies with it," she warned.

"I like my veggies," he protested. "What time?"

"I'm heading out the door in ten, so how about an hour?"

"Sounds good. I should be done with my search by then."

"What search?"

"M. Harrods. I've confirmed the birth records but not

the death records yet.”

“Ah. Okay. Hopefully you’ll have the answers by the time you leave. One hour. Don’t be late.”

“Wait…what kind of wine do you like?”

“I don’t know. Surprise me.”

SURPRISE HER? YEAH, he’d really like to do that. Ward grinned.

“Get that damn grin off your face,” Jeremy snapped humorously. “We need to figure out what to do with your Madge.”

Ward smirked. “You’re just jealous. Besides, we have protocols in place for people like her while we work on finding more. The hospital will follow them.”

“True. But how do these people just go missing and no one reports them gone? I’ve got a grandmother her age, and honestly, all my extended family would be in an uproar if she disappeared.”

Jeremy belonged to a large German family whose ancestors had settled in the area over a hundred years ago like so many others in the community and surrounding area.

“I hear you. By the way, how far back are you looking at reports?”

“I’ve gone back ten years and figured that was way over the top.”

“Try another forty plus years.”

Jeremy shot him a disgusted look. “Really? Isn’t that a bit out of range?”

“Not really. Given her age, she could have been reported missing way back in the sixties, actually.” So far he had a birth date for someone in 1927 and a death recorded as

1958. If she'd just gone missing at that time, she'd be about Madge's estimated age of eighty-eight now.

"Seriously?"

"I'm just thinking. Sari sent me her family tree." He motioned to the screen he had open, explaining the birth record and lack of death record. "That's not official. If Madge disappeared and no one heard any more, I can see the date she disappeared as being the date of her death."

"That kinda makes sense."

"I know."

"Okay, I'll search the old records and see if something pops up."

"Thanks. If I found a record of this person's death that would be a different story, but as it stands now, this tree is the only piece of information that states the person as deceased."

"And the tree also doesn't say if the person is male or female."

Ward shrugged. "Nope. Nothing so helpful." He logged off, shut off his monitor, and stood up.

"You can't leave now – we haven't got this sorted out."

Ward grinned. "I sure can. Heading to the liquor store for a bottle of wine."

"Damn. It was always my love life that was kicking forward at high gear. Now it's yours."

"Trouble in your paradise?" Ward had been so busy lately he'd not gotten the lowdown on his partner's life. Usually Jeremy had a different girl every night, and considering the size of this town, that was a lot of action.

"Naw, not really." But there was something there.

Ward didn't really have time right now, but they'd been partners for a long time and friends since forever. His partner clicked aimlessly through a news feed he had up on his monitor, obviously not reading.

"Since the last thing I heard was about a new girlfriend who was pretty hot stuff and nothing since, it has to do with her."

"Yeah, something like that."

"She broke up with you?" Ward started to grin. That rarely happened. "Sorry, buddy. Thought you had something special going with this one." Of course, Jeremy said that about everyone.

"I did too." Something in Jeremy's tone made Ward stop and look at his old friend. "This one hurts, huh?"

"Yeah. She's different. Not like the others." Jeremy glared at him. "And not just because she dumped me." He turned back to his monitor, brooding.

"Can you talk to her? Ask for another chance?"

Jeremy spun around, a look of shock on his face. "Do guys do that?"

Ward laughed. "If they care, they do."

Disgruntled, Jeremy turned away. "It's not that bad."

Just before reaching the door to leave, Ward grinned and called back, "Yet."

CHAPTER 15

SARI HAPPILY BOUNCED through the fresh produce aisle in the grocery store. She'd already picked up a nice pack of beef. Ward might want red meat, but he was going to get it mixed with vegetables. She loved to cook and she loved stir fry, so that was the menu tonight. Leaving the store with her arms full of bags, she made it out to her small car. A new car had been a luxury she couldn't afford but had anyway. Sometimes a girl just had to make choices. She hit the button to unlock the trunk and stowed her purchases away.

This was her last stop, having dropped her latest sale off at the courier company with all the proper paperwork. Once the money had hit her account, she'd packed it up and taken it with her. Another thing done and gone. Ward should be arriving at her house in about ten minutes. Perfect. He could help make dinner, too.

She got into her car and started it up. She checked her phone but there were no messages. Good, then Ward wasn't likely to be delayed. She pulled into traffic and headed home. She was only a couple of blocks away when she realized a blue truck had been on her tail since leaving the grocery store. She frowned. It was too far away to read the license plate. Making a quick decision, she took a different route for the next couple of blocks. The truck stayed with her.

Shit. Making several more turns away from her house,

she kept watch.

The truck followed. Pulling into a large drugstore parking lot just past her house, she parked. Rather than sitting inside, she hopped out and casually proceeded to enter the store. Once inside, she stepped off to the side of the front door and watched through the front entrance. The truck came in and parked at the far end of the lot.

She dialed Ward.

"Hey, I was just about to call. Red or white wine?"

"I'm being followed," she said abruptly.

Ward was all business. "Where are you?"

She gave him the location, unable to stop from whispering. It wasn't logical. The bad guys were outside. They couldn't hear her. "I'm inside the store. They parked close enough to see me if I leave, but out of the way that I can't see them."

"Don't move. I'm on my way." He hung up. She stared down at the phone, hating the broken connection. As much as she knew he shouldn't drive and talk, she wished he'd kept the phone line open.

Nervous, she huddled at the front door by the magazine rack, too scared to pass the time wandering the store. What if she missed the truck leaving, or worse – what if they came into the store and she didn't know? She needed to see their faces. Could she go out there? No. She immediately dismissed the idea. Ward would shoot her if she did. Better to leave it to the professionals.

Still, she squinted, hoping her eyesight would suddenly zoom to superhuman strength.

"Excuse me. Do you need help?"

Heart slamming in her chest, Sari spun around. An older woman with a name badge proclaiming the store brand and the name of Helen. She smiled, relief washing through her. "Sorry, I'm waiting for someone."

"Oh." Uncertain but willing to be convinced, Helen backed away slightly. "If you're sure everything is all right." She gave Sari a slight smile and moved off down an aisle.

Sari waited until she'd disappeared from view then turned her attention back to the truck outside.

It was gone.

Shit.

She raced out the front door in time to see Ward pull into the parking lot. She ran to meet him. Going to the driver's side, she said, "They just left. I didn't even see them leave."

He frowned, looking around at the parking lot.

She pointed to the far side of the lot. "They were right over there."

He nodded. "I'll drive over there and take a look."

She watched as he pulled forward slowly. She realized that given the truck's location, they would have easily been able to leave via the back exit, pulling onto the main road without her ever knowing it. She reached Ward as he stepped out of the car. She nodded in the direction of the back exit. "They must have driven off that way."

"Can you describe them?"

"The truck? Yes. The driver and passenger? No, not likely. Considering they couldn't have gotten far, can we go looking for them? Maybe drive around a few blocks. If we take your car, they wouldn't know it was me."

He grinned. "Hop in."

She laughed. This was serious stuff, but with Ward at her side, she no longer felt afraid. He was big and solid. He was good for her. Either that, or she'd come to depend on him more than she realized. Something she'd have to think about. She'd always been more independent than not. Depending on someone, loving someone hurt when the person left. Like her father. She'd had relationships before, but not long term as her plan had always been to return home. Now that she was home, she had to wonder if her intuitive plan had been to come back to Ward all this time.

They'd been best buds before. They'd not planned a future. They'd been children, but they were adults now. They were friends again and they hadn't gotten as far as looking at the future. They hadn't had time.

Ward pulled out on the one-way street and drove down several blocks. "You need to give me a description of the truck."

She blurted out everything she could remember. "One of the guys was tall, like I couldn't see the top of his head through the windshield. The other was much shorter and wearing dark sunglasses."

Ward asked several pointed questions and to her surprise, she was able to answer. Yes, it was a full-size truck with the extra-long cab. It had a large chrome bumper with a winch of some sort on the front. It was not all the same color; instead the passenger door was a different color than the rest of the body.

Ward sighed at that. "A truck with that same description was stolen overnight from a construction yard."

Silence. Cautiously, she asked, "Are we assuming it's the same two guys who broke into my house? They were driving a stolen truck then too, weren't they?"

"Yes, they were. And I'd really like to get my hands on them."

She winced, remembering the attack that had knocked

him out. "I bet you would," she murmured.

He shot her a dark grin. "We take a dim view of attacks on a police officer."

"And if they gain another bruise or two while they resist arrest, that wouldn't upset you either, right?"

He cracked his knuckles. "Right."

They drove around for another ten minutes before she sighed. "They're gone, aren't they?"

"Most likely. These guys are pretty canny. If they thought something was off, they'd have bolted to try again another day."

"That's what worries me." She thought about the problem for a moment. "What would they have wanted? They followed me in broad daylight."

"Having searched your place and not finding what they were looking for, it makes sense to follow you and see if you have what they want in your vehicle or on your person."

She gulped at that. "Great." She almost laughed, but it came out closer to a squeak. "As you have spent so much time at my place already, I think you should move into my spare room as a precaution. I really don't want those assholes to return to my house while I'm sleeping," she muttered. "That's presuming I'll ever sleep again."

He shot her a glance. "Did you ever get that security system set up?"

"Yes, but what's the chance these two could bypass it easily?"

He shrugged. "Quite possible, unfortunately."

As he spoke, he turned another block and she realized he'd circled around to her house. He drove up the long winding driveway to park at her front door.

"Of course, parking your truck here might be a good

deterrent, too."

"It might, but we need to retrieve your car."

"After dinner. It's a short walk. Good for our digestion." She tossed him a cheeky grin. A grin that widened at his cry. "Walk?"

"Sure, why not? We drive all the time. I've barely made time for any exercise since moving back to Canada. It's ridiculous. I used to jog in the mornings, walk in the evenings. Yoga most days and now…now I'm lucky if I get up and down the stairs more than a dozen times a day. Hardly noteworthy."

He waited until she unlocked the door. She stepped in and groaned. "We have to go to my car now. The groceries are still in the car."

He shook his head. "Walk or drive?"

"Drive. I'm starving."

He laughed. They made the trip in ten minutes, both racing home to try to park in front of each other. Sari grabbed her bags and led the way through the front door and straight through to the kitchen. She dumped the bags, opened the first one, and found the beef. She turned around and gasped.

A stranger stood in front of her, arm raised.

"Wh—"

She barely felt the blow, but her body collapsed like cooked noodles and she dropped to the floor.

WARD LAUGHED AS Sari ran ahead of him, determined to win the race. He let her. He hadn't seen her this playful since she'd returned home. He loved it. There'd been so much stress in her life lately, this was a wonderful release. For him too.

He followed her into the house, closing the door behind him. He could hear her in the kitchen. He noticed the shop door was open. Normally she kept that door closed, locked. He stuck his head inside. Empty.

Out of habit, he shut the door for her then carried on to the kitchen. He marveled again at the chaotic layout. Double staircase, one on either side of the house. Both rose in different directions. Both were different widths, made of different materials, and ended at different heights. It was a house where additions had been added, with more coming in behind. Someone at a different period in the house's life had coated the place in a uniform color, almost incorporating the additions into the main part, but somehow not quite.

The house had a jagged appearance. Some corners were rounded and others were sharp. Some doorways were standard and others were arched. He grinned as he noticed two separate moldings on the floor and ceiling matching up perfectly at the corners. If nothing else, this house had character. He had no idea about the size of it, but it had to be at least five thousand square feet. A new roof must have cost her a fortune. To put uniform flooring throughout would be another small fortune.

Speaking of which, he had no idea how set she was financially. Sure, she had the roof replaced, installed a security system, and added a new window, but she'd also made a comment about money being tight and needing to do things in stages, and no wonder.

He wandered into the kitchen to find it empty. Where was she? Shaking his head, he went about putting the rest of the groceries away. She'd probably just gone to the washroom. There were at least three bathrooms that he knew of and probably more. The place was full of secrets. Yet it wasn't haunting in any way. It was homey. The changes had been made with love.

Once the food was put away, he didn't know what to do. She should be back soon. He frowned. Walking to the bottom of the closest stairwell, the one leading to her bedroom, he called up.

"Sari? Are you okay?"

There was no answer. He frowned and bolted up the stairs. "Sari? Are you there?"

No answer. He ran down the stairs and back up the other staircase. "Sari?"

Now he switched into panic mode. He raced out back and then through the rooms on the other side of the house. Five minutes later, he slammed his fist into the wall.

Sari was gone.

How? He tried to think logically. She hadn't been but a couple of minutes ahead of him and inside the house at that. She might have gone out the back door, but why…and why wouldn't she have said something to him? Unless she was hiding for fun. Only this didn't feel like fun.

His stomach wanted to heave.

He couldn't get his mind wrapped around it. There'd been no place for her to go. No time for her to have gone. So…someone had to have taken her.

In his mind, he saw her unlock the front door then realize that the groceries were still in the car. They'd left without relocking the front door. And she'd gone in first without him.

Stupid. His fist clenched. He wanted to punch the wall yet again. Instead, he called his partner. "I need you to come to Sari's house."

"What?" Jeremy's voice was surprised but agreeable.

"Okay. Be there in ten."

"Thanks." He hated the relief in his voice, but honest to God, he was barely keeping panic at bay. He should just call it in, but call *what* in? The reporting officer would laugh his ass off. Sure, Sari might have gone out the back door, but why would she? And why would she have gone without saying anything to him? None of this made any sense. Taking his time, he slowly and methodically searched the main level of the house. Feeling stupid but unable to help himself, he opened cupboards and closets and checked inside everything.

Nothing. He returned to the shop and checked there. Nothing. He dropped the ladder and went up to the attic. Nothing appeared disturbed, and there was no sign that Sari had been there lately.

"Damn it." He headed upstairs to her room. There was another bedroom on the same floor as well as multiple closets and another bathroom. The bathroom led to her bedroom. He knocked several times just in case, but she wasn't there. The room was empty. He raced over to her closet and opened the door. The tall narrow doorway stood open ever so slightly. He pulled it open as wide as it could go and stuck his head inside. "Sari?"

No answer. And why would there be? He'd checked out every room.

Hearing a vehicle pull up out front, he raced downstairs to open the door for Jeremy.

"Hey. What's going on this time?" Jeremy's big grin made Ward want to reach out and shake him. But his friend didn't know what was going on.

Then again, neither did he.

Ward motioned his friend inside and quickly explained.

"What? She's gone? Like…*gone* gone?"

"Yes, damn it." He flung his arms wide. "She wasn't out of my sight but five minutes, and she's gone. I've searched the house from top to bottom. There's no sign of her inside or out. She started to make dinner, as in one package of beef was opened, but that's it. The other groceries were still sitting in the bag. I figured she'd gone to the bathroom, so I put the groceries away. Only she never came back. So I went looking. There's no sign of her." He ran his fingers through his hair. "I know it's crazy." Then he realized he hadn't said anything about Sari's earlier call. Quickly he explained.

"Was there a truck here when you arrived?" asked Jeremy. "Could these guys have arrived before you and hidden inside?"

Ward stared at his friend. "I don't know. There was no sign of the truck when we got here, but that doesn't mean it wasn't parked somewhere else. They might have taken her out the back way, too. Jesus. I have to find her."

Jeremy laid a calming hand on his arm. "Look, I'll phone it in. Give the station the description of the truck—"

"No, I already did that. I did it on the way back from delivering Sari to her car. I need to find her." He spun around. "I never thought of a basement. I wonder if this crazy place has one of those, too."

"Let's look."

"Sure, but where? I've searched everywhere downstairs and never came across a door leading below."

Systematically, the two men went back over the same floor and opened doors, cupboards, closets. Nothing. No Sari, no door leading to a basement.

Ward's heart seized. The longer this went on, the worse the chances were of finding her.

He couldn't lose Sari now.

CHAPTER 16

SARI MOANED. HER head pounded and her arms ached. She couldn't figure out what was wrong. She hurt like she hadn't since she fell out of a tree, hitting every branch on the way down. Now that had hurt. Then again, so did this. Waiting for her head to clear, she lay there quietly.

Was she in bed? No, Ward should be here with her. Shouldn't he? He was coming for dinner. No, he was here already.

She couldn't remember. She groaned softly. She should remember. It mattered. She knew it mattered.

"Oh, look who's awake."

"Bloody well time, but keep her quiet."

Sari stifled the groan wanting to burst free. Now she remembered. She'd been attacked in her kitchen. A blow to her head. Unfortunately, he was still here. Wherever here was. She blinked, and light plowed into the back of her eyeballs. She slammed them close. God, that hurt.

"Stop fooling around. We know you're awake."

Great. So there was more than one guy. "Who's we?" she murmured faintly.

"Jed and me."

She didn't recognize the names. Then it hit her. "You two followed me today. In a truck."

"So you did see us? Huh. Wasn't sure. We took off when

you took too long inside."

"I was hardly in there. You should go shopping with females more often. Then you'd understand." She coughed several times then rolled over. She felt like shit. "Did you drug me?"

"Just a couple of drops. They are magnified by being in the crossing."

She stilled. "The crossing?"

"Yeah. You're in a way-station. Inside your house, of all places."

The men laughed, a raucous sound that made her nerves tighten and her stomach heave. Way-station? They'd said inside her house. God, were there more passages she didn't know about? Who'd be crazy enough to do that to their home? She was tempted to raze her house and rebuild.

"I don't suppose you know the history of this place, do you? Victoria is one of the oldest settlements in BC."

Yeah, duh. Even with the blow to her head, she remembered her local history. This house was old along with the city. Out of the main center, the city had finally sprawled out to almost reach her home. She still had enough country to make her feel small town but with all the amenities of the big city within an hour's drive.

And none of it mattered right now.

"This house is sitting on one of the biggest intersecting grid lines. That means that interesting things happen here." That raucous laughter sounded again. She couldn't sort out what he was saying, and the nausea in her stomach was making it all so much worse.

"Interesting things?" she asked cautiously. "Like you breaking into my house in the middle of the night and kidnapping me in daylight? I could do without those interesting things."

"Those are nothing. How about the noises going on inside your house while you're asleep at night? You don't know anything about what goes on here."

The second voice said, "Come on, we're wasting time."

Jed – at least she thought it was Jed – said good-naturedly, "True enough. We're looking for notes, books, answers to help us…and someone else…" he sniggered. "To figure out special markings inside a watch."

She managed to open her eyes and stare at the two men. Both dressed in jeans and t-shirts, both having normal common features. No tattoos or obvious distinguishing marks. Yet they were scary nonetheless. She swallowed. "Why do you care about the markings on the watch?"

"Why do you?"

She swallowed again and managed to push herself into a sitting position. "It's my work, my hobby."

"Well then, it's our hobby too. We have a watch we can't figure out. But you can, although we'd rather have your notes than take you. Still, you didn't leave us a choice. Besides, you must have figured all those markings out a long time ago. After all, you've been obsessed with one in particular, haven't you?"

Her heart turned to ice. What the hell was going on here? How could these two assholes know anything?

She stared. "Is that what you were looking for that first night?"

"No. I wanted the damn book you brought back from France."

Jed smirked. "Jordan thought you might have had it when you moved here until we heard you talking to your mother. And realized she had them."

"You were listening in on my phone calls? How?" She was horrified. But at their exchanged smirks, she realized how close they'd actually gotten and how very dangerous they really were. Had they been in her house during those calls? Physically close enough to listen in? Her blood raced, and she had to close her eyes and work on controlling her breathing.

Sirens sounded in the distance, slightly muffled as if layers of cotton was between her and the noise. "The police are here," she cried out triumphantly.

"Ha, it won't matter. They won't find you here."

Her heart clenched. She had to be found now or else she'd never be found. "You don't understand Ward. I told him about all the hollows and hidden places in this house. He'll come with a sledgehammer and break the wall down if that's what it takes to find me."

Just then a series of knocks and taps could be heard beside them. She grinned. "Like I said."

"Shit." Jed reached out and grabbed her jaw. He pinched her lips open and poured a few drops of something into her mouth.

She struggled against his restraints but she was getting weaker, his face getting blurry. "What did you do?" she whispered. She never heard his answer as the drugs took over and she knew no more.

WARD GROANED AS he repeated the same story over and over again as another cruiser and another team showed up. By rights, Sari needed to be missing for twenty-four hours to be reported as a missing person. But these circumstances were unusual. He didn't know what the hell was going on.

How could she have disappeared just like that? He couldn't stop berating himself for letting her enter the house first. *Think, damn it.*

Jeremy reached across and squeezed his shoulder. Concern radiated from his friend. "How are you holding up?"

Ward dragged a hand down his face. "I'm okay. I just…" Words failed him. Just like he'd failed Sari. "I just can't see how she could have gone anywhere."

"That brings up my next question. I know that you found the one hidden passageway and that weird attic space. Is there any chance that there are more of these so-called hidden spaces in this house?"

"Who knows?" With a head shake, Ward said, "I wouldn't have known about either of the two places we found if it hadn't been for Sari."

"Then let's go room by room and wall by wall and see what we find," Jeremy suggested. With two other friends and officers, they started at the kitchen where Sari had disappeared and systematically searched the entire downstairs. They crawled in cupboards and tapped on back walls. They stood on chairs and rapped on the walls above the cupboards. They opened the pantry and when they found it to be a separate unit, they pulled it away out so they could check the wall behind it.

Nothing. The kitchen done, they moved on to the dining room. Again, nothing. Ward pointed to the stairs going up. "What's the chance there's an open space under there?"

The men swarmed the wall. They tapped, rapped, searched, and listened. Then when all efforts had been exhausted, they turned to face Ward.

Shoulders heaving, head down, desperately trying to think positive, he didn't know what to do next. The team that had gone out looking hadn't reported back. He felt no inclination to go. The house held the secrets. He knew it.

But he couldn't prove it.

Then in the silence, he heard it.

He ran to the wall supporting the rising staircase and put his ear against it.

"Wh—"

"Shh." He motioned to Jeremy to come and listen. The three men surrounded him, ears pressed to the wall.

Ward held his breath, the pulse pounding inside his head interfering. He strained harder. Then almost giving up hope, he heard it again.

A moan, soft and gentle behind the wall. Sari. *Oh thank God.*

Jeremy spoke, determination and relief in his voice, "I heard that. Okay, she's here somewhere. Do we rip out the wall?"

"Can we be sure she's behind the wall? What about below? That last sound was strong enough we could have heard it from several feet away. If there are hidden tunnels, the echo would amplify sounds."

The four men stepped back and walked around the staircase. Built into the wall, there was little to examine. Tight and well-built, there were no doors, obvious breaks in the wall or moveable parts. A carpet runner covered the center of each stair all the way up the first landing. Jeremy ran to the first landing and checked that wall out carefully. Pete, one of the two that had stayed to look, searched the inside wall of the stairs. Stan, the other man, stood back and looked at Ward.

"What's up?"

Ward pointed at the bottom of the stairs. "I'm just remembering the attic and the drop down staircase. If that was true, why can't the reverse be true also? Is there any way those stairs lift?"

"Lift?" Pete stopped what he was doing and stomped on the stair he was standing on. Instead of the solid thunk, there was a hollowness to it.

"Oh, that sounds positive." Pete jumped down.

Ward bent to run his fingers along the bottom seam between the floor and the bottom of the stair. Even as his fingers reached the farthest corner, there was a sharp click and the bottom of the stairs rose slightly.

"Wow." Ward sat back in a crouch and looked up to see Pete grinning and pointing to a button in the ornate support bolted to the wall to hold the railing up. Carefully Ward eased the stairs up, which moved as a single unit upward. They opened up like butterfly wings on an exotic sports car.

Pete whistled. "What a place."

Inside the space, huddled on the floor and tied up, lay Sari.

An hour later, Ward was at Sari's side in the emergency room where she was sleeping off the effects of the knockout drugs.

"Sari." He stepped closer, his hand instinctively reaching out to smooth her hair back off her face. "Sari, it's Ward. Are you awake?"

"Ward?" she whispered.

"Yes." The relief in his voice brought a smile to her face.

"Hi. So glad you found me." She opened her eyes and stared at him. A weak smile emerged as her eyes drifted close.

They stayed closed.

"No. Sari, honey, I know you're tired. I know there are likely drugs in your system. Please fight. Just for a few minutes. We need to know who did this."

She snuggled deeper into the sheets.

"Sari. Please talk to me. Just tell me who did this. Did you recognize the men?"

She yawned, a deep, bone-racking action that made her whole body shake. "Men. Two men," she whispered. "From the truck."

"They were the men who were following you?"

She didn't answer.

He reached over and gently shook her shoulder. "Sari?"

Her voice was so gentle and so soft, he leaned close enough that his ear almost touched her lips. "Yes." Her answer came out on a sigh as she dropped off to sleep.

"Sari?"

A gentle snore was his only answer.

Jeremy piped up, reminding Ward he wasn't alone. "Sounds like she's not going to be much help over the next few hours."

"I know." Ward gently stroked her silky cheek. "I'm just happy we found her."

"I hear you there. Come on, buddy. Let's see if the prints found in her hidden cell led to anything."

"Good idea." Ward smiled, a determined look on his face. "Let's go."

CHAPTER 17

SARI WOKE UP and stretched. She tried to open her eyes, but the bright light hurt. She closed them again and rolled over. Sleep sat beside her, not quite wrapping her in its comforting embrace. She stirred restlessly, and a stiff wrinkling sound followed her movements. She frowned. She wanted to forget.

The voices in her head, the memories prodding at her. She had something important to do. Someone important to see. Now if only she could remember who. She stirred restlessly again then bolted upright. She grabbed her head with both hands.

"Ohh," she whispered. "I shouldn't have done that."

She flopped backwards, gasping at the boom in her head.

"When you wake up, you really snap awake, don't you?"

Ward. She rolled over slowly to face him. "I hadn't expected the massive headache." She winced. "Even now I can't quite believe it. Why?"

"Probably the drugs. The doctors said you'd been given something to keep you quiet."

"Figures," she muttered. "How did you find me?"

"It wasn't easy," Ward snorted. "That house of yours is mad, and the staircase is insane."

A small smile peeped out. "I'd totally forgotten about the hidey-hole under the staircase."

Ward leaned forward, astonishment on his face. "You knew? Jesus. It took us hours to find you."

"I'm just glad you did. The two men asked me a bunch of questions about my father's book. I presume they took it with them."

"A book. That's what this is all about?"

"Maybe. Then again, I wouldn't count on it." She gathered her energy and explained what she'd found in the one book. "I haven't checked the other books out."

"Any idea what the markings mean?"

"No. Some kind of formula. I didn't understand it."

"Formula? As in a chemical compound?"

"No, as in an equation. For time travel." That should do it. He'd really think the knock on her head had done her in.

"Are we back to that? Seriously?"

She closed her eyes as pain radiated from her head down her neck. With difficulty, she tried to focus on Ward's question. "I can't see any other explanation for my father's disappearance or for Madge's appearance." So maybe the drugs were making her say more than she'd intended.

"Time travel."

"Crossing dimensions." She coughed to clear her throat. "The men said my house was a way-station."

"Isn't that the same thing?"

"I'll have to give you some of my books to read."

"A short synopsis would help for now," he suggested quickly. "I can read the books later."

She took a deep breath. "There are conflicting theories—"

He snorted.

She glared at him. "Do you want to know or not?"

"Not. But I need to." He threw up his hands. "I'm sorry.

Please, go ahead."

She sent him a warning look and started again. "I can't go over all the different theories. However, my father and the two men apparently—"

"What? What does this have to do with the two men and your father?"

"Damn it, Ward. Do you want to hear or not?"

He subsided, glaring, arms crossed on his chest. "Proceed."

"If you interrupt me one more time," she warned.

"I won't." He waited, but his glare didn't calm down.

She sighed. "The men mentioned something about the dimensional theory and it sounded something like what my father always said." She took a deep breath. "He believed that at certain parts of the world, places where Earth's meridian lines cross and intersect, the energy was special. Lighter, more vibrant. Thinner. Resonating at a higher frequency than all the other places."

Ward tilted his head. "Don't tell me he said that your house was on one of those lines."

"The whole area is. There are many such places around the world. Take the town of Grand Forks at the Canada/US border. It's long been known to have special energy for a similar reason. Now I haven't found any research to corroborate my father's theory about where I live – in fact, energy being energy, the area in question should be miles across."

"So it's not your house?"

"In his notes, my father talks about a portal originally being opened by an ancestor. Since then…" She shrugged. She winced only slightly this time at the movement. Great. Moving gently, she shuffled higher up the pillows. "In the attic were large piles of belongings. Remember, you helped me bring down some of it." At his nod, she continued. "From what I've seen, each pile belongs to a specific person."

"As in these people stored their stuff there?" His tone of voice said he was trying for patience…and failing.

"Or they died and someone couldn't bear to get rid of it. At least that's what I wondered initially." She took another deep breath. "I'm wondering if these people 'disappeared' and the families put the possessions in the locked up attic."

"Why? So they could forget about them?" he asked incredulously.

"Or for them to have again, should these people come back."

"And you're not thinking that they disappeared as in just having gone out for a walk and never coming home again?"

"Like my father?" At his nod, she shook her head. "I'm thinking my father crossed through this thin veil and is living in another dimension."

"What?" He sat back and stared at her. "Do you really think your father is alive?"

"I believe he is, yes." At the doubt and chagrin on his face, she added, "And I think Madge came from that side. She might have been from here originally and either found her way back or came across accidentally."

"Sari…do you really think your house is some kind of waypoint? A place where people can move between two different realities?" he asked it in such a gentle, reasonable tone of voice that she didn't take any offense.

"I don't know what I believe. Do I want to believe my father is alive and well? Of course I do. Have I spent my whole life wishing it? Of course I have," she cried out. "My mother constantly drilled into me that he was gone. The problem is something that you don't know about. Something my mother refused to ever let me talk about."

Ward leaned forward, his gaze locked on hers.

She smiled wryly. "Yes, we lied to the police all those years ago. But there was a very good reason."

"And that was?" he asked sharply.

"You'd never have believed me," she said simply. "My own mother didn't believe what had happened, and she saw it too."

"Sari," he warned.

She hurriedly added, "This is hard, you know. I've never said this to anyone."

"Just tell me."

She chewed on her bottom lip, undecided. She might as well. Yesterday's event defined who she was today.

If she wanted to see where the relationship went, she'd need to see how he felt about her childhood mystery. She was falling a little bit more in love with him every day. She knew it. She'd had a mad crush on him years ago. That the same feelings had stirred up again only meant they'd been inside all along. Waiting like a buried seed for the right conditions to sprout.

She started to explain about the last day she'd seen her father. "He'd just been fiddling with it, trying to do something according to his notes. He was putting it away to visit with me when the watch fell off the table and we both dove for it, but his arm was longer, his hand bigger. I saw him reach for it..." she stopped, tears even now collecting in her eyes at the memory.

"I heard my mother walk back into the room with the hot chocolate she'd gone to make. I watched as my father's fingers closed over it. He grinned, then something went wrong. His face thinned, became almost see through. He got a really weird look on his face, like he knew something. Something he didn't have time to share. He opened his mouth and said, 'Something's wrong.' Then there was a moment where I could hear everything so loud. And see everything so clear. As if the answer to everything was there at my fingertips. As if the world had stopped and opened up endless possibilities."

She stopped and sniffled.

"And then what?" prompted Ward. She glanced up at him. At least he looked more involved. Less like he wanted to wring her neck.

"Then," she said. "He disappeared."

Silence.

"He disappeared. In front of my eyes. In front of my mother's eyes. He just disappeared into a puff of air. No bells and whistles. No big bang. He just faded from our sight."

Ward stared at her, an unfathomable look in his gaze.

She snorted. "It's true. That's why we couldn't tell the police." She shrugged. "Like they'd have believed us or anything else we'd have had to say back then after that."

She appealed to him. "You haven't said anything. Please believe me."

Silent, he studied her as if considering her words – or that the knock on her head had been worse than first suspected.

He stared at her. "If I believe you, then I have to throw out everything I've believed about reality up until now. I can easily believe a ten-year-old girl who loved her father so very much that she dreamed up something like this, but…"

"But what about my mother?"

He sat back, his hand automatically going to run through his unruly hair. "I don't know what to think." He studied her face. "Will your mother corroborate your story?"

She laughed, a sad, mocking laugh that made him wince. "She might and she might not. She's spent the bulk of my childhood trying to erase that event from my memory and implanting the idea that my father walked out the door and never came back."

"The police version?"

"Yes. Exactly. The police version." She pulled the sheets higher up to her chin. "I guess I can't blame her. I don't know if she knows what happened to him, and out of fear of a reoccurrence, she took me far away." She glanced back over at him. "I just don't know."

"If, and this is a big if, what you saw is really what happened – what does it have to do with those two men who attacked you?"

She grimaced. "I'm wondering if they might have come from the other side."

"For what? To get something? To take you to the other side? To immigrate?" He threw his hands up in the air. "You do realize how crazy this sounds, don't you?"

"Yes." Her voice, full of weary sadness, dropped to a whisper. "That's why I haven't been able to tell anyone. Who'd listen? Who'd believe? No one."

She wanted to hear him say he believed. She needed him to say it. But she had no proof. He was a policeman. He needed proof. To see for himself. What he did say surprised her.

"Wasn't it Arthur Conan Doyle who said, *When you have eliminated **the impossible**, whatever **remains**, however improbable, must be the truth.*"

And he smiled and warmed all the cold lonely places in her heart.

"I DON'T CARE. You're not staying here alone. In fact, I'd feel much better if we stayed at my place. I can't say I feel secure here anymore."

"I do. It's my house, and I don't want to be scared away." She glared at him.

He figured it had more to do with being close to her father in case all these events had something to with his disappearance...and possible return. A crossing spot...like what the hell? No one would believe him. It was too far out there. Too much science fiction for even the strongest believers.

They unloaded the last of the groceries they'd stopped for on the way home from the hospital. As they'd pulled into the driveway, Ward tried again. "Why don't we stay at my house? I have plenty of room."

Sari shot him a disgusted look. "If I run now, then I'm done. I won't want to come back. I need to come in here. Open up all the secret places and check that I'm alone."

"We'll open up all the hidden places. But what if they can cross this dimensional barrier at will? Did you consider that? You could be asleep while they decide to cross over. How would you know?"

"Thanks for that reminder. I think I'll set up cameras."

"Cameras?"

"Inside the attic and inside the staircase. Maybe a few others around the house. Is that being paranoid?"

"Hell no. I wish we'd had them up a few days ago though." He watched as she unlocked her front door and entered. "It would help to identify these two men."

"Only if they are from this dimension. Can you imagine the paperwork headache if they are from another dimension?"

Ward groaned. "Don't even mention it. It's one thing for you and I to joke about it, and…" He held up his hand. "I know you aren't joking. But to even contemplate having to deal with such a concept with my supervisor…" He shuddered. "That is no laughing matter."

She tossed him a grin back over her shoulder. He could see the worry lines on her face as she worked hard to ignore the situation but couldn't quite manage it. Good. He wanted her worried. He wanted her scared. Some assholes were after her, and she needed to be wise and stay safe. Then again, he could talk until his voice went hoarse before she'd listen to reason. He followed her inside the house. He'd been here just a few hours ago. All had been well. He'd also asked his supervisor for protection for her, but hadn't convinced him that this was anything but another case of breaking and entering.

Ward wasn't leaving her alone again. That he could do it and get paid was the compromise he'd made with his boss.

Walking through the front door, he double-checked that the shop door was still as he'd left it. It was.

Sari watched and shook her head. "Are you going to do this every day?"

"Probably. And you're not going to run into the kitchen ahead of me anymore either." He moved past her determinedly and led the way.

He knew she was going to shake her head, but she'd take his lead on this one.

"The whole protector thing is nice in little bits…but…" she said tartly.

"Get used to it. I'm here to stay. There's no way I'm going through what I did yesterday evening."

Her voice softened. "I'm sorry. I know how difficult that must have been."

"You think? I couldn't find you anywhere."

"I know. You went a little nuts, I guess. It all happened so fast. I didn't even have time to warn you."

He spun around. "Warn me? I wasn't worried about me. I wish I'd never let you go ahead of me. Wished that the attacker had found me first. Not you. Then it would have been a different story."

"And maybe you would have been killed. Did you ever think of that? They might also have used you to get to me. I couldn't have stood that."

"Better than me finding out you'd been snatched right out from under my nose. I won't go through that again." He spun around to look at her. "I can't."

She reached up a small palm and laid it gently against his cheek. "I'm sorry."

He closed his eyes. "It's not your fault."

"No, it's not," she admitted softly, the gentle look in her eye his undoing. "But neither is it yours."

She reached up and kissed him gently. "Thank you for finding me."

He wrapped her tight into his embrace and buried his face in her silky hair. She was so precious. He'd come so close to losing her. "I was so scared."

She slipped her arms around his back and stepped closer. They stayed like that for a long moment. She tilted her head back and smiled. "Let's make dinner and then we can relax."

"I'm relaxed right here." He searched her gaze, wondering, questioning. Did she feel like he did? Did she understand the depth of his feelings? Did he understand himself?

"But I'm hungry." She smiled, a mysterious look in her gaze that made his heart race. "Not to worry. We'll come back to this same place after dinner." She reached up and dropped a light kiss on his lips. "I promise."

CHAPTER 18

S ARI STEPPED BACK and busied herself making a simple meal of chicken and veggies. Trying to settle down inside at being back in her kitchen. Her groceries from last night had been put away by someone. Probably Ward.

His gaze followed her every move. She felt it like a warm caress on her back. He was a gentle soul. She knew he was uncertain. Uncertain of her, of taking this next step. Of them. She was too. But she wanted it. She wanted him. She always had. He was the man she'd been waiting for all these years. That it was in the middle of a personally nasty time couldn't be helped. It might have sped up the timetable, but the stress wasn't the cause of the relationship.

It was the catalyst that had brought them to this point tonight. He wanted to sleep here and protect her. She wanted him to sleep here to seduce him.

Now all she had to do was feed him. Assuage one hunger. Then take him to bed. And assuage the other.

And she couldn't wait.

But food came first.

Making dinner together was a fun experience. They laughed and argued. Old times, new times, his times and her times. It was relaxing and peaceful and went with the romantic mellow mood she'd been hoping for, especially after the last stressful couple of days. She really needed this.

So did he.

It was their time.

"A glass of wine?" she asked as she stood up and carried their plates over to the sink.

"I'll get it." Ward stood up and reached for the open bottle. He filled both glasses then helped to clean off the table. "I'll wash up. You cooked. Sit down and enjoy your wine."

He reached over to turn her around and gave her a gentle shove toward the table. "I'm quite capable in the kitchen."

"Nice to know." She patted his cheek. "Thanks."

She sat down. Picking up her glass, she took a sip of wine. "So which bedroom do you want to sleep in tonight?" She smiled at the stiffening of his back. She'd caught him by surprise.

"I don't know. Put me where you want me." He smiled at her over his shoulder.

She smiled back. He thought he'd slipped out from under that one. So not. "You can sleep in my parents' bedroom if you want."

"Your parents' room?" he asked thoughtfully. He rinsed off one plate and put in the draining pan. "That's on the opposite side of the house. Correct?"

"Yes." She waited.

"No way. Either beside your room or in your room." He kept his back to her, but his voice brooked no argument. Good. She didn't want one either.

"Then my room it is." She kept her tone neutral and calm.

Silence. He turned to look at her, soapsuds dripping off his wet hands. "Really?"

"Sure. I'll make you a bed up on the floor. At least that way you'll wake up first if anyone tries to enter."

"True enough." He turned back and studiously kept his gaze down on his job, carefully washing each plate and cup that they'd used.

She waited for him to say more. He didn't.

She yawned. It was late. And she felt more than a little tired after her day in the hospital. It wasn't the most restful place to be. Even when she'd napped from the drugs there was noise, bustle, people coming and going, a light undercurrent of noise that kept her from truly resting.

After he finished washing the dishes, he turned to face her.

"Let's take the wine upstairs and set up my bed. You're exhausted."

She nodded. "I hadn't realized it was as bad as it was until I sat here and let you work. It must be the wine." She took another sip.

"The wine might have something to do with it, but you were tired before that. Come on, let's get you upstairs and into bed before you fall asleep."

He picked up both wine glasses and waited until she double-checked the back kitchen door and preceded him to the front. She checked the front door, the shop door, and set the alarm under his watchful eye.

"Satisfied?" she teased.

"No, but that will have to do."

Wondering what he meant by that, she led the way upstairs. With every step, her legs seemed heavier and heavier.

"Come on. You can do it. We're almost there."

She gave a small laugh. "How come I'm sooo tired now?"

"Doesn't matter. You are. Let's get you to bed."

She kept moving upward. At her bedroom, she headed straight for the bathroom. "I'll be just a moment." In the small room, she willed herself to have enough energy to get through her nightly ritual. By making it short and fast, she managed to wash her face, brush her teeth, and get into her cami top and pj bottoms. Folding her clothes into a neat pile, she realized that somewhere along the way, her plans for a sexy evening culminating in bed had been tossed away in favor of sleep. They had other nights. Right now, she swore if she couldn't lie down and sleep, she'd fall flat on her face any minute.

She opened the door to find the overhead light off and the bedside lamps on. She had a huge queen bed. It was surely big enough for the two of them. She didn't have the energy to make him a bed on the floor.

"Let's get you under the covers. You look ready to drop."

She swayed in place. He rushed over and led her to the side of the bed. He pulled back her duvet and waited for her to slip under then he covered her up again. "Where can I find blankets to make up a bed on the floor?"

She huddled deeper under the covers.

"Sari?"

"Don't bother. Just get in on the other side."

He stilled. "That might be asking for trouble."

"Not tonight it won't. I'm too tired for anything more."

He waited, undecided. She could feel the waves of uncertainty rolling off him. "Are you sure?"

"Yes, I'm sure. It will be fine. Besides, I don't have the energy to make up a bed. So get in. I'm tired."

He bent down and the next thing she knew, she felt his warm lips touch her temple. She smiled. "G'night," she whispered, almost asleep.

"Good night." He left her side. She heard the rustle of clothing then the bed dipped and rocked behind her. So close and yet so far. She smiled. Some things had to happen on their own time. At least in the morning she'd see. Maybe she'd wake him up in her own way.

With that thought on her mind, she drifted off to sleep.

WARD LAY QUIETLY beside Sari. He dared not breathe too hard and rock the bed. He had no idea what kind of sleeper she was. But she needed rest. She rolled over, the movement a gentle shift on the mattress. He glanced over at her. She faced him now. Her face was soft and gentle in sleep, the signs of stress and worry easing as her body reached for the healing it desperately needed.

That those guys had snatched her while he was in the house worried him, more than he'd let on. His profession hadn't allowed him the comfort of ignorance. Horrible things happened to nice people all the time, often for no logical explanation. He was terrified of what was going on in Sari's world.

And the concepts she'd put forward scared him even more. He was no wimp, but the idea of bad guys being able to cross through to another dimension basically at whim, with no fanfare or indication of what they were doing or how, was enough to keep any cop awake. That these supposed dimensional travelers were after Sari made his blood freeze.

She was his. He'd protect her with his life. But he had no way to go to another dimension and haul her back.

Just the thought sent whatever sleep that had been coming his way right back out. No. That this strange phenomenon might have already happened, twice…and could happen again and theoretically many times made the horror all too real.

And if these people had disappeared into another dimension, it couldn't be easy to get back. He knew Sari's father had doted on her to the exclusion of his wife. Or maybe as a result of the coldness of his wife. He didn't know. But he did know that Sari's father would have done anything to get back home to her if he could.

"Stop thinking so loud."

The whisper, so soft and delicate, made him glance over at Sari. Was she even awake?

"See, you're keeping me awake."

"I am not. Go to sleep. You're exhausted."

A tiny smile played at the corner of her mouth. "I am, but your worrying is enough to upset anyone. You need your sleep too. You've had less rest than I have." She reached out a gentle hand and slipped it into his.

He cradled her hand, tugging it gently upwards to kiss her fingers. "Sleep, and then I'll sleep too."

She smiled, her voice drifting off into sleep with the word, "Liar."

He curled up facing her, holding her hand, and drifted off to sleep.

CHAPTER 19

S ARI WOKE UP to the furnace beside her. Warm arms were wrapped around her and her back pressed against a huge bare chest. Ward. She smiled, letting her eyes drift close. The man was a powerhouse. His chest rose and fell in a steady relaxed pattern. She hoped he was having sweet dreams.

As she lay there, she realized she didn't want him to be having sweet dreams about anything other than her, and there was one way to make sure she dominated his dreams.

The tiniest giggle escaped.

His arms tightened in response.

She grinned and gently rolled over.

His arms relaxed then tightened, always keeping her in their loving circle. She burrowed in closer, a happy sigh escaping.

"You okay?" he murmured in a sleepy voice.

"Hmmm." And she was. Good thing she was on the Pill. Although she'd been on for years to stabilize her cycle and not this, it was very convenient. She turned her head slightly and kissed his chest, his neck, his chin.

She slid her hand up his smooth skin, her fingers stopping at his ribs, stroking along the bone and back, loving the feel of his muscles, his strength. On their own, her hands gently explored the taut muscles of his belly, hearing him suck in his breath as they dropped lower and lower until her fingers tangled in the curly hair below his navel. His slow steady breath faltered.

She smirked and slipped her hand yet lower again.

She found the edge of his knit boxers, easing one fingernail along the long edge before slipping a finger under the elastic on the way back.

His chest froze.

She giggled.

"Witch," he said thickly, his arms squeezing her in a tight hug before releasing her.

"It's not my fault. Sleeping with you is like sleeping with fire. You're so hot you woke me up."

"Maybe," he lowered his head to nuzzle her ear, "that was part of my master plan."

She cuddled closer. "Then you're very smart because if that plan had something to do with picking up where we left off earlier – it's working."

And she twisted her head upward and captured his lips in a sweet kiss. With a sigh, she settled back against the pillows and tugged him closer.

He shifted slightly, coming down to rest across her chest, his weight secure on his arms. This time he kissed her. As if knowing the time was theirs with no rush, no pressure, just the promise of what was to come, he kissed her with heart, with such caring it almost brought tears to her eyes.

"Missed you," he whispered, his lips brushing against her. "I missed you so much."

"I'm back now."

"And hopefully to stay." Then as if his actions could make a difference, he kissed her as if he had no plans to ever let her go.

She sank into his embrace, loving the tenderness, loving the possessiveness. She'd missed him so much. She'd not put any thought into a future with him because it had seemed so distant, so impossible. She'd just been waiting. For the right time. The right events to bring her home. Home to him.

She wrapped her arms around his neck and poured all the lost and forgotten emotions now rising up in a wave of longing into her kiss.

And ignited a firestorm.

He responded with all the passion and need she'd felt and hadn't been able to express – and she couldn't get enough. She stroked his back and hips, coming to rest on his hard buttocks, and dug her nails in gently. He moaned and shifted slightly down and away from her hands, but his own slid under her cami to lift the silky knit higher. He lowered his head and nuzzled her ribs, pushing the soft fabric up and out of his way with his head. She grabbed her cami and tugged it over her head. Immediately he palmed her breast, testing the weight, the softness, then groaned and took her nipple into his mouth to suck. She arched her back, whimpering.

"Oh, that feels good," she whispered, her body aching for more. He laved first one breast then the other. His knee lay heavy across her thighs at the heart of her. She slid her hands restlessly up and down his thighs, her fingers sliding under the edge of his boxers before moving up higher.

She tugged his boxers down but he ignored her, his own hands shifting to her pjs, sliding inside the flimsy material, shoving it down off her hips to the floor. She lifted her hips to help him but wanted his boxers off, too. She tugged the elastic down but couldn't reach the other side. She lowered her hand to find the large bulge in front. Sari smiled and clasped the long length of him. The guttural moan from deep inside his chest had her sliding her hand down to cup the sac below. A shudder rippled down his big frame. He shifted away from her.

She tried to follow, only he pushed her back gently. She glared at him. He grinned, bent down, and kissed her on the tip of her nose. "Just a minute."

She pouted, then realizing he was stripping off his boxers, she sat up and reached for him. He caught her hands and flipped her onto her back, stretching her arms above her head. Then he lowered his head and suckled first one nipple then the other. She rolled from side to side, wanting to be free to touch him but not wanting him to stop.

He grabbed both her hands in one of his and secured them tightly in his grasp.

She twisted beneath him then gasped, her shock turning to a groan as his fingers speared through the curls at the juncture of her thighs. He stroked her again, opening her, tormenting her. Her legs shifted restlessly but with his leg once again across hers, she couldn't move far.

He slid one finger inside. She whimpered.

He slid two inside. She groaned.

And bucked against his hand.

"Ward," she cried.

He leaned down to kiss her, his lips hot, mobile, his passion needy. But he wouldn't let her go.

Just when she didn't think she could stand any more, he pulled his hand away and settled himself between her thighs.

She lifted her hips and he plunged deep.

She cried out in joy and need.

He withdrew slightly, repositioned himself, held her hips, and plunged in again. This time he didn't stop; he kept up the rhythm, driving her straight to the edge of the precipice. She hung there, breathless in her frustration, until he lifted her leg over his arm and drove deep into the heart of her.

She shrieked as her world came apart. His movements deepened as he rode her right through the climax rippling through her. She shuddered, her mind a kaleidoscope of sensation, and could only hang on for the ride.

He lowered her leg, grabbed her hips and ground against her. She groaned, buffeted from wave upon wave of feeling as the second crest built. He grabbed her hips and plunged in once more, then eased out as his body shuddered and quaked with his release.

And sent her spinning off again.

Finally, he collapsed on the bed beside her, his breathing hard, his face red, his voice cracking as he whispered, "I missed you so much."

Tears in her eyes, she curled herself around him, over-whelmed by emotion and that one feeling she couldn't quite define. And realized what that emotion was – the sense of rightness. Of being where she belonged. She whispered, "And now I've come home."

Wrapped up tight in his embrace, she fell asleep.

WARD, HIS BREATH still shaky, his lungs still gasping to return to a regular rhythm, hugged Sari close. His heart would take longer to recover.

He'd been devastated when she'd left. It had been hard enough when her father disappeared; he'd gone looking with her for days back then. They'd only been kids, but they'd checked every place within blocks and had searched her house as much as they were allowed. Her mother hadn't been much help. She'd been locked down, almost angry back then. He hadn't understood as a child. He did now.

For Sari though, her world had collapsed.

That he could imagine, but it wasn't until her mother packed them up and took off that he'd really understood.

Ward had tried to pull his world back together again, and as a kid it had been easier to bury himself in everyday life, but something had always been missing.

Sari.

Now fifteen years later, she was back where she belonged.

In his life, in his arms, in his bed. In his heart.

He'd never been happier.

CHAPTER 20

SARI YAWNED AND rolled over. She stretched out a long leg and touched something. She froze, peeked under her lashes. Ward slept beside her. Slow and relaxed, his bare chest moving gently. She lifted her head and checked her watch. Six in the morning. Too early to get up. She was still tired herself. She curled up close to Ward. Unconsciously, he reached out and wrapped an arm around her shoulders, tugging her against his chest as he'd done dozens of times in the night. She smiled and relaxed in his embrace. Just where she wanted to be. Memories of their lovemaking flickered through her tired brain. She'd lost count of how many times they'd made love; it had seemed endless. Her body ached in places she'd long forgotten about.

It was so good to be here at this stage of her life. To have him back in it. She didn't think she'd ever let him go. She snuggled in closer, loving being in his arms. He was so protective – even in sleep. Just as she was drifting off again, she heard a weird sound.

Not worried, she lay there and tried to identify it. It came again. She frowned. With no pets, it could only be the wind. The morning light was bright enough to see it was going to be a clear day here, but she couldn't get a sense of any movement outside. Gusts in Victoria could get downright vicious. And this so didn't sound like wind.

A second muffled bang sounded through the wall. This time, it was followed by an odd shuffling sound. Definitely not wind. Ward's warm body stiffened under her cheek. His heartbeat, slow and steady, sped up. The arm around her shoulder tightened ever so slightly.

"Shh," he murmured against her hair.

Good. He'd heard it too.

She nodded once and rolled back to her pillow. He threw back the covers and sat up. It was the first she'd seen him in the buff. Damn, the man had muscles. Not a cut workout body like the guys who haunted the gym, but like a man used to a physical lifestyle. He came by it naturally. Ward reached for his boxer briefs; smooth, curve-hugging cotton that highlighted muscular cheeks and rock hard thighs. She sighed, wishing she could pull him back down beside her.

He turned back to look at her as he tugged his jeans up and over his hips, pulling up the zipper and closing the snap. He pulled his t-shirt over his head. Lifting a finger, he motioned for her to be quiet. He slipped over to the door, and that was when she finally realized what he was doing.

"Wait," she hissed. "Don't leave me here." She slipped out of bed, then scrambled into jeans and stepped into her shoes, choosing sandals over slippers. She raced over to him, still pulling on her t-shirt.

He shook his head and glared at her. She glared back. "I don't want to be separated. If anything happens to you, I won't know what happened."

He closed his eyes. "I want you to stay hidden. Safe."

"If someone is here, they are going to expect to see me. If I'm not there with you, they will come looking anyway." She had to make him understand. "Please. I don't want to be alone."

"Stay behind me."

He opened the bedroom door, the quiet snick unbelievably loud in the silence. He pulled it open and stuck his head out. He walked to the spare bedroom, the door open, and looked inside. "Nothing there."

"Then they have to be on the other side or..."

"Or?"

"The attic."

He stilled and looked at her. "Can we get there from here?"

She motioned to the closet. "Only through the passageway."

"No." He discarded that idea. "Too noisy."

"Exactly. That's probably what we're hearing as well. Anyone coming from there can't be silent either."

He studied her face for a long moment. Then he glanced at the closet.

"No," she whispered. "There's no point in going that route if we don't know where they are."

He frowned, obviously not wanting to let go of the idea. "It's a great way to sneak up on someone though."

She winced. "Yeah, thanks for that."

"Come on." He tucked her up behind him and slipped out to the hallway. Sari took a deep breath and followed. They checked out the bathroom then crept down the staircase to the first landing. Still, no other sounds anywhere. Could the intruder have left?

They crept down toward the kitchen, silent and vigilant. Sari kept behind him. In the kitchen, they gave the room a quick search. Nothing had been disturbed. She waited to see if he planned to move across the hallway and up the other staircase or down toward the front of the house and the rest of the rooms. He led the way through the living room then sitting room and finally down toward her shop. The morning sun was high enough to give the rooms enough light to see by. There appeared to be no one here. Anywhere.

Less concerned now, Sari reached for the shop door ahead of him. Just as her fingers were about to connect, her hand was grabbed and held. "Wait." He nodded through the glass door. On the other side, she could see a shadow moving.

"Shit," she whispered under her breath. "Now what?"

"I'm going in."

Ward pulled out his gun. The gun she hadn't realized he had tucked into his back. He motioned her back.

"It's locked. I have to unlock it."

He glared at her. "If it's locked, how did this guy get in there?"

She didn't think it was a good time to bring up her parallel universe theory. Ward didn't look like he wanted to hear about bad guys coming though her attic. He reached for the door and turned it. His hand stopped. He shot her a look of frustration.

She grinned and shrugged. Stretching up high to the frame above the door, she pulled down a spare key and, keeping free of the window, she unlocked the door.

Snick.

The sound made her cringe. Ward motioned her out of the way. She flattened against the wall, holding her breath. Ward crouched low, shoved the door open wide, and ran inside.

"Stop. Police!"

Silence.

Then a high-pitched squeal sounded. Jesus. Sari shuddered. Was that even human? She waited a long moment before venturing to look around the corner. When she did, she realized that whatever was in there wasn't bothering Ward. He was running a hand through his hair and staring down at whatever it was on the floor, hidden behind her workbench.

"Ward?"

He glanced over at her, but there was no smile on his face. "Come here, please."

Uh-oh. That tone of voice didn't mean anything good. She flicked on the light switch, noticing as she walked toward him that the security light on the front hall panel flashed red, signaling that all was well. So what the hell had Ward found?

She gave him an inquiring look. "What's the problem?"

Grim faced, he motioned toward the floor. And damn – there sat huddled in a ball was a severely scrawny old man.

Dazed, she stood and stared. "Again?"

"How?"

Ward pointed to the side at something she hadn't noticed at first. "The attic steps were down."

"Oh shit."

They stared at each other in wordless wonder.

"And how am I going to explain this to my partner?" Ward demanded. "How could anyone come from your attic when we've been here all night?"

"We didn't check out the attic when we got home. He could have been hiding in there then," she suggested, approaching the terrified man in front of her.

"And the locked door?"

She shrugged. "Ask Agatha Christie. She loved these

types of mysteries."

"Oh great. That's helpful." He tucked the gun in the back of his pants and bent down to the man. "Hello? Are you okay?"

No response. Sari crouched down and put a hand on the man's leg. With a small cry, he pulled back into a tighter ball. Sari patted his shoulder. Aged enough to have silvery hair and small enough to fit under her desk, she didn't know what to do.

"Maybe call for an ambulance. Give him a bed beside Madge," she suggested.

The silvery head shot up. "Madge?" Blue eyes stared up at the two of them; hope and desperation clung to the gaze. "Do you know Madge?"

"Madge showed up in my house, similar to the way you just have. She wasn't in very good shape. She's in the hospital now and doing a little better, but she's barely talking. Do you know her?" Sari asked gently.

When no answer was immediately forthcoming, Ward leaned forward to ask, "Do you know Madge?"

The old man nodded. "She's my aunt. I have to bring her back."

Sari didn't know what to say. This guy was a senior already, putting Madge into a whole new age category. "Bring her back?" Sari asked. "Bring her back where?"

"Home. I have to. They'll kill me if I don't." The old man's voice rose at the end, panic making him reach out and grab Sari's t-shirt. "Please. Help me."

"Where are you from?"

He looked around in confusion. "Here?"

Ward and Sari stared at each other. She could see the bewilderment in Ward's gaze mirrored in her own. Sari turned back to the shivering man. She studied him. Small and fine boned, he was a similar size and shape to Madge. Dressed in pants and a shirt with socks barely covering his bony feet, she realized he could be anywhere from fifty to ninety. Ageless looking. The same as Madge. "What's your name?"

He frowned. "Mark."

Sari stiffened. Another M name. The family tree.

Just as she was about to stand, Ward prompted, "Mark what?"

Mark frowned, drawing his thick bushy brows together over his confused eyes. "Mark Harrods."

"Harrods?" Sari gasped. Was it possible?

Ward looked at Sari with a question in his eyes. "Sari?"

"I don't know. It's possible." She almost laughed hysterically. After all these years, she'd found relatives. This man had the same last name she did. Jumping up, she ran to her safe and unlocked it. She removed the family tree and opened it up. There listed as deceased was M. Harrods. Again. But beside it, another generation later, was another name – Mark Harrods.

"Christ." She walked the information over to Ward.

"Mark." She waited until he looked at her. "Can you tell me what year this is?"

He frowned. "I can't remember."

"Can you tell me your parent's names?"

His frown deepened. "Julie and Ken."

There it was. Sari held the paper out for Ward. He snatched it up and turned it slightly to read it better. He looked over the paper at Mark then swiveled to stare at Sari.

She raised one eyebrow at him and shrugged. What was she supposed to say?

As far as she was concerned, Mark was the Mark Harrods who'd supposedly died several decades ago.

NO, NO, AND no. No way was he thinking that Mark had appeared out of the air in Sari's attic. "There's no way in hell."

She glanced over at him, a small grin whispering across her face. He glared at her, his mind grappling with a concept so foreign his brain refused to believe it.

Yet how could Mark have gotten in? How could Madge have, for that matter? Then there was the problem of her father disappearing. Except her father hadn't been in the attic. He glanced up to the ceiling and realized the spot Greg had gone missing from was right below.

If the calculations had been slightly off, or slightly sideways, could that have allowed him to cross time or go to an alternate dimension from here? Or was the energy that was generated in something like this so strong that it was actually not a spot of energy, but a column of energy that encompassed this part of the room, too? If he believed any of this was possible, it wasn't hard to believe that the portal would be expanded beyond the one space up above.

If he believed any of this…

"Are you okay?" Sari whispered beside him.

He gave her a strange look. "You're pushing the boundaries of my belief here."

She nodded gravely. "I hear you. I don't know how to prove anything. Maybe Madge can confirm Mark here. And maybe some of his story as well."

Ward studied the frail old man and realized he did need to talk to Madge. But he didn't want to leave Sari alone.

This old man wasn't going to be much of a threat, but that didn't mean someone else couldn't come through whatever doorway he and Madge had used.

And he had no way to close and lock this mythical doorway either. Madge. He'd take ten minutes and try and confirm Mark's story with her, then get back here and sort out the rest of this.

"I'll be half an hour. No longer."

He gave Sari a hard kiss. "Don't leave. Don't open the door outside. Just in case there are more coming, go into the main part of the house and lock the shop tight so no one can get out."

And he left.

CHAPTER 21

AFTER WARD'S QUICK exit, Sari brought Mark into the kitchen and sat him down at the table. She put on coffee and the teakettle. She was still rattled. Who knew what the hell was going on or what they were going to do about it? Mark had been asking questions about Madge incessantly. She hoped a hot drink and a square meal might keep him quiet. She wanted him to talk, but more about how he got here and where he'd been.

So far, none of his answers made any sense.

Glancing out the window for the umpteenth time, she waited for Ward to return. She doubted his half hour time frame, but she hoped. Making tea, she carried the pot and cups over to the table. Mark's face lit up. He positively beamed.

"Oh, I do like a cup of tea."

"Good," she said softly. Knowing Ward would prefer coffee, she finished setting up the coffeemaker and in a moment of positive thinking, she turned it on. He wouldn't leave her alone for long. Not with a second senior appearing in her house.

"Mark, what did you do for a living?"

"Do?" he frowned. "Why, I'm a watchmaker. The same as the rest of the family."

She stared at him. "Is everyone in the family a watchmaker?"

"Yes, of course. We have no choice to be anything but watchmakers. Or timekeepers," he added as an afterthought. He sighed. "Not that we have much choice in that either."

"What does that mean? A timekeeper?"

"If you don't know the answer to that," he said, looking at her strangely, "maybe I should be asking you a question – like what are you doing in my house?"

A surprised laugh slipped free. "I live here. And it's my house, by the way."

Affronted, he stared at her. Then swallowing hard, he reached out and poured himself a cup of tea so hot steam billowed above his cup. Still, he lifted it to his lips.

"It's hot," she warned.

He nodded and blew and sipped and blew and sipped before finally managing a full drink. He closed his eyes and sat back with a happy sigh. "Now that's a decent cup."

Sari watched, fascinated as he drank his full cup, then poured himself a second and repeated the routine.

"I'm glad you enjoyed it."

He set his empty cup down on the table. "Now, where's Madge?"

"In the hospital."

"Is she hurt? Because I need to take her back."

"Back where?"

"To the timekeepers. Where else?"

He sounded so reasonable, so sane, and yet he was making no sense. "Where are the timekeepers?"

Staring at her, one eyebrow raised, he said, "Now I know for sure this isn't your house."

She stared. "Pardon? What does my not knowing about timekeepers have to do with ownership of this house?"

He reached over and lifted the teapot again. Pouring the last of the tea into his cup, he lifted it to his lips and took another sip. "Because all owners of this house are timekeepers."

Now she didn't know what to think. She sat back. "Are the timekeepers in another dimension?" she whispered, unable to help herself from asking the question.

His blue eyes locked onto hers. They stared silently at each other. She knew he was weighing his words carefully, wondering what to tell her.

"Please. Tell me the truth. I lost my father close to fifteen years ago this week. I don't know what happened to him."

The blue eyes widened in astonishment. "Greg? Are you Greg's daughter? If so, why don't you know about this?"

"Yes, yes. He's my father. And I don't know because no one has told me anything." When he just stared at her open mouthed, she gasped in shocked understanding. In a voice barely above a whisper, she said, "Where is he? Have you seen him?"

"He's with the timekeepers."

She closed her eyes then opened them suddenly, shock almost stopping her heart. It hiccupped then raced forward in hope. "Are you saying that he's alive? That he's over in whatever time-space continuum that exists where you used to be? Where Madge came from?"

She stared at him, willing him to tell her the truth. When he didn't answer, she whispered, "Please. I love my father. I've missed him every single day he's been gone."

"Yes." The whisper was so soft and so powerful, yet it threatened to break her.

"Yes, you've seen him?" She caught her breath. "Yes, he's

alive? Yes, he's over there where you have come from?"

"To all those questions…yes."

The first tear slid from the corner of her eye followed closely by a second one. She was scared to hope. Scared to dream that her beloved Poppy might be alive and safe and sound. She swiped at her cheeks with her sleeve. "Can he come home?" she whispered, her eyes gauging his answer, willing it to be the one she wanted to hear.

"I don't know," he admitted softly. "The only reason they brought me here was to bring Madge back. And even then, we can't travel all the time. It's because of the time of year. The lunar eclipse and some other weird planetary alignment means that the distance between the two dimensions or parallel existences can be crossed." He stared at her. "I don't understand how your father came over. It shouldn't have happened." He frowned. "We shouldn't have had another exchange until this week's alignment, but with your father already there, it isn't likely to happen."

She didn't understand. "Are you saying that if my father was meant to go over, it should have happened this year, like next week? Not fifteen years ago?"

"Correct. These things are gauged very closely. Not just anyone can cross, you know. Timekeepers are picked, or chosen you might say. One per generation. But never the only child in the generation."

"One per generation?" She stared at him. "But my father is an only child. As was his father before him."

Mark's gaze narrowed thoughtfully. "And your mother?"

Sari blinked. The concept of her mother in this conversation was just a little too weird. "She's also a single child."

"And what about your grandmother on your father's side? Have there been no more than one offspring per generation?"

"Not for a long time. At least as far as I know."

"Very interesting."

"Why?"

"Because the timekeepers aren't allowed to take the only offspring in a family. And as you're the only offspring, then you can't go to help the timekeepers."

"And therefore neither should my father have been taken…should he have?"

"No." Frowning, Mark shook his head, his eyes downward as if not sure how much to tell her. After a long moment, he tilted his head sideways, his gaze intent, and said, "Maybe your father volunteered – to keep you safe?"

"You mean go so I didn't have to?" She hated that thought. "But I'm an only child, so in theory… Besides, why our family anyway? Why are we needed at all?"

"I'm not sure any of us are needed anymore." He stared down at the table. "Centuries ago, one of our ancestors learned how to cross to the other dimension. That ancestor, whose specialty was time and watches, was naturally treated like a hero. He stayed for a long time to help them as the people over there had only a rudimentary system in place. He built watches, timepieces for them. Showed them how to maintain and repair these items. Teaching them, essentially."

Sari leaned closer, struggling to understand generations upon generations involved. All of them her people.

"For generations, people in our family sworn to secrecy went over to help." He sighed. "And somehow that all changed. Whether it was we refused one time or they wanted more, the system changed from one of goodwill to one of master and slave."

He raised his gaze, sad and looking inward, to Sari.

"When your father came over, there were problems with the portal – it was unstable. It actually broke something in the watch he used. It took years to stabilize it again. There are only the three of us left. Your father has been teaching the younger generation to look after their own issues – he's been trying to resolve the slavery issue so that it would end." His eyes glistened. "But I don't know. The old timekeepers said it's always been done this way, and that's the way it will stay."

"Did everyone go over from this house? Madge?"

"Absolutely. We all did." He leaned back to stare at her. "We grew up knowing one person would have to go over. And if we didn't – well, the consequences would be severe. Not only were we forced over there, but now they've learned how to travel here."

A horrid thought. "So you were forced to sacrifice one person."

He nodded. "But it was never to be the only child in that generation."

"Apparently that changed with my father." She glared out the window. To know that he was alive, a prisoner so close and yet impossibly far away, was intolerable. "Why didn't the family move? Get away from here?"

"Several reasons." He stared out the window. "Tron, the boss, would have done everything he could have to find us, and he would have succeeded. But more than that, it would have left the door open for him to come and take other people. Other things. He'd have had a one-way door to our world. By keeping us there, he agreed to leave our world alone."

"And you believed him?" At his nod, she sank back, her mind working furiously. They've been indoctrinated into this mindset for generations. She could hardly blame them for fearing something she didn't understand. Hell, she was afraid enough already from the little bit she did know. That one man could come to her world and do whatever he wanted with no repercussions and no one knowing it was him terrified her.

She said abruptly, "I want to bring my father home."

"They might not let him go. He's become very important to them."

"They don't need him. He's spent fifteen years helping them. I need him now," she cried out passionately. "I'm the one that grew up without a father." She glared at him bitterly. "Did you leave children behind when you went over?"

He shook his head. "No. Neither did Madge. They always choose single people without families. In your father's case, maybe there was no one else. Maybe he had no choice. I don't know."

"And I don't care." She stood up and walked over to the window. "It's time for him to come home."

"And who'd replace him? Madge and I are worn out. Old. Look at Madge. She shouldn't have to go, but I have to bring her back. Leaving permanently isn't an option." He ran a tired hand over his face. "Madge was supposed to come home when I went over, but they wouldn't let her." He frowned. "It's the master, Tron. He changed the rules when he came into power."

"And if you don't go back, what then?" She spun around. "Can't we close the door? Stop them from coming back here?"

"No. I don't know any way. They'll just come and take who and what they want regardless."

Sari didn't want to hear that last part. She'd latched onto one thing. Her father was alive. She wanted him to come home. To return to the life he'd lived before he disappeared. And she was going to find a way to make that happen.

And stop those bastards from stealing her kin – forever. Somehow.

She stiffened. She shouldn't. The idea was crazy. Stupid, even. And yet…

She spun around to face him. "I want to go over there with you. Instead of Madge."

WARD HAD PARKED outside the hospital and almost ran inside. He was only just realizing Madge might still be sleeping – something she obviously needed. Then again, remembering his hospital stay and the number of times the nurses came in to check up on him, he realized he'd barely gotten any sleep. Hopefully he'd catch her awake and alert.

Remembering her fear last time, he slowed his pace as he approached her room. He needed her calm and cooperative and to go in like a madman…he'd get nowhere.

The main light was off when he walked in, but the small lamp at the head of the bed was on. The curtains around her bed were closed. He hesitated. "Madge? Are you awake?"

Behind the curtain, he could hear the rustle of sheets.

"Madge? I have to tell you that Mark arrived in the attic this morning."

He heard a shocked gasp. He stepped forward. "Madge?" He reached over to pull the curtain back slightly. She stared at him, her eyes huge from above the covers. His heart ached. She was absolutely terrified. He took several steps closer but stayed at the end of her bed.

"I'm sorry. I know you want this to go away, but Sari is in danger now. Mark helped you come home." He waited, trying to gauge her reaction, but she stared unblinking at him. "Correct?"

She shuddered, but there was a barely perceptible nod.

"Okay. Good. So that part of his story checks out. Now he's been found out…and has been sent back to take you home again."

She squealed in fear.

"Stop. You're safe here." He held up his hand. "We're not letting him take you back. You can stay here." He took a step closer, hating to see her frail shoulders quiver like this. Whatever was over there had been incredibly hard on her. She was safe, but she had no reason to believe him.

"I need to know what goes on over there so we can figure out how to close the door forever. I can't let Sari be taken too."

Madge's wispy hair waved gently as she shook her head. "She won't be."

As much as he was delighted to hear her speak, he wished she'd explain.

"Greg took her place."

Jesus. "Greg is alive?"

Madge nodded. "It was him who figured out how to send me back."

"Well, thank heavens for that. Wait until Sari hears." Ward winced. As she was talking to Mark right now, chances were good she already knew.

"Why didn't he come back with you?"

But of course he knew. Greg had adored Sari. That had never been in question. If he'd gone over to keep her safe, he'd never come home if he knew it would put his only child and beloved Sari in danger.

Ward understood.

CHAPTER 22

SHE KNEW HER father would have done anything to save her. She could do no less. She had to find a way to save him and bring him home safely, then find a way to close that door forever.

"What about Madge?" He sipped his cup and looked at her over the rim. "I came for her."

"And maybe you can get her." She crossed her fingers in childish protection against her lie. "But I want to see my father."

"I don't want to go back, but I have to. I helped Madge escape and I was caught." His shoulders sagged. "Although why they'd care, I don't know. We're both done."

"So tell me, how is the one person per generation picked?"

He dropped his gaze.

Ahh. Shooting in the dark, she probed further. "Does the rest of the family vote?"

He lifted his gaze, startled. "Now what made you say that?" he said, aggrieved, trying to appear affronted.

She leaned back and studied him. "A lucky guess."

He glared at her. "You make it sound like my family didn't want me."

"If they voted you as the one to cross over, then maybe it was an honor." The longer she studied him, the more his glare turned to real anger.

"So what if the family did vote? I was the only one not married. The only one without a family to support. I was the logical choice."

She nodded. A tough decision on everyone's part. "And Madge?"

He drew circles on the tabletop. "Same. She was unmarried – a spinster, and the only one in her generation not necessary to the rest of the family."

"And my father?"

He looked up at her. This time honest puzzlement gleamed. "I really don't know. Normally we aren't approached one by one. It's done ahead of time. We have warning. A chance to say goodbye. This system has been in place for a long time. It's not a sudden event."

"Is there no other way to stop one person from our generation going over there?" She was never going to have kids if that were the case. As both she and her father were the only one of their respective generations, had their agreement been thrown out the window?

"I think that's what your father has been trying to do. Teach them to help themselves, to understand the portal. Then they wouldn't need anyone from our family as a slave."

Her heart stopped. "A slave? Just exactly what is your lifestyle like there? Is my father a prisoner?"

Mark looked around her kitchen. "It's a very similar environment to here. Houses, people running around crazy like ants. Everyone works every day and the sun rises and sets every day as well."

She nodded. "But..."

"But we are prisoners. We don't have our families. We can't have relationships. We are not allowed to go anywhere anytime. The family treats us as second class citizens." He stared out the window. "We aren't free. And that makes all the difference."

"How did Madge escape?"

He sighed. "Your father, mostly. She wasn't doing so well. She's been over there a long time. It was well past time for her to come home, but they wouldn't let her."

"How could he help her and not help himself? If she'd been able to go over…"

"It's not that easy." Mark said, his voice rising. "Greg managed to fix the watch that had taken him to the other side and he'd tried several times with no luck, then he figured out the problem in time for me to sneak Madge across."

"Then you all could have come home," she cried. "At the same time."

"And they'd have come after us and likely taken you as well."

Shit. She sat back, bitter and pissed. "Sounds like time for them to go forward on their own and leave us alone."

"It's time, but it won't happen as long as they have access to us through this house."

"Let's burn the house down then," she snapped.

He raised an eyebrow. "That's been tried before. Many times."

She laughed in disbelief. "Really? Is that when all those oddball wings were built?"

"The ones I know about, yes. The attic is the crossing point. Of course, that's why it was never open to the rest of the house. To make sure they never came in the middle of the night and stole someone they weren't supposed to take."

"How hard is the crossing to make?" she asked, more

determined than ever to rescue her father and wondering about the hidden passageway out of the attic. Someone tried to build an escape. It looked like it didn't work. "Does it take days to recover?"

"No. As you can see, I'm sitting here just having a cup of tea like normal. You could go and come back as if you made a trip to the store, but only if you know how and if it's the right time of the year – and you have the right watch with the correct settings. Otherwise, you can do anything you want and it won't happen."

She sighed. "That's why all attempts to reach my father in the past fifteen years have failed. I wasn't here in this house." Damn her mother for leaving. She might have saved her father years of servitude.

"Exactly. Now Madge's escape was a good example. Your father figured out roughly when to try it. But we didn't know if it would work. You say she is sick and in bad shape. I don't know how much of that might have been caused by the crossing. She was in a bad way before, but she was mentally sound and strong. But her spirit had failed her lately. She wanted to come home to die."

"And that's why you helped her?" At his nod, she added, "And if it is, then why are you insisting on returning her? You know she's safe here. That she'll get help here. So why take her home?"

His face darkened, his features aging before her. "Because they know I helped. Even now the clock is ticking. If I don't go back, I'm not sure what they will do."

"Well, I can tell you." Ward's voice interrupted. Hard and forceful, his tone of voice matched. "They would come and take back whoever and whatever they can. Like they have done every other time."

"Ward." Sari hopped up off her chair and threw herself into his arms. "Finally you're back."

He wrapped her up in a tight embrace. "I tried to make it as fast as possible."

Setting her off to one side, he kept a tight grip on her hand. "I spoke to Madge."

Mark's face lit up. Turning her attention back to Ward, she asked quietly, "How is she?"

"Terrified of being forced to go back. She was a little unclear where 'back' was though."

Mark nodded as if he'd been expecting that. Sari's heart hardened against him. He'd still take her back even knowing this. Then again, how could she judge? She didn't know what these people were capable of doing.

"According to Mark, they have both come from a parallel dimension. It's similar in looks and actions to this one but where they – and my father – are slaves."

Ward sent her a narrow-eyed look, but he didn't look terribly surprised. He turned to face Mark, who shrugged.

"She's right," Mark said. "Apparently the only people that can cross over are those from my family. I was sent over decades ago, and Madge was sent over before me."

"And yet they will come after you if you don't return? That makes no sense."

"They can travel here with the watches, too. I don't have that knowledge. They kept that to themselves," Mark said bitterly.

"That explains the clothes, the belongings sitting here waiting for the people to come back. Or in hopes of them coming back," Sari amended. "And maybe just easiest to keep together, like a memorial of those gone but not forgotten." And not being dead, she could understand the families not wanting to get rid of the personal belongings. She wondered if they'd been allowed to take anything with them or if they went with just the clothes on their back.

Sari stared. "How is it these people can cross when they want and we can't?"

Mark, his voice earnest said, "They can't. They are held to the same timeframe we are. The only reason they brought me over was to retrieve Madge – and the watch she used. Your father fixed it but didn't tell Tron, so he wants it now."

"But they don't appear to be limited to the same family rule? They're allowed to cross over though, aren't they?"

He shook his head. "It doesn't appear to be."

"Do you know these men?" Sari quickly described the two who'd held her captive under the stairs.

Mark's face darkened. "They are the enforcers. Tron's sons – Jed and Jordan."

Ward leaned forward, grabbed a kitchen chair, and sat down on it. "Tell me everything. Don't leave anything out. I want to know how I can get Sari's father back and close the door between the two dimensions forever."

"It's never going to happen," Mark grumbled in defeat.

"Yes. It. Will." Ward glared at Mark. "Now start talking so I can figure it out."

With a deep sigh, Mark got started repeating most of what he'd told Sari.

She watched as Ward fumed. The longer Mark talked, the angrier he appeared to get. Finally, Mark went silent. Sari hated what she'd heard, and yet wasn't it typical. Help someone over and over again and they got to expect it. Then take away that help and they got mad. "I have to help my father."

"You're not going. You could get stuck over there."

"Like my father has been? Fifteen years. It's time he came home. If Madge and Mark are here, then he needs to be as well."

"Madge won't be going anywhere but to a home where she can be cared for in her last years." Ward assessed Mark. "Mark, how old are you? Sixty? Seventy? And Madge has to be that much older again."

"I'm sixty-six and Madge, the dear girl, is almost ninety."

"And my father would be in his late forties, early fifties by now."

Mark nodded. "Exactly. One a generation. Madge is my aunt. And Greg, your father, is my nephew."

"The others in the family are gone, you know." Sari said. "My father was an only child. His parents were killed in a car accident along with several family members. Through one thing or another, my father grew up mostly without family. By the time he married, he was alone. I never met any grandparents or aunts and uncles."

"There was only my brother," Mark said. "Every generation we had less and less children. Probably to avoid this exact problem."

"I understand. I certainly won't have any until I know this problem is solved."

"And that's going to be very soon," Ward interrupted. "Mark. Tell me about the place you stayed at and the security that kept you there."

"And while you explain that all to him, I'm going to make a quick trip upstairs to the bathroom. Back in a minute."

The other two men, buried deep in their conversation, barely noticed and never responded. Sari raced upstairs, her mind churning with the information. Time was running out for her father. Now that she knew her father was a prisoner, she couldn't stand it. She knew Ward was trying to work out some plan of rescue, but *he* couldn't cross. Only she could. And Mark. And Madge. And that was no good. Both of them had done their time. They shouldn't be forced to go back. Still, if Mark stayed here, where would he live?

Here with her? The same for Madge? Not that Madge would have many years left, not if she was close to ninety. Still, her father was her prime concern.

And how was she going to convince Ward to let her go over?

She walked into her bedroom

And was snatched from behind.

She never had a chance to do more than struggle weakly. Something was stuffed into her mouth, then the two men wrestled Sari to the ground. Her arms and legs secured, she was picked up and shoved into the closet passageway. She fought harder.

"Damn it. Knock her out or something," gasped the man trying to contain her feet.

Pain slammed into her temple as darkness washed through her, and she slumped boneless to the ground.

WARD WROTE DOWN the last of the notes on the parallel dimension, shaking his head that he was actually doing so. "A week ago I'd never have listened to this."

Mark sat back, his gaze hardening. "No one would unless you'd been living my life or my family's life. For us, it's been something we've been raised with. Something hanging over our heads. Something we couldn't escape."

"Until now."

The look in Mark's gaze narrowed. After a long pause, he nodded, whispering, "Until now."

Thinking of Sari, he looked around the kitchen asking, "Did you see where Sari went?"

"Upstairs." Mark lowered his head to his arms on the table and closed his eyes. "I need to close my eyes for a few minutes. Just a short rest."

Ward stood up and walked away. He had to hold his personal feelings back until this mess was sorted out. He knew Sari wouldn't rest until her father had been rescued. He also knew there was no way to convince his supervisor of this parallel dimension. Not a hope in hell. He ran his fingers through his hair. He had no idea what to do. Except keep Sari safe.

At the base of the staircase, he called up, "Sari? Are you coming down?" He wondered if she'd gone to lie down and had fallen asleep. He glanced at Mark, who hadn't moved, then took the stairs two at a time. At the open door to Sari's room, he stopped. Peering around the corner of the doorway, he checked to see if she slept.

She wasn't there. What the hell? "Sari?"

No answer.

He walked through the room quickly. There was no sign of her. He retreated to the hallway and quickly checked the other rooms. There was no sign of her. Bordering on panic, he raced down the stairs, recognized that Mark still hadn't moved, and ran up the opposite stairwell calling out, "Sari? Where are you?" as he went. Upstairs again, he went through the same routine, panic fueling his steps as he raced through the house looking for Sari.

Ten minutes later, he found himself at the door to the

shop. "Damn." The door was locked. Of course it was. He reached up and found the spare key on the top of the frame. He grinned. Snatching it up, he unlocked the door and rushed in. The room was empty. That didn't mean the attic was. He dropped the ladder and called up, "Sari?"

He was up inside in seconds. The attic was empty, but the door that led to her bedroom was ajar. He raced over, crouching down to pull it open. Had she come in here? Been forced to come in here? Or had they left it open last time they'd explored that weird hallway? He dove in. Maybe she'd come out on her bedroom side while he'd been calling. Desperately hoping, he crawled through the secret hallway to Sari's closet. He pushed open the door and peered out. It was empty.

He bowed his head and tried to still the panic inside. What could he have missed? Had there been any sign of where she'd gone? He couldn't help but wonder if she'd been taken. How could he know for sure?

He crept back out the hallway and back into the attic. He took a quick look around and realized that he wouldn't know the difference if Sari had just been in here or not. He quickly descended to the shop.

"About time you got back down."

Ward stiffened. He didn't know that voice. He turned slowly to face the intruder.

Two men were there, holding a shaky Mark between them. Two men that fit Sari's description of the ones who'd followed her. The same ones who'd broken into her house and had attacked him and left him lying on the road outside.

"So there you are," he commented mildly. "I wondered when you'd show up."

The taller of the two, a carrot top with an ugly busted

nose, grinned at him. "Oh, we've been here all the time."

Ward speared him with his gaze. "I know. You've been playing games across dimensions."

The shorter, swarthy-skinned male dressed all in black spoke up, "So you do understand. And you aren't freaking out. Interesting."

Ward stared at him coolly. Whatever these men wanted it wasn't good. "Not as interesting as finding out where you've taken Sari."

The redhead smacked his partner. "Look at him. Thinks he knows everything."

The sly smile on the other man's face made Ward's stomach clench and his skin go cold. They had taken her somewhere safe where he couldn't get her back. *The other side.* Shit. What had Mark said, only his family line could cross over? Meaning he couldn't.

So how had these two assholes made it across? That was the hole in Mark's logic. Logic that had probably been used to keep Mark's family in line. Fear was a powerful motivator for believing all kinds of things.

"I suppose you're planning on taking Mark here back with you, too?"

The redhead laughed. "Yeah, we are. We brought him over to do a specific job. He didn't do it."

This time the nasty smile was on his face. Ward was starting to hate these two. Somehow he had to go back with them.

"Then you might as well take me along, too. I'm not letting you two out of my sight until I find her."

They both shook their heads. The redhead gave Mark a shake. The older man shuddered, taking a hard gasping breath. His color had drained, leaving him looking like every inch what he was – an old man desperate to save himself. Ward felt sorry for him. This wasn't over yet, and he didn't know who'd survive what was to come.

"See, you can't go with us. It doesn't work that way. And your girlfriend – well, she's already gone." The shorter male grinned a nasty smirk. He pulled out a gun, a type Ward had never seen before. He eyed it cautiously. Who knew what kind of damage that thing could do?

"And if I don't believe you?"

"Hey, Jed, let him come. The trip is likely to kill him anyway."

The redhead laughed. "Sure, why not?" He pulled out a matching weapon from his pocket. "Upstairs."

"This way?" asked Ward curiously, pointing up to the attic.

"Sure. Let's go this way. It doesn't matter to us."

Ward raced into the attic ahead of the two men. Mark made his way upstairs without help, but he looked shaky. He sent Ward a warning glance that Ward couldn't interpret. Standing off to one side, Ward waited for the men to reach the floor level. They came up fast, well used to the ladder. He frowned, not liking that aspect. "So can you come and go at will? Any time of day or night?"

"At the moment, but there are a few restrictions on travelling. We only have today and tomorrow. After that, the doorway closes again."

So Mark had spoken the truth. "How long have you been here yourselves?"

"Just over a month. We can travel three to four times a year."

At their words, he shook his head at the concept of assholes like these two coming and going and taking what they wanted. "And you always come in and out of the attic?" Ward shrugged. "What's with that?"

"It's the doorway. A portal. It's not supposed to be open like this though. Some idiot put a window in."

"What difference does the window make?" He didn't want Sari to get in trouble for such a simple thing. "And what about Greg? He didn't go by the portal."

"Travel is safer in total darkness." Jed shrugged. "The portal is stronger at different times. We're right below and still within the power grid."

Ward nodded as if that made sense. In truth, nothing these two had said made any sense. All that mattered was that they were key to getting Sari back. But maybe their words explained Greg leaving from the shop and not the attic.

"I want to see Sari."

"If you survive the crossing, you can. Of course, you'll also be a slave."

"Hurry up. That's enough talking," Jordan snapped. "We still have to return for Madge and that damn watch she used to get here."

What watch? Ward's blood ran cold. "She's an old woman who's almost at the end of her life. Why do you have to take her back?"

"The boss wants her back. No one ever escapes, and definitely not with one of his precious watches."

"She did though." Mark mustered a dark smile. "I did."

"And that's the first time this has ever happened, and look how well it went. A disaster. A fucking disaster. People coming and going as if they had the right."

The men brought out two timepieces from their pockets. Ward's gaze widened as he recognized them. "Those are

Sari's."

"Not quite."

He stepped forward to take a closer look, but the men pulled back so he couldn't see them. "Is that what you were looking for in Sari's house that night?"

"A different one." The redhead spoke up. "There are five we know of, but there should be more. The boss needs them so he doesn't have to worry about anyone crossing over without his permission. He controls the portal."

"Sounds like criminals are the same on both sides of the portal," Ward snorted. "Your boss wants to control something that isn't his to control."

"Sure it is. He's been in charge for a long time. He doesn't plan on giving it up."

"Then let's go meet him."

Jed said, "I'll take Mark back. You," he glanced over at who Ward assumed was Jordan. "You bring this guy across."

"Except he might not make it."

The redhead shrugged. "That's his problem. He's not going to come back, we know that for sure."

The two men smiled evilly. "True enough."

Ward checked his own wristwatch. "Let's go then. I want to be home in time for dinner." He shot the two men a confident look.

"Sure." The redhead smirked. "The boss will be surprised to see you. He's 'visiting' with Sari now."

Ward muttered under his breath only loud enough for Mark to hear. "Not for long."

CHAPTER 23

S ARI WOKE SLOWLY, shifting her legs and whimpering. Her muscles ached and throbbed. What the hell? What had happened to her? She hadn't done anything that she could remember to cause these aches and pains. She rolled over slightly and opened her eyes. Her gaze scanned the small closet-sized room and frowned. Where was she? She went to push herself into a sitting position when she realized she couldn't. She glanced down and froze.

She had straps tied to her wrists with about a foot of play, enough to allow her to move about but not get out of bed. She had a light blanket covering her. She lifted it to see her feet were similarly tied up. She could roll around or scrunch up into a tight ball, but she couldn't leave the bed. Her heart pounded. She was a prisoner. How and why, she didn't remember.

Wait. She closed her eyes as images of two men attacking her in her bedroom came to her. They'd done something to her. They had to have. She'd never have gone with them willingly.

She lifted a hand to her throat and realized how dry and sore her mouth was. That's right. They'd stuffed a cloth in her mouth to muffle the sounds of her screaming.

Ward had been downstairs. With Mark. Had they heard her struggle? Did they even know she'd been taken? God, she hoped so.

Then it hit her. What if she'd been taken through that damn portal? Ward couldn't come after her. If she'd crossed the portal, then her father should be here.

Her heart lightened and she wanted to squeal. After spending a lifetime looking for him, to think he might actually be on the other side of that doorway made excitement pulse through her. He was here. She knew it.

Now to get free. She studied the odd straps on her wrists. They weren't a locking system she knew. Neither did they look difficult. She checked out the way they were attached to the bed. That appeared more difficult.

Except her feet were small and the loops around her ankles were slightly loose. Slipping off the sandals, she could just about wiggle her bare feet through. There. Flushed with success, she tucked her legs up under her crossed-legged and returned to studying the bands on her wrist. They loosened as well, but not quite enough to slip her wrist through. She studied the odd knots and frowned. They should just open up. She wasn't sure if they were meant to keep her as a prisoner or just restrained until she was of sound mind. She played with the closure system a little more and smiled. The band on her left hand dropped off.

Good. Only one more to go. Diligently she went to work on that one. Watching it drop sent her spirits soaring. She hopped off the bed and looked under it. Nothing. Dragging her sandals out from the blanket, she put them back on. Standing up, she surveyed the small room.

There appeared to be a closet of some kind against the opposite wall. Again the opening was foreign to her but once she realized it was a pressure release, she had it open in seconds. There was a second blanket in the closet and that was it. She frowned, closing it. A spare room? A prison. It certainly lacked the homey comforts of a room commonly lived in. Unless one was a slave…

She turned to the door, afraid and nervous but terrified that her father wasn't going to be here after all. Stupid. After fifteen years, his disappearance still dictated her emotions. Then again, she loved her father.

Taking a deep breath, she reached out and turned the latch on the door. It opened easily under her hand.

WARD WATCHED THE sly smirk on the shorter, dark-haired man as the redhead, with a firm grip on Mark's shoulder, walked through a spot in front of the window and disappeared in front of him. What the hell? He stepped over and ran his hand through the space. Nothing. Nothing to see or feel. The air was no lighter, hotter, or seemingly thinner. How could anyone know it existed? "How?" he asked, "did he do that?"

The man grinned and held up the watch. "It's a trick of the timepieces to correlate with the GPS location on the other side. That's what the other markings are on the watch."

GPS. It had never occurred to him. "Did you guys make these?"

The other man shook his head. "No. We've lost track of how it all started, but someone on your side made the first one. We keep trying to find another family member who could recreate them."

Ward nodded as if he understood. Like hell. "Is this the only portal?"

"In this part of the world, yes. There are others, but they

don't seem to function the same."

"So if this one is closed, you guys can't come back and forth." Ward grinned.

"True. But you can't close it. The controls are on our side. And to close it means you can't get back either."

Damn. Didn't that figure?

"Now let's go." The other man grabbed his shoulder and shoved him into the portal.

CHAPTER 24

S ARI STEPPED OUT of the tiny quarters into a large circular room where all the walls were made from wood. Around the perimeter were many other small doors leading, she presumed, into other small rooms like the one she'd woken up in. Like prisoner or slave quarters. Would her father be in one of those rooms? Should she check? She stood, undecided, when she heard noises behind her. She slipped to the door beside hers and opened it. Sticking her head inside and realizing it was empty, she slipped inside, leaving the door open a crack. She glanced around the new room. This one looked lived in. Books were on a shelf. The bed was made with several blankets. The closet door was open enough to see that there were items inside. Nothing she recognized, but nothing so far different as to be foreign.

Someone lived in this room.

She peered through the crack left by the open door. She couldn't see anyone, but voices were getting louder. Mark? Maybe. She hunched her shoulders. She had no doubts she had traveled to the other dimension. Now if only she knew how to get home.

The voices became louder, clearer.

"Work will continue later. I want you to stay in your room for the rest of the day. We have visitors, and I need to deal with them." The strong, arrogant voice jarred her. She didn't recognize it, yet in a way she did. She frowned and strained to hear his next words. She missed the early part of his statement, hearing only, "Mark is returning now as well."

"And Madge?"

Sari stiffened, shock and delight making her gasp. Was that her father? She squinted, trying to make out the faces to go with the voices.

"Haven't heard yet."

She heard sounds of muffled murmurs; whether they were of assent or dissent, she didn't know. The doors opened and closed, followed by retreating footsteps. She pulled the door open wider, catching sight of a large man leaving through a larger door at the end of the room. She hadn't seen it earlier. Now which door had the other person gone into? She eyed the ones to the left of her. The first one was the room she'd woken up in; after that was a second and third. Had she heard one or two voices?

She slipped out to the common area and headed to the first door. Placing an ear to the closed door, she listened for sounds within. Nothing. She hadn't expected there to be as that had been hers. She walked to the next one. A muffled rustling said someone was inside. Would they help her or turn her in? She didn't have much time. She knew the portal would be at prime position tonight and after that, she'd be stuck here. And that she didn't want to happen.

She opened the door softly. An astonished face peered at her. An older man. Sari slipped inside his room, her finger to her lips to keep him quiet.

"Sari?" the shaky voice whispered.

Oh my God! She opened her mouth to answer, only no words came out.

Mute, she nodded. Tears collected in the corner of her

eyes as she stared at her beloved father. She whispered, "Hello, Poppy."

Tears ran down his face. He opened his arms.

She ran into them, grateful to feel the rough fabric under her cheek, the warmth and strength she so remembered of those arms as they held her tight against him. Memories and emotions washed over her.

It was true. *This really was her father.* Alive and holding her.

She closed her eyes and burrowed deeper, the young child still looking for reassurance.

After all these years, she'd finally found him.

WARD KEPT HIS eyes opened, knowing he might or might not survive the journey. Yet for all that he could tell, crossing into another dimension was akin to walking into another room. He didn't feel any air pressure change. His breathing wasn't affected, nothing. He looked down at his hands and feet. Normal. If they hadn't said that he'd crossed a dimension, he'd never have believed them. Even now he wasn't so sure.

Except…he looked around. There was no way they were still in Sari's attic. He was in a long hallway space. Bare, no windows and with wooden floors, he could see nothing to identify his new location. He watched as his companion checked his watch, clicked an odd pointed button at the top of it, and then put the item away in his pants pocket. Ward filed that information for later.

"Move. We're here already, so stop your gawking and get going. The boss is waiting for us."

Ward obliged by taking several steps, waiting for the

other man to lead the way. The boss, huh? Good – that's just the man Ward wanted to see.

They walked down the long hallway and into a chamber type room with a tall ceiling. This room was furnished with couches and desks. A comfortable working room. At the end, seated behind a large desk, sat a man. Large, swarthy, likely related to the man beside him and scowling.

"Jordan. What is the meaning of this?"

"Father," the man started, bowing his head slightly, giving the impression that more of a ruler than a father sat before him. "We felt it best to bring this man to you."

Father stood tall in front of Jordan, anger vibrating through his spine. "We don't bring strangers across. We can't control the portal if we let other people know about it."

"He already knew."

Father's scowl deepened. "How?" he barked.

"From Sari," Ward said calmly, in a slightly amused voice as if he knew more than he let on.

"And who are you?" snapped Father.

"I'm Ward, Sari's fiancé, and the man who's going to make you pay for all the pain she's suffered."

CHAPTER 25

G REG TOOK A step back. Wiping tears from his eyes, he sniffled several times then tried to clear his voice. "I wish you hadn't come."

Sari started. Tears threatened again. He wished she'd never come while she'd spent her whole life getting to this point. "Why?" she cried out. "I've been looking for you for years. You disappeared in front of me, remember? How could I not be obsessed with finding you?"

"But you were safe over there. Here you are a prisoner." He placed both hands on either side of her cheeks. "You've grown into a beautiful woman. I want you to have a future. A life."

"My whole life has been trying to find you," she whispered. "There was no life. You were on my mind every single day. Trying to find you. Trying to figure out what had happened. Trying to not feel guilty because I couldn't stop it. Whatever *it* was." The tears slid down her cheeks. "Don't you understand? When you left, my life came to a stop. Sure, I grew up, there are some things that carry on – but in many ways I never did. I missed you terribly. The way you disappeared was traumatizing to a level I couldn't deal with."

His deep blue eyes clouded with tears. "I'm so sorry," he whispered brokenly. "I'd have done anything to have been there for you. To protect you. To watch you grow up. You were my life."

"And you were mine!" she cried. "I couldn't function for a long time. Did you think I'd forget about you?"

"No, but I'd hoped you'd recover and move on." He ran his fingers down over his face. "If I could have found a way to return and still keep you safe, I would have." He closed his eyes. "And if I hadn't done the job properly, they'd have come after me – and likely taken you as well."

"How is it these people know about this and we didn't?" She shook her head. She didn't like anything about this place. And she wanted to go home.

"What started as a business arrangement to benefit both sides ended up as a tyranny as things went wrong. Each generation, the father and now the son have taken slaves from our side. Our family. They are feudal here. The one lord and many serfs. Serfs can have families, but essentially they live on the whim of Tron. There are four generations of males from the same family here, each indoctrinating the next one down."

He pulled her tight into his embrace again. "As much as I wish you weren't here, I'm so very happy to see you. But you have to realize – there is no escape."

"We'll see about that. Did you know today is the lunar eclipse? If we can get back to the portal today, tonight…we can all go back home."

"They won't let us. Don't you see? We're not here just because of the portal. Our being here keeps the rest of you safe." He shook her shoulders gently. "I had to make sure you stayed safe."

"Well, they came after me anyway. So now we can both leave," she said, determination in her voice.

"What? They went after you? They brought you here?"

At her nod, anger infused his features, turning his pale aging skin to a deep red. "That's a different story. If he's broken his word, then the rules have changed."

He stood, deep in thought. She studied him, looking for the man she knew. The beloved, in-control father figure. It was hard to see him inside this aging man. He wasn't old by any means, but these last many years hadn't been easy on him. Her protective instincts rose even as she watched the changes in him. He stood straighter. His shoulders squared. The years seemed to fall away from his features. Anger had given his pale blue eyes a sharper glint.

That was when she saw it. That one flash sent her back into herself. *My God, it really is him!* She could hardly speak, she was so overcome with emotion. She closed her eyes as warmth and unbelievable amounts of love swelled through her. *She'd finally found him.* On the heels of that thought, one shocking realization swept through her. They weren't safe.

She could so easily lose all that she'd found.

Determination and anger at all the two of them had suffered filled her heart. There was no way she was going to stay here. And he was coming home with her.

Today was their one window of chance.

Her father spoke up. "We'll need the watches to cross. The boys carry them with them all the time."

She frowned. "The boys?" she asked. "Do you mean the redhead and the black-haired man?"

"Jed and Jordan. Both sons of Tron. Both from different mothers."

"They are the two that kidnapped me from home and brought me here."

Anger rippled across her father's face. "Did they?" he

asked softly. "Well now. That's good to know. They will pay for that."

She snorted. "Stand in line. Ward wants first crack at them. They broke into the house one night looking for something and then attacked him as they were escaping. They've followed me around town, kidnapped me, and stashed me under the damn stairs. And I'd forgotten about that place until I woke up in there with Ward hunting for me." She shrugged. "At that point, things had gone beyond coincidental."

Her voice came to a stop at the odd look on his face.

"Ward? They kidnapped you while you were home?" His voice grew faint. "I'd forgotten the cupboard under the stairs. That was one of your favorite places."

"As a child," she answered gently, slipping her arm through his. "But after you left, so did we. I only returned to the house two months ago. It's been empty ever since. Sure, Mom had people go through and do whatever maintenance was necessary and she continued to pay the taxes but the house, for all intents and purposes, was left for your return." She tugged him toward the closed door. They needed to make a move.

"No. It wasn't supposed to happen that way. She was supposed to stay. Raise you. Stop Tron from having access."

Sari stopped in mid-step. She spun slowly until she could look her father in the eye. "Are you saying Mom knew? About you coming here?"

Confusion clouded his gaze for a moment, but clarity still shone through. "Yes, of course. We didn't know when or that it would even happen, but we discussed the possibilities at length once we found out Lisbeth was pregnant for the second time. For that reason, I was content here. I knew she understood." He motioned with his hand. "Oh, I knew she wasn't happy about it, but she is my wife." He hesitated, a pinched look on his face. "Unless she has remarried."

Pregnant? For a second time. Sari didn't know what to say. She was shocked. Horrified. Talk about a betrayal of horrific proportions. Speaking slowly, as if the answers she was seeking would show up by the time she was through, she said, "Mom has not remarried. She, as far as I know, hasn't even had you declared legally dead."

And that was the strongest piece of confirmation that Sari could imagine. Her mother was all about gain. If there was something to gain from declaring her husband dead, then she would have done so. So why hadn't she? Because she knew he wasn't dead. She knew he might come back. One day.

She'd known.

And she hadn't said anything to Sari. She gasped silently as the blows kept coming. She could understand her mother keeping the news secret when Sari had been little, but any time after she'd turned sixteen would have been good. Or how about after Sari had moved back to the very house her father had disappeared from? The final straw was the realization that last supposedly very heart-to-heart conversation she'd shared with her mother when she'd gone to pick up her father's things was false. Her mother had known then, but she didn't say a word.

"Dad, I don't have a sibling. If she was pregnant, she lost it soon after." She couldn't remember ever seeing her mother with a pregnant belly. In fact, she couldn't see her mother ever allowing her figure to get out of shape a second time. Suspicious, she wondered if her mother had pretended to be pregnant.

The color drained from his face. He said sadly, "I'd hoped that having a second child would have made up for losing me. I knew her parents would make sure she never needed anything." He sighed. "Don't blame her."

"Why the hell not?" Frustrated, Sari tried to rein in her temper. "Not only did she know all these years, but she just gave me your books back that you'd asked her to take care of. And we had a long talk. Still, she never said anything."

"Your mother loves you…" he started and stopped at her long look. He tried again. "She does. It's just that she can't deal with many things. She does this ostrich thing and tries to pretend that nothing happened."

"Now I know you're my father," Sari laughed. "She still does that. It drives me crazy."

He smiled. "She did me, too. And still I love her."

Sari lost her smile. She thought of all her mother's boy-friends over the years. It was so hard not to judge her. Her husband had been gone for fifteen years. That was a long time to be alone and not know if her husband would ever return. Sari had to admit it would be hard for anyone. Plus, her mother wasn't strong in moral fiber. She sighed, and some of the anger relaxed. Her mother was who she was. Right now, Sari had something more important to think about than her mother's character – getting her father home.

"Come on, we have to get out of here."

"How? We need those watches," he protested as she pulled him to the door. "We can't just go out there right now." He tugged his arm free. "Sari, we'll be caught."

She stared at him. How could she get him to throw off the prisoner mentality and understand they had to do something before that small window of opportunity closed and they were stuck here?

"We are caught already!" She struggled with her next words. "We are in a bad way. We have to do something and we have to do it now. This is not the time for quibbling. This *is* our window of escape."

She opened the door and stuck her head out. Immediately, voices filled the small room.

JED'S FATHER LAUGHED. "Like hell. Sari is now my prisoner as is the rest of her family." His tone turned grim. "So are you." He waved toward his son. "Jordan had no business bringing you over. But you can't be allowed to return, so my choices at this point are limited." He glared at Ward. "As for Sari, she won't be allowed to have any relationships, so you can forget that. Slaves have no rights here."

It was all Ward could do to hold back from killing this man. But he had no idea where Sari was. That had to be first. Find her and her father, and then he'd make sure he took out this asshole who dared to consider Sari's family as his personal property.

Oddly enough, he hadn't been searched before being brought through the crossing. He still had his gun in the small of his back.

Good thing.

The last thing he planned on becoming was some asshole's slave. And he'd never let that fate happen to Sari. This bastard had ruined her life enough.

Time for him to get a reality check.

And Ward was just the person to give it to him.

CHAPTER 26

SARI JUMPED BACK inside the room and closed the door as much as possible without actually closing it. She kept one eye on the room outside. Her father crowded behind her. His hand was a tight clamp on her arm.

She waited as the voices swelled. Whoever it was, they were coming closer. She strained her hearing. Did she recognize them? She thought it might be the redhead that had followed her. Jed? Was that his name? A deeper voice mingled with the others. A deeper voice that made her eyes wide. *No, surely, not.* It couldn't be possible. That sounded like Ward. *No.* They'd said only her family could cross.

The voice came again. She closed her eyes, now understanding her father's feeling. She was relieved and delighted that Ward was here. At the same time, she wished he were anywhere but here. She wanted him safe.

"Damn," she whispered as the voices came closer. Her heart picked up as she heard a third voice mingled in. Probably Jordan. And Mark. She banged her head lightly against the doorframe. Everyone was here.

Madge? She peered through the crack in the door as the first of the men entered. Jed. Jordan. Mark and Ward. Her heart lightened. It was so good to see him.

She watched to see where they'd go. She should have asked her father how many men were here. Did an army exist, or with fear being the controller, was it not necessary? Mark walked to a door beside her and disappeared from sight, presumably inside. Her father gasped behind her.

She shot him an inquiring look. "What's up?"

He whispered against her ear, "Look, Jed is holding the watch. If we could get it…"

Sari understood. And action was required. She opened the door and walked out.

WARD COULDN'T BELIEVE how purely normal this dimension appeared to be. He walked on floors in a corridor that could have been any typical hallway in his world. Wood and tile were the materials of choice from what he could see. Mark's steps slowed the farther down the hallway he made it.

He nudged Mark. "Are you okay?"

Mark shuddered. "Don't want to be here." His voice was so low and faint it was hard for Ward to hear.

"I know. I don't either. But I have to help Sari."

"No helping her. Everyone is stuck now." Mark's shoulders drooped, his face despondent. "Accept it. You're here now."

"Hey, stop talking."

Ward straightened, turning slightly to look behind him. "Or what?"

He almost laughed at the look on Jed's face. They weren't used to defiance. He tucked that note away in the back of his mind. He was also way bigger than Sari's family. Ward bowed his head slightly, turning to face forward. He kept pace with Mark. He knew he could take these two jackasses. He just had to do it before too many more came and joined him. Two he could overpower; more than that and it would get dicey. He also needed to make sure he acted while Jed still had the damn watch in his possession. He didn't know how this system worked, but he'd trust Sari and Greg to get him home. Especially as Mark had snuck Madge out.

"See," Mark whispered, "it's over."

Not bloody likely.

It was just beginning.

"Ward!" Sari called to him.

Ward spun around. His face split into a wide grin and his arms opened wide. "There you are."

She raced into his arms, laughing, to bury her face against his shoulder. His arms closed tight around, holding her close. "You've got to stop disappearing like that."

Her lips against his ear she whispered, "We have to make a move now before they bring more people. We need the watches the men have on them."

"Done." He squeezed her tight then released her.

"Hey, enough of that. You two separate. Now." Jordan smacked Ward on the back, jerking Ward backwards. With a half-smile, Ward let his weight fall back. Catching himself at the last minute, he looked like he was going to tumble to the floor.

Jed laughed. "God, look at him."

Jordan grinned – until Ward's fist plowed into Jordan's front teeth. Sari gasped as the dark man's head snapped back. He fell to the ground, blood streaming from his mouth. Ward was on him in an instant.

Jed screamed. "Jordan. Damn it, how did that bastard get the drop on you?" He ran over to his brother and launched himself onto Ward's back.

Sari didn't want to dog pile on top, but the choices were

limited. They needed both men down and out. She slipped off her shoe, only a sandal, but it was a weapon of sorts. She ran behind Jed, who had his arm around Ward's throat trying to choke him. Reaching back in her best imitation of a batter up to the plate, she grasped her shoe with both hands and swung. Hard.

She hit Jed on the ear with enough force to knock him off Ward, collapsing to the ground, screaming as he clasped his hands over his head.

Sari jumped on him, sliding her arms around his elbows and pulling them farther back behind his head.

Ward came to help her. "Easy. Let me have him." Sari released her hold, Jed's arms smacking to the ground. Jed came up off the floor in a rush and connected with Ward's right-handed fist.

Jed collapsed to the ground unconscious.

Ward straightened, spinning around to see if Sari was okay. She ran into his arms. "That was almost too easy."

"I know." He kissed her hard then released her. "But we're not home free yet."

She dropped down beside the unconscious Jed and tugged the watch free from his pocket. "We need the second one, otherwise they can still travel to our world."

"That's never going to happen again." Ward walked over to Jordan and systematically went through his pockets. "The days of enslaving your family are over."

"God, I do hope so," said a strange voice.

"Ward, this is my father."

Ward spun around, shock on his face. Jesus. It really was Greg. He searched the older man's features, then saw the young man in the face in front of him. Ward grinned. "Sir, am I glad to see you."

Greg smiled, a warm caring expression that made Sari's breath catch. She still couldn't believe he was here in front of her. "Ward, it's so good to see you again. You've grown up into a fine young man." Then a sparkle twinkled in his eyes. "I presume you learned how to spell aquarium sometime during the last fifteen years."

Ward's lips quirked crookedly at the reference to the spelling bee contest he'd lost to Sari in a way that made her heart jump. Damn, she wanted to get home and haul him into her bedroom. They had to get back there first.

"Indeed I have," Ward said.

"Dad, can you get Mark please? Is there anyone else here?"

Greg shook his head. "With Madge on the other side, that will be all of us."

"Good." Ward held up the second watch. "Let's go home."

Greg was about to knock on Mark's door when he understood Ward's comment.

He spun around, his hand still in mid-air. "Not quite."

Ward groaned. "Why not?" He just knew he wasn't going to like what Greg was about to say. He was still struggling with the whole concept that the man who'd been missing for fifteen years had been found safe and sound. It made him wonder about the other hundred missing person files in the precinct.

"Because I was building another watch for them. That's what I was brought over for. To make new ones. I made several but could never get the markings correct. But if we leave all my work, they might easily finish it successfully. Especially now that they have the books."

Sari winced. "They grabbed them from the shop, didn't

they?"

"They were supposed to. I haven't seen if they did or not."

Mark said, "They grabbed them after grabbing me."

"That's no good." Sari stared at Ward. "They could possibly figure out how to do this again."

"That can't be allowed to happen." Ward turned to Greg, who had opened Mark's door. "Where would they be? And your work – how can we retrieve it and get back here in time?"

Sari checked her watch. "I don't know if time is the same here or not, but our window is closing."

"How long? Never mind." Ward swore softly. He didn't really want to know. "So where is your workshop, Greg? And how many men are we likely to come up against getting there?"

Mark and Greg looked at each other. They weren't old in years, but they'd had enough suffering that they both looked aged. Ward wouldn't be able to depend on them for help. Somehow he had to get everyone home safe and sound …fast.

"If we don't make too much noise, it's possible we might make it there and back without alerting anyone," Mark suggested hopefully.

Greg pursed his lips. "Except Tron will be waiting for these two to return. They will come looking soon."

"Then let's go." Ward nodded toward the old pair. "Greg, you lead."

He nodded, then held out a hand to Sari and walked to the main door. "It's through here."

CHAPTER 27

A T THE DOOR, GREG tried to tuck Sari behind him. She resisted until he explained, "We don't know who's out there. They're going to be expecting me. Not you."

Subsiding, but not happy about it, Sari waited until her father opened the door casually as if he were allowed to move about freely. She watched the look on his face. Nothing changed. Good…so no unpleasant surprises there.

She urged him forward. They had no time to spare.

He led the way out into the next room and down yet another hallway to a set of double doors. He paused, then waited until they were all clustered around. Then with a click, he led the way into the workshop.

Sari stood at the entrance, Ward at her side. No windows, no natural light, just a dark hole with several large desks. Odd-looking instruments hung over them, along with a lamp of a kind she didn't understand.

"Hurry, Father. Grab your stuff." She watched both her father and Mark grab items off the tables. There appeared to be no drawers to store stuff and limited writing utensils or notepads. She frowned, wondering why these people had not taken advantage of the technology as well when they grabbed her people. Did they consider her world more primitive? Or had they taken what they wanted? And the slaves weren't entitled to own or use anything of such value?

She had so many questions and so little time.

Her father tucked items into his pockets at a furious rate. "Dad, I have pockets here. Give me something to carry."

He rushed over, his hands full. He handed her several watch pieces, tools, and some kind of notes. Ward reached over and took several items and stuffed them into his pockets. Mark showed up with his hands full. Everyone repeated the process until all items were stowed away. Walking back out, Sari found her father's books that Jed and Jordan had stolen from her shop sitting on a bench. She snatched them up and held them close. If they contained vital information worth the number of attempts the men had gone through already, then there was no way she could afford to leave them behind.

"Let's go." Sari turned to walk down the hallway again and the others followed close behind. At the door, she turned to look back at her father.

He nodded and stepped up. He opened the door and walked through. The two men were still lying on the floor.

"We should have locked them up somewhere safe."

Ward laughed, a dark sound that held no humor. "I hope we're a long ways away before then."

"Too bad then," said a dark voice promising retribution behind them, "for your hopes will be dashed."

Sari stiffened then turned slowly. A strange-looking man wearing odd clothing stood in front of them. Henchmen flanked him on both sides. They appeared to be carrying weapons of some kind. She just didn't know what they did for damage.

Ward placed his hands on the small of Sari's back. She leaned into it. Her mind raced furiously. What could they do? They needed weapons. A plan of action.

What kind of skills did Ward have? As a police officer, he had to have had hand-to-hand combat training. Could he have martial arts? She didn't. She'd taken a self-defense class, but that was all. Not much help against three men. Ward would be good for two of them, and maybe she and her father could take the third one? Except for the weapons.

"Greg. What's going on here?" The commanding voice said it all. This man was used to being in control. To giving orders and having them obeyed instantly. He used fear to get his own way. Preyed on people weaker than him. He was despicable.

Her father stepped forward. "Tron, my apologies. I was just showing the new arrivals the layout – helping them to get settled." He motioned to the rooms.

Tron's lips quirked, but there was no humor in the movement. He motioned to the henchmen. Both men ran over to the fallen men. The one at Jed's side said, "He's out cold but alive."

"So is Jordan."

If she hadn't been watching, Sari might have missed the slight relaxing of Tron's shoulders. Now that he knew his sons were safe, fear subsided, only to be replaced by anger. Rage that someone dared to do this.

So this was the man responsible for keeping her father here.

She glanced up at Ward, but he was watching the man beside Jed. Of course. The men were on the ground. Vulnerable. She nodded slightly. Keeping her eyes on Tron standing so boldly and arrogantly in front of her, she waited and watched for him to make a move.

The first man grabbed Jed's shoulders, trying to lift him up slightly so as to drag him toward his father.

"Greg, help him."

Greg immediately walked over and picked up Jed's feet. Ward quietly walked over and picked up Jordan's feet, and they manhandled the boys to their father. They laid them down again on the floor.

One of the henchmen asked, his voice polite and subservient, "Where do you want them?"

"We'll take them to their rooms in a moment. First I want to deal with these people." Tron smiled, and something unidentifiable flickered across his face.

Ward caught just a flash. But it was enough. There wasn't going to be any easy answer. Options. What were the damn options? None. He moved back as if to rejoin the group, then spun and lashed out in a high kick that slammed Tron in the middle of the chest.

Gasps sounded. Then all hell broke loose. He didn't have time to worry about it. His attention was fully on the guy he'd attacked. The man might be a leader here, but it wasn't an empty title. Damn, the man could fight.

He kicked, punched, and grappled to the point he was afraid he was outmatched. Then the other man went down and Ward was on him in an instant. He had his arm around his neck in a chokehold he didn't dare release. Gritting his teeth, he dug deep and clenched tighter, mentally counting, and just when he didn't think he could hold on anymore, the man went limp.

Thank God. Ward bowed his head. He pulled his gun free from his lower back and turned to look around.

Jesus.

Sari had her damn shoe off again and was whaling away on one of the henchmen. The second henchman was sprawled out cold on his back. He clambered to his feet and raced over to Sari. One hard clip of his fist against the henchman's temple and he was down, too.

Sari leaned back, gasping for air.

"About time."

He grinned. "Why? You were doing just fine."

She laughed.

You had to appreciate a woman who could smile at a time like this.

She stood up and ran to her father, who was trying to catch his breath off to the side. "Dad, we need to go. Now."

"Yes." He straightened and slapped Mark over the shoulder. "Come on, Mark."

Ward took one look around. "Do we need anything from here?"

He walked over to Tron, bending to search his pockets, and pulled out a timepiece. He held it up. "This is the third."

"Good." Sara held out the other two. "Let's go. We're out of time."

They needed no urging. The four raced down the hallway.

"Is there something special we have to do?"

Sari frowned. "I don't know." She glanced over at her father. "Dad, is there?"

"Yes." Greg held out his hand for one of the watches she held. She handed both over, watching as he fiddled with dials, even opening the first one to make an adjustment on the inside. Then he repeated his actions with the second one.

There were so many questions whirling around in her head, she didn't know what to say. First things first, they needed to go home and fast.

As if hearing her unspoken urgings, he said, "I'm trying.

I'm trying."

Sari held back the panic threatening to overwhelm her. She wanted to be gone. Their window of opportunity was now, but only if they could take it. She bit her lip and focused on her breathing.

Then he held out his hand for Tron's watch.

Ward gave it to him and her father fiddled with it. Just as she was about to say something to him, Ward placed a restraining hand on Sari's shoulder. "Easy," he whispered. "Give him time."

She closed her eyes and nodded. "Sorry," she whispered.

He squeezed gently, reassuringly.

Sari couldn't stop glancing over her shoulder. The men could arrive at any time. She closed her eyes and found prayers slipping through her mind. *Please let them make it. Please let them go home safely. Please.*

Another long few minutes and her father said, "Done."

She opened her eyes to find him grinning at her.

"Let's go home."

CHAPTER 28

S ARI LAUGHED.

She stood in the middle of her kitchen spinning and dancing and laughing like a wild woman. She was home. Safe and sound. Ward stood, grinning wildly, at the entrance. Both her father and Mark were sitting, exhaustion, euphoria, and a sense of disbelief still on their faces. Her father rubbed both hands down over his face. She didn't know if he was rubbing away tears or fatigue. For at least the fifth time, she ran over and hugged her father. Then she danced toward Ward and caught him up in a close hug.

"It's so good to know that's all over."

Ward interrupted. "That's the question I was going to ask. Is it over? Can we know that for sure?"

Sari glanced at him in surprise. "Yes, of course. We're all home. The watches are all here. Jed and Jordan can't cross over anymore."

"But I thought there was mention of a fifth watch?"

At the silence in the room, she spun around to stare at her father. "Dad?"

He threw up his hands. "I think it's over. I can't be sure there aren't more watches."

The silence was deafening. Both Mark and Greg stared at each other.

Sari hated this. The silence. The odd looks between the

men. The unknown. That's what really bugged her. There was something she didn't understand. And it was important.

"Damn it. What aren't you telling her?"

Ward walked over to stand beside her. He wrapped an arm around her. She leaned into his strength. Craving it. Wanting so much more. He faced the two seated men. "Are you saying that we are still in danger?"

"I don't know." Greg tried to smile. "I *think* we're safe."

"Except for the fifth watch." Ward pursed his lips. "Something was bugging me. Jed and Jordan have been here for a month this time. Where do they stay? How do they live?"

He glanced over at Mark's blank look, then at Greg, and nodded. "Greg, one of them lives on this side, correct?"

Sari glanced from Ward to her father and back. Slowly, his words filtered through her brain. "It has to be. It's the only way they'd be able to come back and forth and not stand out. Someone coached them. Gave them a place to stay. A way to live. To understand our way of life." She sat down heavily. "Oh my God. Father, do you know who this person is?"

Her father ruffled his hair. "Tron's brother."

"What brother?"

Once again Greg and Mark looked at each other. They turned as one to face Sari and Ward. "Tron's brother has lived here for decades. Since Mark went over."

"Jesus."

Sari didn't have anything to say. She didn't know why she hadn't considered such a thing. After all, she'd wondered why they hadn't taken technology from this world over to that world. It only made sense that one of them wanted to travel and possibly stay here. She just couldn't get her mind wrapped around the problem of whether that was a good thing or a bad thing. The issue appeared to be if he could come and go at will.

"Oh shit." Ward stared at Sari's father. "Does this man have the capability to cross dimensions at will?"

"No, not at will. It's all dependent on timing. But he goes home several times a year."

She tilted her head. "Via the house?"

Her father nodded. As she'd never been here and the house had been empty for the last fifteen years, that made a sick kind of sense. No one had been here, so it had been easy to travel. In fact, with the shop out in the front of the house, no one would have heard intruders coming and going quietly over the years. And that was yet another reason for her mother to move a long ways away.

As family loyalty and trust went, it made sense. She doubted Tron trusted many. "Is he the only one that you know of?"

Both older men nodded.

"Why?" Sari asked. "Why would he want that? What's in it for him?"

"He gets to live here." Greg gave her a crooked smile. "Away from Tron – a hard man for anyone to take."

"What's to stop this man from closing the door forever and locking his brother on the other side?" She was struggling with the idea that one man controlled the gate between two worlds. Surely both societies could have used the knowledge. Not just the one man.

"We need to have a talk with him, see if he's interested in closing the door forever. If not, we need to find a way to send him home without a watch."

"That won't work. He'd have to have a watch to travel

home, and that will leave a watch on their side, keeping the door to our house open as well."

"Oh God." Sari poured tea. The mindless activity occupied her hands while her mind raced.

"Then he can go home, hand over the watch and stay, or die and stay here anyway."

Sari glanced over at Ward. The cop personae stood in front of her like she hadn't seen before. He wasn't going to tolerate anything but this door between the two worlds being closed permanently.

She had to admit it was the only solution she could live with herself. Her family had been traumatized for centuries. Enough was enough.

Ward said, "Let me get this straight. Tron kept one of his family over here all the time just to keep tabs on Sari's family?"

"No, not just for that." Greg shook his head. "Also to keep Tron in the loop about our technology and weapons, government, etcetera. He didn't want his people knowing about this world as he figured he'd lose control. But they've learned from us."

"Bizarre," Sari murmured. And way too much to take in all at once. The implications were horrific.

"So this brother is the only person we need to worry about?" At the older men's nods, Ward asked, "Does he have a family?"

"No. He didn't want one."

Sari couldn't help but stare. "So he has no family but he lives like a spy here, going home once a year with new ideas, concepts, and inventions that he can take over to his brother?"

Mark nodded.

"Who is he?" Ward asked, "The brother? And where does he live?"

Mark frowned, his gaze locked onto the top of the tabletop.

Greg cleared his throat. "Um…you know him too."

He opened his mouth to speak when a voice behind her spoke first. She spun around.

"It's me."

"Brodin Wilson?" She sat back in shock, her mind still adjusting to his surprise appearance. But as she thought back over the years, the one man who'd been here on the spot, the one man who hadn't doubted the crazy story both Sari and her mother had told…it had to be him.

Ward was on his feet in a flash, his small handgun out and ready.

"That won't be necessary." Brodin stood in front of him, a small pistol directed at Ward.

Sari gasped. Ward closed his eyes. "God damn it," he said savagely.

"Now move over closer to Sari. Carefully."

Ward started to move.

"Slowly," Brodin ordered. "I don't have a problem shooting you, but I'd just as soon not deal with the mess afterward."

Ward snorted. "No problem. Just drag the bodies to your world. What do you care if your brother gets to deal with the mess? He's good at cleaning up. Isn't he?"

"He is at that," Brodin grimaced. "What my brother puts up with from his sons is nothing short of a miracle considering his attitude toward everyone else. Still, he's my brother. And it's my home."

"A home you're planning on returning to, I presume."

"Never." Brodin smiled sadly. "It's not like here. My brother rules like a dictator. He gives no one any freedom. I might not be a slave, but I was a prisoner to his whims no less." He glanced over at both Mark and Greg and smiled forlornly.

Greg stood shakily and walked over to Brodin. "You don't need a gun here. Not in my home."

"What about him?" Brodin said, waving the gun at Ward, who still held his own gun at the ready. "I don't know him. Therefore, I don't trust him."

"And yet you're happy to force men from here to be slaves for your brother?" Sari asked in outrage. "How could you?"

"I had no choice, any more than your father did. He went over to save you." He took a shuddering breath. "I helped him once I understood that Lisbeth was pregnant, making you or the unborn child Tron's next slave."

Greg reached out and took the gun from his hand. Brodin didn't argue. Sari watched Ward lower his slightly. Something had shifted here, and she had to understand what that was.

"But was she?" Sari asked, her heart heavy. The possible duplicity of one she loved threatened to overwhelm her. Even knowing her mother's character, the enormity of this betrayal was so huge, so devastating, that it was unforgiveable. "Are you *sure* she was pregnant?"

"Of course. It's the only reason I went over there," her father said. "Once I had the second child, one of you belonged to Tron." Her father choked back a sob. "I couldn't let that happen, so Brodin contacted Tron and set it up, but I didn't know when it would happen."

"No," she whispered with such love, "I do understand."

"Lisbeth thought it would be easier without a difficult goodbye for Sari. So after talking to Tron, I set the watch for it that afternoon, knowing when I returned, he'd be gone. In fact," Brodin looked miserable. "I didn't leave. I went to the attic to meet him on the other side. Make it easier for him."

"Easier for him? And this was to be easier for me?" Sari asked, shocked. Brodin dropped his gaze to the table. "How could this be easy for me?"

But she knew. There was only person this was easier for. She hoped she was wrong, but… She pulled her cell phone out and while everyone watched, she dialed her mother.

"Hello, Lisbeth," Sari glanced over at her father, his gaze wide and shocked. He studied the phone in her hand. "I have a question, an odd thought, but…"

"What is it, Sari?" her mother asked impatiently. "I'm busy." In the background, there were sounds of others around her mother. As if she had company over, a dinner party possibly.

"Of course you are," Sari murmured. She clicked the speaker button on the phone. "The question just occurred to me – did you ever have a second child?"

"What? What kind of question is that? Of course not. You were there, you should know," her mother said waspishly. "And why would you possibly ask me that right now?"

Sari persisted. "And a second pregnancy – were you ever pregnant a second time while you were married?"

"Like I'd go through that again?" She gave a delicate snort. "No, of course not. I was unhappy to begin with. Why would I compound the situation with a second child?"

"So telling Brodin and my father that you were pregnant accomplished what? Setting up my father to sacrifice the rest of his life while giving you the freedom you craved, all with a viable excuse so your parents would take you back in?" Sari cried, her voice hard and hurting. "Is that the kind of selfish, self-serving bitch you are?"

She stared blindly as the four men stared back at her, the phone shaking in her hand.

"Brodin?" her mother's voice broke. "What…what has this got to do with him?"

"He's here with me."

"He's lying," Lisbeth shot back immediately. "You can't believe a word he says."

"And me, Lisbeth," Sari's father said painfully. "Am I not believable either?"

A shocked silence filled the air.

"Greg?" Lisbeth asked in a dazed whisper. "No, that can't be!"

"Why, because you sent him over to never return?" Sari snapped. "Sorry to tell you, but I went over there and brought him back. Something I'd have done years ago if I'd known what you'd done."

"No, wait…" Lisbeth cried out. "I can explain!"

"Right now I don't wish to even hear your voice – it makes me sick!" Sari tossed the phone on the table. She glared at the men assembled in front of her, their gazes focused on the phone. "I think we should ship her over to Tron."

Her father winced. She knew it would take him a long time to deal with his wife's perfidious nature, but he'd heard the truth from her now. He couldn't be blind to what she was. Angered at what her mother had put the two of them through, she glared at Brodin, the only target in front of her.

"And you helped that bitch crucify my father," she snapped, hating him in that moment.

"Whoa, I didn't know she wasn't pregnant – how could I?" he protested.

"He's right, Sari. Brodin helped at my request."

Brodin had dropped his gaze to the table. "Actually, I wasn't going to help you. I didn't want to send you over there. I'd hoped to keep the second child a secret from Tron. But it was only after Lisbeth begged me so that she could rest at night knowing her children would be safe did I finally buckle under and agree to help. As it was, the portal had become unstable and you were Tron's best hope of fixing it."

Greg nodded sadly. "And I did. I should have left it broken."

"Wow," Mark said. "I'd always hated that I'd never had a chance at a normal life with a wife and kids." He motioned to the phone. "It's just possible that I've been given a lucky escape."

On the heels of his words, Sari's phone rang. She picked up her phone, saw it was her mother, and blocked the caller, then tossed the now silent phone back onto the table. She couldn't even begin to deal with such a monumental betrayal.

Ward reached over to wrap an arm around her shoulders, tugging her close. "Sorry," he whispered.

There was nothing to say. She glanced over at her father, but he stared at the phone like he didn't know what to do with it. Then again, why would he? His wife had arranged for his life sentence as a slave.

"I was happy over there, you know. Because I knew it kept you safe." He tore his gaze away from the phone to stare at Sari.

"I know," she whispered. She reached across the table to clasp his hand in hers. "But it was all so unnecessary."

"Then," Ward said, "let's make something good come out of this. Let's close the door forever." He directed his gaze at Brodin. "This side or Tron's side?"

"You'd have a hard time fitting in over there again, wouldn't you?" Sari's soft voice eased the aggression rising in the room.

"I never fit in. You don't know what my brother is like. Look what he does to people." He motioned toward Greg. "He steals them, enslaves them by threatening harm to their loved ones, and puts them to work until they are too old to work anymore." Brodin turned to Mark. "You, did you ever explain about Madge? Why it was important to return her home before it was too late? Before she died?"

"She's not dying," Sari cried out. "She's going to be fine."

"Now that she's here, yes, at least for whatever days she has left." Mark shook his head. "I heard Tron discussing her fate. She was to be taken out into the wilds and left for the animals like he does every other person of no value."

Ward stared at Brodin. "Let me get this straight. You know what he's like. You know he's planning on enslaving Sari and the rest of her family, and yet you still helped him?" He paused for a long moment, staring at the smaller man like he'd stare at a unique bug. "What does that make you?"

"Desperate," snapped Brodin. "You don't understand. He'll kill me if I don't do as he wants. Those sons of his come and go and do as they please."

Sari shook her head. "No, he won't. He'll never be able to find you. Not if you hand the watch over for us to destroy. Then he and his men can never come here and you can never return there."

"No," Brodin said, shaking his head violently. "You

don't know him. What he wants he gets. You'd have to kill him to get him to stop."

"With pleasure." Cold and brutal, Ward's words hung heavy in the air.

Brodin stared. His mouth worked, but no sound came out.

Sari laughed. "The way I see it, you can either stay here and stay out of trouble, or you can go back and face your brother. Without us. And good luck with Ward and the rest of the police force if you ever try to come back."

Brodin's desperate gaze went from Greg to Mark, then back to Ward before finally landing on Sari. "I didn't want to keep going over there. He'd send Jed and Jordan to get me if I was even a little bit late. And I always had to take back something he'd like. I spent so much of my time trying to find something to make him happy so he wouldn't stop me from coming back. I had to go – he had the watches. Any number of his people could come looking for me."

"They no longer have the watches." Sari smiled. "And neither do they have Mark's or my father's pieces in progress or their notes. Or my father's old books that they stole from me." Her smile deepened with satisfaction. "They will have to start from scratch and figure it out for themselves if...if you hand over the final timepiece."

He looked broken, like a man who'd have to look over his shoulders for the rest of his life.

Greg spoke for the first time. "Brodin, I don't hate you or him. But I'd like to see you stand up for once and do what's right. Hand over everything and leave your brother and his evil ways locked on the other side. Everyone who is supposed to be here is here. You are the only one who's not. Now if you want to go home and stay there – fine, then I will take my chances and walk you across and leave you there. Otherwise, I suggest you make a deal to stay here." He laughed. "Honestly. What choice is there? We'll treat you so much better here than we were ever treated over there."

With a heavy thump, Brodin sat down one of the kitchen chairs. He looked like a weight had fallen off his shoulders. Sari realized that although his life had been easier than her father's, they'd both been prisoners.

Ward said, "I suggest you people get the rest of the watches and materials that you need to destroy so we can close this chapter and get some rest tonight."

Brodin emptied his pockets. He had his watch. "I don't have anything else. I'm not like them," he nodded toward Mark and Greg. "I like to fiddle, but with jewelry, not watches."

He grinned boyishly. "Actually, Greg and I spent hours making jewelry pieces for Sari here."

Greg smiled, warmth and happiness on his face. "And we will again, old friend. We will again."

CHAPTER 29

T HE AFTERMATH WAS anticlimactic, with the biggest
issue being to find the watch Madge had used to cross
over. After talking with her at the hospital, they searched the
attic and found the box she'd thrown it into for safekeeping.

When they were sure that they had them all, the watches
were disassembled, the pieces mixed up and then taken to a
local foundry to be melted. Sari and Ward had elected to stay
and watch as the metal pieces dissolved into nothing but a
pool of molten metal. Her father hadn't wanted to come. He
knew the watches needed to be disposed of, but the watchmaker in him had wanted them preserved safely somehow.

There'd been much discussion as to the outcome of the
little attic room, but no resolution as yet. Considering they
were likely to have Mark, her father, and possibly even
Madge living in her house – her father's house – life was
about to get very interesting.

Then there was Ward.

Walking back out into the sunshine a little later, surprised by the sadness inside, Sari asked Ward, "Do you think
it's all over?"

He dropped a kiss on her forehead. "No. It's just the
beginning."

Author's Note

Thank you for reading Time Thieves! If you enjoyed my book, I'd appreciate it if you'd leave a review.

Dear reader,

I love to hear from readers, and you can contact me at my website: www.dalemayer.com or at my Facebook author page. To be informed of new releases and special offers, sign up for my newsletter or follow me on BookBub. And if you are interested in joining Dale Mayer's Reader Group, here is the Facebook sign up page.
http://geni.us/DaleMayerFBGroup

Cheers,
Dale Mayer

Tuesday's Child

Book 1 of the Psychic Vision Series

Get this book at your favorite vendor.

What she doesn't want…is exactly what he needs.

Shunned and ridiculed all her life for something she can't control, Samantha Blair hides her psychic abilities and lives on the fringes of society. Against her will, however, she's tapped into a killer—or rather, his victims. Each woman's murder, blow-by-blow, ravages her mind until their death releases her back to her body. Sam knows she must go to the authorities, but will the rugged, no-nonsense detective in charge of tracking down the killer believe her?

Detective Brandt Sutherland only trusts hard evidence, yet Sam's visions offer clues he needs to catch a killer. The more he learns about her incredible abilities, however, the clearer it becomes that Sam's visions have put her in the killer's line of fire. Now Brandt must save her from something he cannot see or understand…and risk losing his heart in the process.

As danger and desire collide, passion raises the stakes in a game Sam and Brandt don't dare lose.

Dangerous Designs
Book 1 of the Design Series

Get this book at your favorite vendor.

Drawing is her world…but when her new pencil comes alive, it's his world too.

Her…Storey Dalton is seventeen and now boyfriendless after being dumped via Facebook. Drawing is her escape. It's like as soon as she gets down one image, a dozen more are pressing in on her. Then she realizes her pictures are almost drawing themselves…or is it that her new pencil is alive?

Him…Eric Jordan is a new Ranger and the only son of the Councilman to his world. He's crossed the veil between dimensions to retrieve a lost stylus. But Storey is already experimenting with her new pencil and what her drawings can do – like open portals.

It … The stylus is a soul-bound intelligence from Eric's dimension on Earth and uses Storey's unsuspecting mind to seek its way home, giving her an unbelievable power. She unwittingly opens a third dimension, one that held a dangerous predatory species banished from Eric's world centuries ago, releasing these animals into both dimensions.

Them… Once in Eric's homeland, Storey is blamed for the calamity sentenced to death. When she escapes, Eric is ordered to bring her back or face that same death penalty. With nothing to lose, can they work together across dimensions to save both their worlds?

About the Author

Dale Mayer is a *USA Today* best-selling author, best known for her SEALs military romances, her Psychic Visions series, and her Lovely Lethal Garden cozy series. Her contemporary romances are raw and full of passion and emotion (Broken But … Mending, Hathaway House series). Her thrillers will keep you guessing (Kate Morgan, By Death series), and her romantic comedies will keep you giggling (*It's a Dog's Life*, a stand-alone novella; and the Broken Protocols series, starring Charming Marvin, the cat).

Dale honors the stories that come to her—and some of them are crazy, break all the rules and cross multiple genres!

To go with her fiction, she also writes nonfiction in many different fields, with books available on résumé writing, companion gardening, and the US mortgage system. All her books are available in print and ebook format.

Connect with Dale Mayer Online

Dale's Website – www.dalemayer.com
Twitter – @DaleMayer
Facebook Page – geni.us/DaleMayerFBFanPage
Facebook Group – geni.us/DaleMayerFBGroup
BookBub – geni.us/DaleMayerBookbub
Instagram – geni.us/DaleMayerInstagram
Goodreads – geni.us/DaleMayerGoodreads
Newsletter – geni.us/DaleNews

Also by Dale Mayer

Published Adult Books:

Psychic Vision Series

Tuesday's Child

Hide'n Go Seek

Maddy's Floor

Garden of Sorrow

Knock, Knock...

Rare Find

Eyes to the Soul

Now You See Her

Shattered

Into the Abyss

Psychic Visions Books 1–3

Psychic Visions Books 4–6

Psychic Visions Books 7–9

By Death Series

Touched by Death – Part 1

Touched by Death – Part 2

Touched by Death – Parts 1&2

Haunted by Death

Chilled by Death

By Death Books 1–3

Second Chances...at Love Series

Second Chances – Part 1

Second Chances – Part 2

Second Chances – complete book (Parts 1 & 2)

Charmin Marvin Romantic Comedy Series

Broken Protocols

Broken Protocols 2

Broken Protocols 3

Broken Protocols 3.5

Broken Protocols 1-3

Broken and... Mending

Skin

Scars

Scales (of Justice)

Broken but… Mending 1-3

Glory

Genesis

Tori

Celeste

Glory Trilogy

Biker Blues

Biker Blues: Morgan, Part 1

Biker Blues: Morgan, Part 2

Biker Blues: Morgan, Part 3

Biker Baby Blues: Morgan, Part 4

Biker Blues: Morgan, Full Set

Biker Blues: Salvation, Part 1

Biker Blues: Salvation, Part 2

Biker Blues: Salvation, Part 3

Biker Blues: Salvation, Full Set

SEALs of Honor

Mason: SEALs of Honor, Book 1

Hawk: SEALs of Honor, Book 2

Dane: SEALs of Honor, Book 3

Swede: SEALs of Honor, Book 4

Shadow: SEALs of Honor, Book 5

Cooper: SEALs of Honor, Book 6

Markus: SEALs of Honor, Book 7

Evan: SEALs of Honor, Book 8

Mason's Wish: SEALs of Honor, Book 9

SEALs of Honor, Books 1–3

SEALs of Honor, Books 4–6

Collections

Dare to Be You…

Dare to Love…

Dare to be Strong…

RomanceX3

Standalone Novellas

It's a Dog's Life

Riana's Revenge

Published Young Adult Books:

Family Blood Ties Series

Vampire in Denial

Vampire in Distress

Vampire in Design

Vampire in Deceit

Vampire in Defiance

Vampire in Conflict

Vampire in Chaos

Vampire in Crisis

Vampire in Control

Vampire in Charge

Family Blood Ties Set 1–3

Family Blood Ties Set 1–5

Family Blood Ties Set 4–6

Family Blood Ties Set 7–9

Sian's Solution – A Family Blood Ties Short Story

Design series

Dangerous Designs

Deadly Designs

Darkest Designs

Design Series Trilogy

Standalone

In Cassie's Corner

Gem Stone (a Gemma Stone Mystery)

Time Thieves

Published Non-Fiction Books:

Career Essentials

Career Essentials: The Résumé

Career Essentials: The Cover Letter

Career Essentials: The Interview

Career Essentials: 3 in 1

www.ingramcontent.com/pod-product-compliance
Lightning Source LLC
Chambersburg PA
CBHW071225210726
48293CB00002B/586